Praise for *The Solitude of Prime Numbers*

"Mesmerizing ... Out of a mathematical conceit the Italian writer Paolo Giordano has drawn a mesmerizing portrait of a young man and woman whose injured natures draw them together over the years and inevitably pull them apart ... What is even more distinctive, and transforming, is the writing. The author works with piercing subtlety. He manages—to move from math to physics—an exquisite rendering of wh~~~ ings at the subatomic level, emo

Times

"Seductive and unnerving

—*Entertainment Weekly*

"Giordano's passionate evocation of being young and in despair will resonate strongly." —*USA Today*

"[D]ark, funny, elegiac and affecting." —*The Globe and Mail*

"This starkly rendered coming-of-age tale about Alice and Mattia, two alienated, damaged children, is a painful but beautiful novel that belies its debut status." —*Winnipeg Free Press*

"The elegant and fiercely intelligent debut novel by 27-year-old physicist Paolo Giordano, *The Solitude of Prime Numbers*, which won Italy's Strega prize, revolves around Mattia and Alice, friends since high school—'twin primes, alone and lost, close but not close enough to really touch each other,' wherein resides the seductive enchantment of this singular love story." —*ELLE*

"Moving ... masterful ... his eye for the telling detail brings the reader closer to the characters' drama."

—*The Times Literary Supplement*

"This compelling debut shows a remarkable sensitivity and maturity in the depiction of its damaged soul mates. A fragile, unconventional love story by a talent to watch." —*Kirkus Reviews*

"Deeply soulful, powerful and honest, like a forgotten childhood memory, one of those rare books you love in an instant."

—Andrew Sean Greer, author of *The Confessions of Max Tivoli* and *The Story of a Marriage*

"Paolo Giordano is a writer of freakish talent. Readers of this post-traumatic love story will not be surprised to learn that its author is also a physicist: his storytelling has momentum; his characters, magnetism; his insights, gravity. *The Solitude of Prime Numbers* is beautiful right down to the subatomic level. Introverts, outsiders and lone wolves alike will find a kindred spirit here."

—Koren Zailckas, bestselling author of *Smashed*

"Surprising, intimate and deeply moving, *The Solitude of Prime Numbers* takes the reader on a hypnotic journey through an unexpected love affair. Paolo Giordano writes with grace and elegance of gentle but damaged characters, using inventive language to create a story unlike anything in recent fiction. This is everything a debut novel should be and leaves one longing for the books that will follow."

—John Boyne, author of *The Boy in the Striped Pajamas*

"Paolo Giordano is an expert on loss and sorrow. He understands and reveals the hidden hollows of the heart. His story is a quiet one, but his strong writing and unforgettable characters make his book a page turner. *The Solitude of Prime Numbers* is sad, dark and perfect."

—Mary Pipher, author of *Seeking Peace: Chronicles of the Worst Buddhist in the World*

"What a shock to open a novel written by a young physicist in Italy and find myself there, on every page. No wonder Giordano's readers can be counted in the millions; this astute, aching contemplation of solitude has a power to make us all feel a little less alone. A love story told with astonishing perceptiveness and remarkable subtlety, *The Solitude of Prime Numbers* is an extraordinary affirmation of the reasons we read."

—Stefan Merrill Block, author of *The Story of Forgetting*

"A deeply touching debut. Beautiful and affecting ... it reads easily, due in part to the almost seamless translation. An intimate psychological portrait of two 'prime numbers'—together alone and alone together." —*Booklist*

"Cerebral yet touching." —*Publishers Weekly*

"The year's most important debut." —*La Repubblica*

"Genius ... everybody can find in Giordano's book a small piece of himself." —*Il Giornale*

"The story is moving, to say the least ... Giordano's masterful handling of free indirect discourse, as well as his eye for the telling detail, brings the reader closer to the characters' dramas."

—*The Times Literary Supplement*

"Very accomplished ... a melancholic, but strangely beautiful, read ... similar to Goethe's *The Sorrows of Young Werther*."
—*The Guardian*

"We follow the destinies of these two wonders and are guided through their hearts and minds with a delicate but insightful analysis of human nature, its weakness, passions and helplessness ... A promising hope for the future of Italian literature."
—*The Independent*

"A novel of rare acuity and invention. Giordano is adept at capturing the forthright nature of teenagers' contorted thought processes: simultaneously judgmental and insecure. The prose is toned and precise ... a quite wonderful debut." —*The Spectator*

"A delicately nuanced meditation on the nature of loneliness. In clear, heartbreakingly precise prose, the youngest ever winner of the prestigious Premio Strega explores the way that trauma and guilt can capsize emotional stability and leave the vulnerable floundering in a wash of unease and loss. Giordano posits the possibilities of ballast, connection and hope ... A stunning achievement." —*Daily Mail*

PENGUIN CANADA

THE SOLITUDE OF PRIME NUMBERS

PAOLO GIORDANO is the youngest-ever winner of Italy's prestigious literary award, the Premio Strega, for his debut novel *The Solitude of Prime Numbers*, which has been translated into more than thirty languages worldwide. He has a PhD in theoretical physics and lives in Italy.

Paolo Giordano

THE
SOLITUDE
OF
PRIME
NUMBERS

PENGUIN
CANADA

PENGUIN CANADA

Published by the Penguin Group

Penguin Group (Canada), 90 Eglinton Avenue East, Suite 700, Toronto, Ontario, Canada M4P 2Y3
(a division of Pearson Canada Inc.)

Penguin Group (USA) Inc., 375 Hudson Street, New York, New York 10014, U.S.A.
Penguin Books Ltd, 80 Strand, London WC2R 0RL, England
Penguin Ireland, 25 St Stephen's Green, Dublin 2, Ireland (a division of Penguin Books Ltd)
Penguin Group (Australia), 250 Camberwell Road, Camberwell, Victoria 3124, Australia
(a division of Pearson Australia Group Pty Ltd)
Penguin Books India Pvt Ltd, 11 Community Centre, Panchsheel Park, New Delhi – 110 017, India
Penguin Group (NZ), 67 Apollo Drive, Rosedale, Auckland 0632, New Zealand
(a division of Pearson New Zealand Ltd)
Penguin Books (South Africa) (Pty) Ltd, 24 Sturdee Avenue, Rosebank, Johannesburg 2196, South Africa

Penguin Books Ltd, Registered Offices: 80 Strand, London WC2R 0RL, England

Published in Penguin Canada paperback by Penguin Group (Canada), a division of Pearson Canada Inc., 2010.
Simultaneously published in the United States by Pamela Dorman Books/Viking Penguin, a member
of Penguin Group (USA) Inc.

Translation copyright © Shaun Whiteside, 2009

Originally published in Italian as *La Solitudine dei Numeri Primi* by Arnoldo Mondadori Editore, Milan.
Copyright © 2008 Arnoldo Mondadori Editore S.p.A. This English translation published by arrangement
with Transworld Publishers, a division of The Random House Group Limited.

Published in this edition, 2011

  2 3 4 5 6 7 8 9 10 (WEB)

"Grey Room" Testo e Misica di Damien Rice © 2006 by Warner Chappell Music Publishing Ltd.

Designed by Carla Bolte

*Publisher's note: This book is a work of fiction. Names, characters, places and incidents either are the product of the author's
imagination or are used fictitiously, and any resemblance to actual persons living or dead, events, or locales is entirely
coincidental.*

Manufactured in Canada.

LIBRARY AND ARCHIVES CANADA CATALOGUING IN PUBLICATION

Giordano, Paolo, 1982-
   The solitude of prime numbers / Paolo Giordano.

Translation of: Solitudine dei numeri primi.
ISBN 978-0-14-317745-6

   I. Title.

PQ4907.I57S6413 2011   853'.92   C2011-904906-6

Visit the Penguin Group (Canada) website at www.penguin.ca

Special and corporate bulk purchase rates available; please see
www.penguin.ca/corporatesales or call 1-800-810-3104, ext. 2477.

To Eleonora,

because in silence

I promised it to you

Acknowledgments

This book wouldn't have existed without Raffaella Lops.

I would like to thank, in no particular order, Antonio Franchini, Joy Terekiev, Mario Desiati, Giulia Ichino, Laura Cerutti, Cecilia Giordano, my parents, Giorgio Mila, Roberto Castello, Emiliano Amato, Pietro Grossi, and Nella Re Rebaudengo. Each of them knows why.

Her old aunt's elaborately trimmed dress was a perfect fit for Sylvie's slender figure, and she asked me to lace it up for her. "The sleeves are plain; how ridiculous!" she said.

—Gérard de Nerval, *Sylvie*, 1853

SNOW ANGEL

1983

Alice Della Rocca hated ski school. She hated getting up at seven-thirty, even during Christmas vacation. She hated her father staring at her over breakfast, his leg dancing nervously under the table as if to say hurry up, get a move on. She hated the woolen tights that made her thighs itch, the mittens that kept her from moving her fingers, the helmet that squashed her cheeks, and the big, too tight boots that made her walk like a gorilla.

"Are you going to drink that milk or not?" her father insisted again.

Alice gulped down three inches of boiling milk, burning her tongue, throat, and stomach.

"Good, today you can show us what you're really made of."

What's that? Alice wondered.

He shoved her out the door, mummified in a green ski suit dotted with badges and the fluorescent logos of the sponsors. It was 14 degrees and a gray fog enveloped everything. Alice felt the milk swirling around in her stomach as she sank into the snow. Her skis were over her shoulder, because you had to carry your skis yourself until you got good enough for someone to carry them for you.

"Keep the tips facing forward or you'll kill someone," her father said.

At the end of the season the Ski Club gave you a pin with little stars on it. A star a year, from when you were four years old and just tall enough to slip the little disk of the ski lift between your legs until you were nine and you managed to grab the disk all by yourself. Three silver stars and then another three in gold: a pin a year, a way of saying you'd gotten a little better, a little closer to the races

3

that terrified Alice. She was already worried about them even though she had only three stars.

They were to meet at the ski lift at eight-thirty sharp, right when it opened. The other kids were already there, standing like little soldiers in a loose circle, bundled up in their uniforms, numb with sleep and cold. They planted their ski poles in the snow and wedged the grips in their armpits. With their arms dangling, they looked like scarecrows. No one felt like talking, least of all Alice. Her father rapped twice on her helmet, too hard, as if trying to pound her into the snow.

"Pull out all the stops," he said. "And remember: keep your body weight forward, okay? Body weight forward."

"Body weight forward," echoed the voice in Alice's head.

Then he walked away, blowing into his cupped hands. He'd soon be home again, reading the paper in the warmth of their house. Two steps and the fog swallowed him up.

Alice clumsily dropped her skis on the ground and banged her boots with a ski pole to knock off the clumps of snow. If her father had seen her he would have slapped her right there, in front of everyone.

She was already desperate for a pee; it pushed against her bladder like a pin piercing her belly. She wasn't going to make it today either. Every morning it was the same. After breakfast she would lock herself in the bathroom and push and push, trying to get rid of every last drop, contracting her abdominal muscles till her head ached and her eyes felt like they were going to pop out of their sockets. She would turn the tap full blast so that her father wouldn't hear the noises as she pushed and pushed, clenching her fists, to squeeze out the very last drop. She would sit there until her father pounded on the door and yelled so, missy, are we going to be late again today?

But it never did any good. By the time they reached the top of the first ski lift she would be so desperate that she would have to crouch down in the fresh snow and pretend to tighten her boots in order to take a pee inside her ski suit while all her classmates looked on, and Eric, the ski instructor, would say we're waiting for Alice, as usual. It's such a relief, she thought each time, as the lovely warmth trickled between her shivering legs. Or it would be, if only they weren't all there watching me.

Sooner or later they're going to notice.

Sooner or later I'm going to leave a yellow stain in the snow and they'll all make fun of me.

One of the parents went up to Eric and asked if the fog wasn't too thick to go all the way to the top that morning. Alice pricked up her ears hopefully, but Eric unfurled his perfect smile.

"It's only foggy down here," he said. "At the top the sun is blinding. Come on, let's go."

On the chairlift Alice was paired with Giuliana, the daughter of one of her father's colleagues. They didn't say a word the whole way up. Not that they particularly disliked each other, it was just that, at that moment, neither of them wanted to be there.

The sound of the wind sweeping the summit of the mountain was punctuated by the metallic rush of the steel cable from which Alice and Giuliana were hanging, their chins tucked into the collars of their jackets so as to warm themselves with their breath.

It's only the cold, you don't really need to go, Alice said to herself.

But the closer she got to the top, the more the pin in her belly pierced her flesh. Maybe she was seriously close to wetting herself. Then again, it might even be something bigger. No, it's just the cold, you don't really need to go again, Alice kept telling herself.

Alice suddenly regurgitated rancid milk. She swallowed it down with disgust.

She really needed to go; she was desperate.

Two more chairlifts before the shelter. I can't possibly hold it in for that long.

Giuliana lifted the safety bar and they both shifted their bottoms forward to get off. When her skis touched the ground Alice shoved off from her seat. You couldn't see more than two yards ahead of you, so much for blinding sun. It was like being wrapped in a sheet, all white, nothing but white, above, below, all around you. It was the exact opposite of darkness, but it frightened Alice in precisely the same way.

She slipped off to the side of the trail to look for a little pile of fresh snow to relieve herself in. Her stomach gurgled like a dishwasher. When she turned around, she couldn't see Giuliana anymore, which meant that Giuliana couldn't see her either. She herringboned a few yards up the hill, just as her father had made her do when he had gotten it into his head to teach her to ski. Up and down the bunny slope, thirty, forty times a day, sidestep up and snowplow down. Buying a ski pass for just one slope was a waste of money, and this way you trained your legs as well.

Alice unfastened her skis and took a few more steps, sinking halfway up her calves in the snow. Finally she could sit. She stopped holding her breath and relaxed her muscles. A pleasant electric shock spread through her whole body, finally settling in the tips of her toes.

It must have been the milk, of course. That and the fact that her bum was freezing from sitting in the snow at six thousand feet. It had never happened before, at least not as far as she could remember. Never, not even once.

But this time it wasn't pee. Or, not only. As she leaped to her feet she felt something heavy in the seat of her pants and instinctively touched her bottom. She couldn't feel a thing through her gloves, but it didn't matter—she had already realized what had happened.

Now what, she wondered.

Eric called her but Alice didn't reply. As long as she stayed up there, the fog would hide her. She could pull down her ski pants and clean herself up as best she could, or go down and whisper in Eric's ear what had happened. She could tell him she had to go back to the lodge, that her knees hurt. Or she could just not worry about it and keep skiing, making sure to always be last in line.

Instead she simply stayed where she was, careful not to move a muscle, shielded by the fog.

Eric called her again. Louder now.

"She must have gone to the ski lift already, silly girl," a little boy said.

Alice could hear them talking. Someone said let's go and someone else said I'm cold from standing here. They could be just below her, a few yards away, or up at the ski lift. Sounds are deceptive: they rebound off the mountains and sink in the snow. "Damn . . . let's go see," Eric said. Alice slowly counted to ten, suppressing her urge to vomit as she felt something slither down her thighs. When she got to ten, she started over again, this time counting to twenty. Now all was silent.

She picked up her skis and carried them under her arm to the trail. It took her a little while to work out how to position them at right angles to the fall line. With fog that thick you can't even tell which way you're facing.

She clipped into her skis and tightened the bindings. She took off her goggles and spat inside them because they had misted up. She could ski down to the lodge all on her own. She didn't care that Eric was looking for her at the top of the mountain. With her pants caked in shit, she didn't want to stay up there a second longer than she absolutely had to. She went over the descent in her head. She had never done it alone, but, after all, they had gone only as far as the first ski lift, and she'd been down this slope dozens of times.

She began to snowplow. Just the day before, Eric had said if I see you doing one more snowplow turn, I swear I'm going to tie your ankles together.

Eric didn't like her, she was sure of it. He thought she was a scaredy-pants and, as it turned out, events had proved him right. Eric didn't like her father either, because every day, at the end of the lesson, he pestered him with endless questions. So how is our Alice coming along, are we getting better, do we have a little champion on our hands, when are we going to start racing, on and on. Eric always stared at a spot somewhere behind her father and answered yes, no, well . . .

Alice saw the whole scene superimposed on her foggy goggles as she gently edged her way down, unable to make out anything beyond the tips of her skis. Only when she ended up in the fresh snow did she understand that it was time to turn.

She started singing to herself to feel less alone. From time to time she wiped away her snot with her glove.

Keep your weight uphill, plant your pole, turn. Lean on your boots. Now shift your body weight forward, okay? Bo-dy weight for-ward. The voice was partly Eric's and partly her father's.

Her father would probably fly into a rage. She had to come up with a lie, a story that would stand up, no holes or contradictions. She didn't even dream of telling him what had really happened. The fog, that was it, blame it on the fog. She was following the others onto the big slope when her ski pass had come off her jacket. No, that's no good, no one's ski pass ever blew away. You'd have to be a real idiot to lose it. My scarf. My scarf blew away and I went back to find it, but the others didn't wait for me. I called them a hundred times but there was no sign of them; they had disappeared into the fog and so I went down to look for them.

And why didn't you go back up? her father would ask.

Of course, why hadn't she? On second thought, it was better if she lost her ski pass. She hadn't gone back up because she'd lost her ski pass and the man at the ski lift wouldn't let her.

Alice smiled, pleased with her story. It was flawless. She didn't even feel all that dirty anymore. She would spend the rest of the day in front of the TV. She would take a shower and put on clean clothes and slip her feet into her furry slippers. She would stay inside, in the warmth, all day. Or she would have, if only she'd looked up from her skis long enough to see the orange tape with the words TRAIL CLOSED. Her father was always telling her look where you're going. If only she'd remembered that in fresh snow you shouldn't put your body weight forward and if only Eric, a few days before, had adjusted her bindings better, and her father had been more insistent in saying but Alice weighs sixty pounds, won't they be too tight like that?

The drop wasn't very high. A few yards, just long enough to feel a slight void in your stomach and nothing beneath your feet. And then Alice was facedown in the snow, her skis pointing straight up in the air, and her fibula broken.

She didn't really feel that bad. To tell the truth, she didn't feel a thing. Only the snow that had slipped under her scarf and into her helmet and burned her skin.

The first thing she did was move her arms. When she was little and woke up to find it had snowed, her father would wrap her up tight and carry her downstairs. They would walk to the center of the courtyard and, hand in hand, would count to three and fall backward like a deadweight. Then her father would say make an angel, and Alice would move her arms up and down. When she got up and looked at her outline sculpted in the white, it really did look like the shadow of an angel with outspread wings.

Alice made a snow angel, just like that, for no reason, just to prove to herself that she was still alive. She managed to turn her head to one side and start breathing again, even though it felt as if the air wasn't going where it was supposed to. She had the strange sensation of not knowing which way her legs were turned. The very strange sensation of no longer having legs at all.

She tried to get up, but she couldn't.

If it weren't for the fog, someone might have seen her from above, a green stain splayed at the bottom of a gully, a few steps from the spot where a little waterfall would start flowing again in the spring, where, with the first warmth, wild strawberries would grow, and if you waited long enough they'd ripen, as sweet as candy, and you could pick a basketful in a day. Alice cried for help, but her thin voice was swallowed up by the fog. She tried to get up again, or at least to turn over, but it was no use.

Her father had told her that people who freeze to death feel very hot and, just before dying, have an urge to get undressed. Almost everyone who dies of cold is found in their underwear. And hers were dirty.

She was starting to lose feeling in her fingers as well. She took off her glove, blew into it, and then put it back on her clenched fist, to warm it up. She did the same with her other hand. She repeated this ludicrous gesture two or three times.

It's your extremities that get you, her father always said. Your toes and fingers, your nose and ears. Your heart does everything in its power to keep the blood to itself, leaving the rest to freeze.

Alice imagined her fingers turning blue and then, slowly, her arms and her legs. She thought about her heart pumping harder and harder, trying to keep in all the remaining warmth. She would go so stiff that if a wolf passed by it would snap off one of her arms just by stepping on it.

They must be looking for me.

I wonder if there really are any wolves around here.

I can't feel my fingers anymore.

If only I hadn't drunk that milk.

Bo-dy weight for-ward.

Of course not, wolves would be hibernating now.

Eric will be furious.

I don't want to race.

Don't be stupid, you know very well that wolves don't hibernate.

Her thoughts were growing more and more circular and illogical.

The sun sank slowly behind Mount Chaberton as if nothing was the matter. The shadow of the mountains spread over Alice and the fog turned completely black.

THE ARCHIMEDES PRINCIPLE

1984

2

When the twins were small and Michela was up to one of her tricks, like throwing herself downstairs in her baby walker or sticking a pea up one of her nostrils, so that she had to be taken to the emergency room to have it removed with special tweezers, their father would always say to Mattia, the firstborn, that his mother's womb was too small for both of them.

"God only knows what the two of you got up to in there," he said. "I reckon all those kicks you gave your sister did her some serious damage."

Then he laughed, even though it was no laughing matter. He lifted Michela in the air and buried his beard in her soft cheeks.

Mattia would watch from below. He would laugh too, letting his father's words filter through him by osmosis, without really understanding them. He let them settle at the bottom of his stomach, forming a thick, sticky layer, like the sediment of wine that has aged for a long time.

His father's laughter turned into a strained smile when, at two and a half, Michela still couldn't utter a single word. Not even *mommy* or *poo-poo* or *sleepy* or *woof*. Her inarticulate little cries rose from such a solitary, deserted place that they made their father shiver every time.

When she was five and a half a speech therapist with thick glasses sat Michela down in front of a board with four different shapes cut out—a star, a circle, a square, and a triangle—and the corresponding colored pieces to place into the holes.

Michela looked at them with wonder.

"Where does the star go, Michela?" asked the speech therapist.

Michela stared at the puzzle but didn't touch anything. The doctor put the yellow star in her hand.

"Where does this go, Michela?" she asked.

Michela looked everywhere and nowhere. She put one of the points in her mouth and began to chew on it. The speech therapist took the object out of her mouth and asked the question yet again.

"Michela, do what the doctor tells you, for God's sake," snarled her father, who couldn't quite manage to stay seated, as he'd been told.

"Signor Balossino, please," the doctor said in a conciliatory voice. "Children need time."

And Michela took her time. A whole minute. Then she let out a heartrending groan that might have been of joy or of despair, and resolutely jammed the star in the square hole.

In case Mattia had not already figured out for himself that something was not right with his sister, his classmates didn't hesitate to point it out to him. Simona Volterra, for example, during the first year of school. When the teacher said Simona, you're going to sit next to Michela this month, she refused, crossing her arms, and said I don't want to sit next to her.

Mattia let Simona and the teacher argue for a while, and then said Miss, I can sit next to Michela again. Everyone had looked relieved: Michela, Simona, the teacher. Everyone except Mattia.

The twins sat in the front row. Michela spent the whole day coloring, meticulously going outside the lines and picking colors at random. Blue children, red skies, all the trees yellow. She gripped the pencil like a meat pounder, pressing down so hard that she often tore the page.

At her side Mattia learned to read and write, to add and subtract, and was the first in the class to master long division.

His brain seemed to be a perfect machine, in the same mysterious way that his sister's was so defective.

Sometimes Michela would start squirming on her chair, waving her arms around crazily, like a trapped moth. Her eyes would grow dark and the teacher, more frightened than she was, would stand and look at her, vaguely hoping that the retard really might fly away one day. Someone in the back row would giggle, someone else would go shhh. So Mattia would get up, picking up his chair so that it wouldn't scrape on the floor, and stand behind Michela, who by now was rolling her head from side to side and flailing her arms about so fast that he was afraid they would come off.

Mattia would take her hands and delicately wrap her arms around her chest.

"There, you don't have wings anymore," he'd whisper in her ear. It took Michela a few seconds before she stopped trembling. She'd stare into the distance for a few seconds, and then go back to tormenting her drawings as if nothing had happened. Mattia would sit back down, head lowered and ears red with embarrassment, and the teacher would go on with the lesson.

In the third year of primary school the twins still hadn't been invited to any of their classmates' birthday parties. Their mother noticed and thought she could solve the issue by throwing the twins a birthday party. At dinner, Mr. Balossino had rejected the suggestion out of hand. For heaven's sake, Adele, it's already embarrassing enough as it is. Mattia sighed with relief and Michela dropped her fork for the tenth time. It was never mentioned again. Then, one morning in January, Riccardo Pelotti, a kid with red hair and baboon lips, came over to Mattia's desk.

"Hey, my mom says you can come to my birthday party," he blurted, looking at the blackboard.

"So can she," he added, pointing to Michela, who was carefully smoothing the surface of the desk as if it were a bedsheet.

Mattia's face went red with excitement. He said thank you, but Riccardo, having gotten the weight off his chest, had already left.

The twins' mother immediately became anxious and took them both to Benetton for new clothes. They went to three toy shops, but Adele couldn't make up her mind.

"What sort of things is Riccardo interested in? Would he like this?" she asked Mattia, holding up a jigsaw puzzle.

"How would I know?" her son replied.

"He's a friend of yours. You must know what games he likes."

Mattia didn't think that Riccardo was a friend of his, but he couldn't explain that to his mother. So he simply shrugged.

In the end Adele opted for the Lego spaceship, the biggest and most expensive toy in the store.

"Mom, it's too much," her son protested.

"Nonsense. And besides, there are two of you. You don't want to make a bad impression."

Mattia knew all too well that, Lego or no Lego, they would make a bad impression. With Michela, anything else was impossible. He knew that Riccardo had invited them only because he'd been told to. Michela would cling to him the whole time, spill orange juice on herself, and then start whining, as she always did when she was tired.

For the first time Mattia thought it might be better to stay at home.

Or rather, he thought it might be better if Michela stayed at home.

"Mom," he began uncertainly.

Adele was looking in her bag for her wallet.

"Yes?"

Mattia took a breath.

"Does Michela really have to come to the party?"

Adele suddenly froze and stared into her son's eyes. The cashier observed the scene indifferently, her hand open on the conveyor belt, waiting for the money. Michela was mixing up the candy on the rack.

Mattia's cheeks burned, ready to receive a slap that never came. "Of course she's coming," his mother said, and that was that.

Riccardo's house was less than a ten-minute walk away, and they were allowed to go on their own. At three o'clock on the dot Adele pushed the twins out the door.

"Go on, or you'll be late. Remember to thank his parents," she said.

Then she turned to Mattia.

"Take care of your sister. You know she shouldn't eat junk."

Mattia nodded. Adele kissed them both on the cheek, Michela for longer. She tidied Michela's hair under her hair band and said enjoy yourselves.

On the way to Riccardo's house, Mattia's thoughts kept time with the Lego pieces, which shifted back and forth inside the box like the tide. Michela, tagging a few feet behind him, stumbled as she tried to keep up, dragging her feet through the mush of dead leaves stuck to the pavement. The air was still and cold.

She's going to drop her potato chips on the rug, thought Mattia. She'll grab the ball and she won't want to give it back.

"Will you hurry up?" he said, turning to his twin sister, who had suddenly crouched down in the middle of the pavement and was torturing a long worm with her finger. Michela looked at her brother as if seeing him for the first time in ages. She smiled and ran to him, clutching the worm between her fingers. "You're disgusting. Throw it away," Mattia ordered, recoiling.

Michela looked at the worm again for a moment and seemed to be wondering how it had ended up in her hand. Then she dropped it and launched into a lopsided run to join her brother, who had already walked on ahead.

She'll grab the ball and won't want to give it back, just like at school, he thought to himself.

Mattia looked at his twin, who had his same eyes, same nose, same color hair, and a brain that belonged in the trash, and for the first time he felt genuine hatred. He took her hand to cross the street, because the cars were going fast, and it was then that the idea came to him.

He let go of Michela's hand in its woolen glove, instantly thinking that it wasn't right.

Then, as they were walking by the park, he changed his mind again and convinced himself that no one would ever find out.

Just for a few hours, he thought. Just this once. He abruptly changed direction, dragging Michela by an arm, and entered the park. The grass was still damp from the night's frost. Michela trotted behind him, muddying her brand-new white suede boots. There was no one in the park; it was so cold that no one would have felt like going for a walk. The twins came to an area with trees, three wooden tables, and a barbecue. They had eaten lunch there once, in year one, when the teachers had taken them to collect dry leaves from which they made ugly table decorations to give to their grandparents for Christmas.

"Michela, listen to me," said Mattia. "Are you listening?"

With Michela you always had to check that her narrow channel of communication was open. Mattia waited for his sister to nod.

"Good. So, I have to go away for a little while, okay? But I won't be long, just half an hour," he explained.

There was no reason to tell the truth, since to Michela there was little difference between half an hour and a whole day. The doctor had said that her spatiotemporal perception development had been arrested at a preconscious stage, and Mattia understood perfectly well what that meant.

"You sit here and wait for me," he said to his twin. Michela stared gravely at her brother and didn't reply, because she didn't know what to say. She gave no sign of having really understood, but her eyes lit up for a moment, and for the rest of his life when Mattia thought of those eyes he thought of fear.

He took a few steps away from his sister, walking backward to make sure she didn't follow him. Only prawns walk like that, his mother had yelled at him once, and they always end up crashing into something.

He was about fifteen yards away and Michela had already stopped looking at him, engrossed in trying to pull a button off her woolen coat.

Mattia turned around and started to run, tightly clutching the bag with the present. Inside the box more than two hundred little plastic blocks crashed into one another. It was as if they were trying to tell him something.

"Hi, Mattia," Riccardo Pelotti's mother said as she opened the door. "Where's your little sister?"

"She has a temperature," Mattia lied. "A mild one."

"Oh, what a shame," the woman said, not seeming displeased in the slightest. She stepped aside to let him in.

"Ricky, your friend Mattia is here. Come and say hello," she called, turning toward the hall.

Riccardo appeared, sliding along the floor, an unpleasant expression on his face. He stopped for a second to glance at Mattia and look for traces of the retard. Relieved, he said hi.

Mattia waved the bag with the present under the woman's nose. "Where shall I put this?" he asked.

"What is it?" Riccardo asked suspiciously.

"Legos."

Riccardo grabbed the bag and disappeared down the hall.

"Go with him," Mrs. Pelotti said, pushing Mattia. "The party's down there."

The Pelottis' living room was decorated with bunches of balloons.

On a table covered by a red paper tablecloth were bowls of popcorn and chips, a tray of dry pizza cut into squares, and a row of still unopened soda bottles of various colors. Some of Mattia's classmates had already arrived and were standing in the middle of the room guarding the table.

Mattia took a few steps toward the others and then stopped a few yards away, like a satellite that doesn't want to take up too much room in the sky. No one paid him any attention.

When the room was full of children, an entertainer with a red plastic nose and a clown's bowler hat made them play blindman's buff and pin the tail on the donkey. Mattia won first prize, which consisted of an extra handful of candy, but only because he could see out from under the blindfold. Everyone shouted boo, you cheated, as he shamefacedly slipped the candy into his pocket.

Then, when it was dark outside, the clown turned out the lights, made them sit in a circle, and began to tell a horror story. He held a flashlight under his chin.

Mattia didn't think the story was all that scary, but the face, lit up like that, sure was. The light shining from below turned it all red and revealed terrifying shadows. Mattia looked out the window to keep from looking at the clown and remembered Michela. He hadn't ever really forgotten about her, but now for the first time he imagined her all alone among the trees, waiting for him, and rubbing her face with her white gloves to warm up a bit.

He got to his feet just as Riccardo's mother came into the dark room carrying a cake covered with candles, and everyone started clapping, partly for the story and partly for the cake.

"I've got to go," Mattia said to her, without even giving her time to set the cake down on the table.

"Right now? But the cake."

"Yes, now. I've got to go."

Riccardo's mother looked at him from over the candles. Lit up like that, her face was full of threatening shadows, just like the clown's. The other kids fell silent.

"Okay," the woman said uncertainly. "Ricky, walk your friend to the door."

"But I've got to blow out the candles."

"Do as I say," his mother ordered, still staring at Mattia.

"You're such a drag, Mattia."

Someone started laughing. Mattia followed Riccardo to the front door, pulled his jacket from the pile, and said thanks, bye. Riccardo didn't even reply, quickly shutting the door behind him to run back to his cake.

In the courtyard of Riccardo's building, Mattia glanced back at the lit window. His classmates' muffled cries filtered out like the reassuring hum of the television in the living room when his mother sent him and Michela to bed in the evening. The gate closed behind him with a metallic click and he began to run.

He entered the park, but after ten yards or so the light from the street lamps was no longer enough for him to make out the gravel path. The bare branches of the trees where he had left Michela were no more than slightly darker scratches against the black sky. Seeing them from a distance, Mattia was filled with the clear and inexplicable certainty that his sister was no longer there.

He stopped a few yards from the bench where Michela had been sitting a few hours before, busily ruining her coat. He stopped and listened, catching his breath, as if at any moment his sister were bound to pop out from behind a tree saying peekaboo and then run toward him, fluttering along with her crooked gait.

Mattia called Michela and was startled by his own voice. He called again, more quietly. He walked over to the wooden tables and laid a hand on the spot where Michela had been sitting. It was as cold as everything else.

She must have gotten bored and gone home, he thought.

But if she doesn't even know the way? And she can't cross the road on her own either.

Mattia looked at the park, which disappeared into the darkness. He didn't even know where it ended. He thought that he didn't want to go deeper and that he didn't have a choice.

He walked on tiptoes to keep from crunching the leaves under his feet, turning his head from side to side in the hopes of spotting Michela crouching behind a tree to ambush a beetle or who knows what.

He walked into the playground. He tried to remember the colors of the slide in the Sunday afternoon light, when his mother gave in to Michela's cries and let her have a few goes, even though she was too old for it.

He walked along the hedge as far as the public toilets, but wasn't brave enough to go inside. He found his way back to the path, which was now just a thin strip of dirt marked by the coming and going of families. He followed it for a good ten minutes until he no longer knew where he was. Then he started crying and coughing at the same time.

"You're so stupid, Michela," he said under his breath. "A stupid retard. Mom told you a thousand times to stay where you are if you get lost. . . . But you never understand anything. . . . Nothing at all."

He went up a slight slope and found himself looking at the river that cut through the park. His father had told him its name loads of times, but Mattia could never remember it. A bit of light from who knows where was reflected on the water and quivered in his teary eyes.

He went over to the riverbank and sensed that Michela must be somewhere close by. She liked the water. His mother always told how when they were little and she gave them a bath together, Michela would shriek like mad because she didn't want to get out, even once the water was cold. One Sunday his father had taken them to the riverbank, perhaps even to this very spot, and taught him to skip stones across the water. As he was showing him how to use his wrist to spin the stone, Michela leaned forward and slipped in up to her waist before their father caught her by the arm. He smacked her and she started whining, and then all three of them went home in silence, with long faces.

The image of Michela playing with a twig and breaking up her own reflection in the water before sliding into it like a sack of potatoes ran through his head with the force of an electric shock.

Exhausted, he sat down a couple of feet from the river's edge. He turned around to look behind him and saw the darkness that would last for many hours to come.

He stared at the gleaming black surface of the river. Again he tried to remember its name, but couldn't. He plunged his hands into the cold earth. On the bank the dampness made it softer. He found a broken bottle, a sharp reminder of some nighttime festivity. The first time he stuck it into his hand it didn't hurt, perhaps he didn't even notice. Then he started twisting it into his flesh, digging deeper, without ever taking his eyes off the water. He expected Michela to rise to the surface from one minute to the next, and in the meantime he wondered why some things float while others don't.

ON THE SKIN AND
JUST BEHIND IT

1991

3
────

The horrible white ceramic vase, with a complicated gold floral motif, which had always occupied a corner of the bathroom, had been in the Della Rocca family for five generations, but no one really liked it. On several occasions Alice had felt an urge to hurl it to the floor and throw the countless tiny fragments in the trash can in front of the house, along with the Tetra Pak mashed-potato containers, used sanitary napkins—although certainly not used by her—and empty packets of her father's antidepressants.

Alice ran a finger along the rim and thought how cold, smooth, and clean it was. Soledad, the Ecuadorean housekeeper, had become more meticulous over the years, because in the Della Rocca household details mattered. Alice was only six when she first arrived, and she had eyed her suspiciously from behind her mother's skirt. Soledad had crouched down and looked at her with wonder. What pretty hair you have, she had said, can I touch it? Alice had bit her tongue to keep from saying no and Soledad had lifted one of her chestnut curls as if it were a swatch of silk and then let it fall back. She couldn't believe that hair could be so fine.

Alice held her breath as she slipped off her camisole and closed her eyes tightly for a moment.

When she opened them again she saw herself reflected in the big mirror above the sink and felt a pleasurable sense of disappointment. She rolled down the elastic of her underpants a few times, so that they came just above her scar, and were stretched tightly enough to leave a little gap between the edge and her belly, forming a bridge between the bones of her pelvis. There wasn't quite room for her index finger; but being able to slip her little finger in made her crazy.

29

There, it should blossom right there, she thought.

A little blue rose, like Viola's.

Alice turned to stand in profile, her right side, the good one, as she would tell herself. She brushed all her hair forward, thinking it made her look like a child possessed by demons. She pulled it up in a ponytail and then scooped it higher up on her head, the way Viola wore hers, which everyone always liked.

That didn't work either.

She let her hair fall on her shoulders and with her usual gesture pinned it behind her ears. She rested her hands on the sink and pushed her face toward the mirror so quickly that her eyes seemed to form one single, terrifying Cyclops eye. Her hot breath formed a halo on the glass, covering part of her face.

She just couldn't figure out where Viola and her friends got those looks they went around with, breaking boys' hearts. Those merciless, captivating looks that could make or break you with a single, imperceptible flicker of the eyebrow.

Alice tried to be provocative with the mirror, but saw only an embarrassed girl clumsily shaking her shoulders and looking as if she were anesthetized. The real problem was her cheeks: too puffy and blotchy. They suffocated her eyes, when all the while she wanted her gaze to land like a dagger in the stomachs of the boys whose eyes it met. She wanted her gaze to spare no one, to leave an indelible mark.

Instead only her belly, bum, and tits got slimmer, while her cheeks were still like two round pillows, baby cheeks.

Someone knocked at the bathroom door.

"Alice, it's ready," her father's hateful voice rang out through the frosted glass.

Alice didn't reply and sucked in her cheeks to see how much better she would be like that.

"Alice, are you in there?" her father called.

Alice puckered her lips and kissed her reflection. She brushed her tongue against its image in the cold glass. Then she closed her eyes and, as in a real kiss, swayed her head back and forth, but too regularly to be believable. She still hadn't found the kiss she really wanted on anyone's mouth.

Davide Poirino had been the first to use his tongue, in the third year of secondary school. He'd lost a bet. He had rolled it mechanically around Alice's tongue three times, clockwise, and then turned to his friends and said okay? They had burst out laughing and someone had said you kissed the cripple, but Alice was happy just the same, she had given her first kiss and Davide wasn't bad at all.

There had been others after that. Her cousin Walter at their grandmother's party, and a friend of Davide's whose name she didn't even know, and who had asked her in secret if he could please have a turn too. In a hidden corner of the school playground they had pressed their lips together for a few minutes, neither of them daring to move a muscle. When they had drawn apart, he had said thank you and walked off with his head held high and the springy step of a real man.

But now she was lagging behind. Her classmates talked about positions, love bites, and how to use your fingers, and whether it was better with or without a condom, while Alice's lips still bore the insipid memory of a mechanical kiss in third year.

"Alice? Can you hear me?" her father called again, louder this time.

"Ugh. Of course I hear you," Alice replied irritably, her voice barely audible on the other side of the door.

"Dinner's ready," her father repeated.

"I heard you, damn it," Alice said. Then, under her breath, she added, "Pain in the ass."

———

Soledad knew that Alice threw away her food. At first, when Alice started leaving her dinner on her plate, she said *mi amorcito,* eat it all up, in my country children are dying of hunger.

One evening Alice, furious, looked her straight in the eyes.

"Even if I stuff myself till I burst, the children in your country aren't going to stop dying of hunger," she said.

So now Soledad said nothing, but put less and less food on her plate. But it didn't make any difference. Alice was quite capable of weighing up her food with her eyes and choosing her three hundred calories for dinner. The rest she got rid of, somehow or other.

She ate with her right hand resting on her napkin. In front of the plate she put her wineglass, which she asked to be filled but never drank, and her water glass in such a way as to form a glass barricade. Then, during dinner, she strategically positioned the saltshaker and the oil cruet too. She waited for her family to be distracted, each absorbed in the laborious task of mastication. At that point she very carefully pushed her food, cut into small pieces, off the plate and into her napkin.

Over the course of a dinner she made at least three full napkins disappear into the pockets of her sweatpants. Before brushing her teeth she emptied them into the toilet and watched the little pieces of food disappear down the drain. With satisfaction she ran a hand over her stomach and imagined it as empty and clean as a crystal vase.

"Sol, damn it, you put cream in the sauce again," her mother complained. "How many times do I have to tell you that I can't digest it?"

Alice's mother pushed her plate away in disgust.

Alice had come to the table with a towel wrapped like a turban around her head in order to justify all the time she had spent locked away in the bathroom.

She had thought for a long time whether to ask them for it. But she'd do it anyway. She wanted it too much.

"I'd like to get a tattoo on my belly," she began.

Her father pulled his glass away from his mouth.

"Excuse me?"

"You heard," said Alice, defying him with her eyes. "I want to get a tattoo."

Alice's father ran his napkin over his mouth and eyes, as if to erase an ugly image that had run through his mind. Then he carefully refolded it and put it back on his knees. He picked up his fork again, trying to put on all his irritating self-control.

"I don't even know how you get these ideas into your head," he said.

"And what kind of tattoo would you like? Let's hear," her mother broke in, the irritable expression on her face probably due more to the cream in the sauce than to her daughter's request.

"A rose. Tiny. Viola's got one."

"Forgive me, but who might Viola be?" her father asked with a bit too much irony.

Alice shook her head, stared at the middle of the table, and felt insignificant.

"Viola's a classmate of hers," Fernanda replied emphatically. "She must have mentioned her a million times. You're not really with it, are you?"

Mr. Della Rocca looked disdainfully at his wife, as if to say no one asked you.

"Well, pardon me, but I don't think I'm all that interested in what Alice's classmates get tattooed on them," he pronounced at last. "At any rate you're not getting a tattoo."

Alice pushed another forkful of spaghetti into her napkin.

"It's not like you can stop me," she ventured, still staring at the vacant center of the table. Her voice cracked with a hint of insecurity.

"Could you repeat that?" her father asked, without altering the volume and calm of his own voice.

"Could you repeat that?" he asked more slowly.

"I said you can't stop me," replied Alice, looking up, but she was unable to endure her father's deep, chilly eyes for more than half a second.

"Is that so? As far as I know, you're fifteen years old and this binds you to the decisions of your parents for—the calculation is a very simple one—another three years," the lawyer intoned. "At the end of which you will be free to, how shall I put it, adorn your skin with flowers, skulls, or whatever you so desire."

The lawyer smiled at his plate and slipped a carefully rolled forkful of spaghetti into his mouth.

There was a long silence. Alice ran her thumb and forefinger along the edge of the tablecloth. Her mother nibbled on a bread stick and allowed her eyes to wander around the dining room. Her father pretended to eat heartily. He chewed with rolling motions of his jaw, and at the first two seconds of each mouthful he kept his eyes closed, in ecstasy.

Alice chose to deliver the blow because she really detested him, and seeing him eat like that made even her good leg go stiff.

"You don't give a damn if no one likes me," she said. "If no one will ever like me."

Her father looked at her quizzically, then returned to his dinner, as if no one had spoken.

"You don't care if you've ruined me forever."

Mr. Della Rocca's fork froze in midair. He looked at his daughter for a few seconds, seemingly distressed.

"I don't know what you're talking about," he said, a slight quaver to his voice.

"You know perfectly well," Alice said. "You know it'll be all your fault if I'm like this forever."

Alice's father rested his fork on the edge of his plate. He covered his eyes with one hand, as if thinking deeply about something. Then he got up and left the room, his heavy footsteps echoing across the gleaming marble hallway.

Fernanda said, oh Alice, with neither compassion nor reproach, just a resigned shake of the head. Then she followed her husband into the next room.

Alice went on staring at her full plate for about two minutes, while Soledad cleared the table, silent as a shadow. Then she stuffed the napkin filled with food into her pocket and locked herself in the bathroom.

4

Pietro Balossino had stopped trying to penetrate his son's obscure universe long ago. When he would accidentally catch sight of Mattia's arms, devastated by scars, he would think back to those sleepless nights spent searching the house for sharp objects left lying around, those nights when Adele, bloated with sedatives, her mouth hanging open, would sleep on the sofa because she no longer wanted to share the bed with him. Those nights when the future seemed to last only till the morning and he would count off the hours, one by one, by the chimes of distant church bells.

The conviction that one morning he would find his son facedown on a blood-soaked pillow had taken root so firmly in his head that he was now used to thinking as if Mattia had already ceased to exist, even at times like this, when he was sitting next to him in the car.

He was driving him to his new school. It was raining, but the rain was so fine that it didn't make a sound.

A few weeks before, the principal of Mattia's science high school had called him and Adele to his office, *to inform them of a situation*. But when the time came for the meeting, he skirted the issue, dwelling instead on the boy's sensitive temperament, his extraordinary intelligence, his solid 90 percent average in all subjects.

Mr. Balossino had insisted on his son being present for the discussion, for reasons of correctness, which doubtless interested him alone. Mattia had sat down next to his parents and throughout the whole session he had not raised his eyes from his knees. By clenching his fists tightly he had managed to make his left hand bleed slightly. Two days before, Adele, in a moment of distraction, had checked only the nails on his other hand.

Mattia listened to the principal's words as if he were not really talking about him, and he remembered that time in the fifth year of primary school when, after not uttering a word for five days in a row, his teacher, Rita, had made him sit in the middle of the room, with all the other kids arranged around him in a horseshoe. The teacher had begun by saying that Mattia clearly had a problem that he didn't want to talk to anyone about. That Mattia was a very intelligent child, perhaps too intelligent for his age. Then she had invited his classmates to sit close to him, so that they could make him understand that they were his friends. Mattia had looked at his feet, and when the teacher asked him if he wanted to say something, he finally opened his mouth and asked if he could go back to his chair.

Once the plaudits were finished, the principal got down to business. What Mr. Balossino finally understood, although only a few hours later, was that all of Mattia's teachers had expressed a peculiar unease, an almost impalpable feeling of inadequacy, with regard to this extraordinarily gifted boy who seemed not to want to form bonds with anyone his age.

The principal paused. He leaned back in his comfortable armchair and opened a folder, which he didn't need to read. Then he closed it again, as if remembering all of a sudden that there were other people in his office. With carefully chosen words he suggested to the Balossinos that perhaps the science high school was not capable of responding fully to their son's needs.

When, at dinner, Mattia's father had asked him if he really wanted to change schools, Mattia had replied with a shrug and studied the dazzling reflection of fluorescent light on the knife with which he was supposed to be cutting his meat.

"It isn't really raining crooked," said Mattia, looking out the car window and jerking his father out of his thoughts.

"What?" said Pietro, instinctively shaking his head.

"There's no wind outside. Otherwise the leaves on the trees would be moving as well," Mattia went on.

His father tried to follow his reasoning. In fact none of it meant anything to him and he suspected that it was merely another of his son's eccentricities.

"So?" he asked.

"The raindrops are running down the window at an angle, but that's just an effect of our motion. By measuring the angle with the vertical, you could also calculate the fall velocity."

Mattia traced the trajectory of a drop with his finger. He brought his face close to the window and breathed on it. Then, with his index finger, he drew a line in the condensation.

"Don't breathe on the windows, you'll leave marks."

Mattia didn't seem to have heard him.

"If we couldn't see anything outside the car, if we didn't know we were moving, there would be no way of telling whether it was the raindrops' fault or our own," said Mattia.

"Fault for what?" his father asked, bewildered and slightly annoyed.

"For them coming down so crooked."

Pietro Balossino nodded seriously, without understanding. They had arrived. He put the car in neutral and pulled on the hand brake. Mattia opened the door and a gust of fresh air blew inside.

"I'll come and get you at one," said Pietro.

Mattia nodded. Mr. Balossino leaned slightly forward to kiss him, but the belt restrained him. He leaned back into the seat and watched his son get out and close the door behind him.

The new school was in a lovely residential area in the hills. It had been built in the Fascist era, and in spite of recent renovations, it remained a blot on the landscape amid a row of sumptuous villas; a parallelepiped of white concrete, with four horizontal rows of evenly spaced windows and two green iron fire escapes.

Mattia climbed the two flights of steps leading to the main door but kept his distance from all the little groups of kids who were waiting for the first bell, getting wet from the rain.

Once inside, he looked for the floor plan with the layout of the classrooms, so that he wouldn't have to ask the janitors for help.

F2 was at the end of the corridor on the second floor. Mattia took a deep breath and entered. He waited, leaning against the back wall, with his thumbs hooked in the straps of his backpack and the look of someone who wanted to disappear into the wall.

As the students were taking their seats, their new faces glanced at him apprehensively. No one smiled at him. Some of them whispered in each other's ears and Mattia was sure they were talking about him.

He kept an eye on the desks that were still free, and when even the one next to a girl with red nail polish was taken, he felt relieved. The teacher came into the classroom and Mattia slipped onto the last empty chair, next to the window.

"Are you the new boy?" asked his neighbor, who looked just as alone as he did.

Mattia nodded without looking at him.

"I'm Denis," he said, extending his hand.

Mattia shook it weakly and said nice to meet you.

"Welcome," said Denis.

5

Viola Bai was admired and feared with equal passion by her classmates, because she was so beautiful she made people uneasy, and
because at the age of fifteen she knew more about life than any of
her contemporaries did; or at least that was the impression she gave.
On Monday mornings, during break, the girls congregated around
her desk and listened greedily to the account of her weekend. Most
times this was a skillful reimagining of what Serena, Viola's older
sister by eight years, had told her the day before. Viola transferred
the stories to herself, but embellished them with sordid, and often
completely invented, details, which to her friends' ears sounded mysterious and disturbing. She talked about this or that bar, without
ever having set foot in them, and she was capable of giving minute
descriptions of the psychedelic lighting, or of the malicious smile
that the bartender had flashed at her as he served her a Cuba libre.

In most cases she ended up either in bed with the bartender or
out behind the bar, among the beer kegs and the cases of vodka,
where he took her from behind, covering her mouth with his hand
to keep her from screaming.

Viola Bai knew how to tell a story. She knew that all the violence
is contained in the precision of a detail. She knew how to work the
timing so that the bell rang just as the bartender was busy with the
fly of his name-brand jeans. At that moment her devoted audience
slowly dispersed, their cheeks red with envy and indignation. Viola
was made to promise that she would go on with her story at the next
bell, but she was too intelligent to actually do it. She always ended
up dismissing the whole thing with a pout of her perfect mouth, as
if what had happened to her was of no importance. It was just one

more detail in her extraordinary life, and she was already light-years ahead of everyone else.

She had actually tried sex, as well as some of the drugs whose names she liked to list, but she had been with only one boy, and only once. It had happened at the shore. A friend of her sister's who had smoked and drunk too much that evening to realize that a little thirteen-year-old girl was too young for certain things. He had fucked her hastily, in the street, behind a trash bin. As they walked back, heads lowered, to rejoin the others, Viola had taken his hand but he had snatched it away and asked what are you doing? Her cheeks burned and the heat still trapped between her legs had made her feel alone. In the days that followed the boy didn't say a word to her and Viola had confided in her sister, who had laughed at her naïveté and said wise up, what did you expect?

Viola's devoted audience was made up of Giada Savarino, Federica Mazzoldi, and Giulia Mirandi. Together they formed a compact and ruthless phalanx: the four bitches, as some of the boys at the school called them. Viola had chosen them one by one and had demanded a little sacrifice from each of them, because her friendship was something you had to earn. She alone decided if you were in or out, and her decisions were obscure and unequivocal.

Alice observed Viola on the sly. From her desk two rows back, she fed off the broken sentences and fragments of torrid tales; then in the evening, alone in her room, she savored every detail.

Before that Wednesday morning Viola had never spoken a word to her. It was a kind of initiation and had to be done properly. None of the girls ever knew for sure whether Viola was improvising or whether she planned the torture in advance—but they all agreed that it was brilliant.

Alice hated the locker room. Her oh-so-perfect classmates stood around for as long as possible in their bras and underwear so as to make the others envious. They assumed stiff, unnatural poses, sucking in their stomachs and thrusting out their tits. They sighed at the cracked mirror that covered one of the walls. Look, they'd say as they sized up their hips, which could not have been better proportioned or more seductive.

On Wednesdays Alice wore her shorts under her jeans so that she wouldn't have to get completely undressed. The others would look at her suspiciously, imagining the horrors that were surely hidden under her clothes. She would turn her back to take off her sweater so they wouldn't see her belly.

She would put on her sneakers and tuck her shoes, neatly parallel, against the wall, and then carefully fold her jeans. Her classmates' clothes, in contrast, tumbled chaotically from the wooden benches, their shoes scattered about and upside down because they had yanked them off with their feet.

"Alice, do you have a sweet tooth?" Viola asked.

It took Alice a few seconds to convince herself that Viola Bai was actually talking to her. She was sure she was invisible to her. She pulled the two ends of her shoelaces, but the knot came untied between her fingers.

"Me?" she asked, looking around uneasily.

"I don't see any other Alices."

The other girls giggled.

"No. Not particularly."

Viola got up from the bench and came closer to her. Alice felt those marvelous eyes on her, bisected by the shadow of her bangs.

"But you like gumdrops, don't you?" Viola continued in her honeyed voice.

"Yeah. I guess. Pretty much."

Alice bit her lip and chided herself for being so wishy-washy. She pressed her bony back against the wall. A tremor ran down her good leg. The other remained inert, as always.

"What do you mean pretty much? Everyone likes gumdrops. Isn't that right, girls?" Viola addressed her three friends without even turning around.

"Mm-hmmm. Everyone," they echoed. Alice noticed a strange trepidation in Federica Mazzoldi's eyes as she stared at her from the other end of the locker room.

"Yes, actually, I do like them," she corrected herself. She was starting to feel frightened, even though she didn't yet know why.

In the first year, the four bitches had grabbed Alessandra Mirano, the one who ended up being thrown out and going to beautician school, and dragged her into the boys' locker room. They shut her inside and two boys pulled their cocks out in front of her. From the corridor Alice had heard the four torturers egging them on and laughing hysterically.

"I thought so. Now, would you like a gumdrop?" Viola asked.

If I say yes, who knows what they're going to make me eat, Alice thought.

If I say no, Viola might get pissed off and I'll end up in the boys' locker room as well.

She sat in silence like a moron.

"Come on. It's not such a hard question," Viola said mockingly. She took a handful of fruit candies from her pocket.

"You girls back there, what flavor do you want?" she asked.

Giulia Mirandi came over to Viola and looked into her hand. Viola didn't take her eyes off Alice, who felt her body crumpling under the gaze like a sheet of newspaper burning in the fireplace.

"There's orange, raspberry, blackberry, strawberry, and peach," Giulia said. She threw a fleeting, apprehensive glance at Alice, without letting Viola see.

"I'll have raspberry," said Federica.

"Peach," said Giada.

Giulia tossed them their candies and unwrapped the orange one for herself. She slipped it into her mouth and then took a step back to return the stage to Viola.

"Blackberry and strawberry are left. So do you want one or not?"

Maybe she just wants to give me a candy, Alice thought.

Maybe they just want to see whether I eat or not.

It's just a candy.

"I prefer strawberry," she said quietly.

"Damn it, that's my favorite too," Viola said, giving a terrible performance of disappointment. "But I'll happily give it to you."

She unwrapped the strawberry candy and let the paper fall to the ground. Alice held out her hand to take it.

"Wait a minute," Viola said. "Don't be so greedy."

She bent down, holding the candy between her thumb and index finger. She rubbed it along the filthy locker room floor. Walking with her knees bent, she dragged it slowly along the whole length of the room to Alice's left, close to the wall, where the dirt had co-agulated in balls of dust and tangles of hair.

Giada and Federica were dying of laughter. Giulia nervously chewed on her lip. The other girls had figured out where things were going and left, closing the door behind them.

When she got to the corner, Viola headed for the sink, where the girls splashed their armpits and faces after gym. With the candy she wiped up the whitish slime that lined the inside of the drain.

Then she turned to Alice and held the revolting object under her nose.

"There," she said. "Strawberry, just what you wanted."

She wasn't laughing. She had the serious, determined look of one who is doing something painful but necessary.

Alice shook her head no. She pressed herself even closer to the wall.

"What? Don't you want it anymore?" Viola asked her.

"Go on," Federica cut in. "You asked for it and now you can eat it."

Alice gulped.

"What if I don't?" she summoned the courage to say.

"If you don't eat it, you'll accept the consequences," Viola replied enigmatically.

"What consequences?"

"You can't know the consequences. Ever."

They want to take me to the boys, Alice thought. Or else they'll strip me and not give me back my clothes.

Trembling, but almost imperceptibly, she held her hand out toward Viola, who dropped the filthy candy into her palm. She slowly brought it to her mouth.

The others had fallen silent, and seemed to be thinking, no, she's not really going to do it. Viola was impassive.

Alice put the gumdrop on her tongue and felt the hairs that were stuck to it dry up her saliva. She chewed only twice and something squeaked between her teeth.

Don't throw up, she thought. Do not throw up.

She choked back an acidic spurt of gastric juices and swallowed the candy. She felt it as it went down, like a stone, along her esophagus.

The fluorescent light on the ceiling gave off an electrical hum and the voices of the kids in the gym were a formless mixture of shouts and laughter. Here in the basement the air was heavy and the windows were too small to allow it to circulate.

Viola stared solemnly at Alice. Without smiling she nodded her head as if to say now we can go. Then she turned around and left the locker room, passing the other three without so much as a glance.

6

There was something important you had to know about Denis. To tell the truth, Denis thought it was the only thing about him worth knowing, so he'd never told anyone.

His secret had a terrible name, which settled like a nylon cloth over his thoughts and wouldn't let them breathe. There it was, weighing heavily inside his head like an inevitable punishment with which he'd have to come to terms sooner or later.

When, at age ten, his piano teacher had guided his fingers through the D major scale, pressing his hot palm on the back of Denis's hand, Denis had been unable to breathe. He bent his torso slightly forward to hide the erection that had exploded in his sweatpants. For his entire life he would think of that moment as true love, and would fumble around every corner of his existence in search of the clinging warmth of his teacher's touch.

Each time memories like this surfaced in his mind, making his neck and hands sweat, Denis would lock himself in the bathroom and masturbate fiercely, sitting backward on the toilet. The pleasure lasted only a moment and radiated just a few inches beyond his penis. But the guilt rained down on him from above like a shower of dirty water. It ran down his skin and nestled in his guts, making everything slowly rot, the way that damp eats away at the walls of an old house.

During biology class, in the basement lab, Denis watched Mattia dissect a piece of steak, separating the white fibers from the red. He wanted to stroke his hands. He wanted to discover whether that cumbersome lump of desire that had taken root in his head would really melt like butter simply through contact with the classmate he was in love with.

They were sitting close to each other. Both rested their forearms on the lab bench. A row of transparent flasks, beakers, and test tubes separated them from the rest of the class and deflected the rays of light, distorting everything beyond that line.

Mattia was intent on his work and hadn't looked up for at least a quarter of an hour. He didn't like biology, but he pursued the task with the same rigor he applied to all subjects. Organic matter, so violable and full of imperfections, was incomprehensible to him. The vital odor of the soft piece of meat aroused nothing in him but a faint disgust.

With a pair of tweezers he extracted a thin white filament and deposited it on the glass slide. He brought his eyes to the microscope and adjusted the focus. He recorded every detail in his squared notebook and made a sketch of the enlarged image.

Denis sighed deeply. Then, as if taking a backward dive, he found the courage to speak.

"Mattia, do you have a secret?" he asked his friend.

Mattia seemed not to have heard, but the scalpel with which he was cutting another section of muscle slipped from his hand and rang out on the metal surface. He slowly picked it up.

Denis waited a few seconds. Mattia sat perfectly still, holding the knife a few inches above the meat.

"You can tell me; you can tell me your secret," Denis went on. His veins pulsed with trepidation. Now that he had pushed himself over the edge and into his classmate's fascinating intimacy, he had no intention of letting go.

"I've got one too, you know," he said.

Mattia cleanly sliced the muscle in half, as if he wanted to kill something that was already dead.

"I don't have any secrets," he said under his breath.

"If you tell me yours, I'll tell you mine," Denis pressed. He moved his stool closer and Mattia visibly stiffened. He stared, expressionless, at the scrap of meat.

"We have to finish the experiment," he said in a monotonous voice. "Otherwise we won't be able to finish the chart."

"I don't give a damn about the chart," said Denis. "Tell me what you did to your hands."

Mattia counted three breaths. Light molecules of ethanol stirred in the air, and some of them penetrated his nostrils. He felt them rising, a pleasant burning sensation along his septum, up to a point between his eyes.

"You really want to know what I've done to my hands?" he asked, turning toward Denis but looking at the jars of formalin lined up behind him: dozens of jars containing fetuses and amputated limbs of all sorts of animals.

Denis nodded, quivering.

"Then watch this," said Mattia.

He gripped the knife in his fist. Then he plunged it into the hollow of his other hand, between his index and middle fingers, and dragged it all the way to his wrist.

7

On Thursday Viola was waiting for her outside the gate. Alice, head lowered, was walking past her when Viola grabbed her by the sleeve. Viola startled her, calling out her name. She remembered the candy and was dizzy with nausea. Once the four bitches had you in their sights, they didn't let you go.

"I've got a math test," Viola said. "I don't know anything and don't want to go."

Alice looked at her uncomprehendingly. She didn't seem hostile, but Alice didn't trust her. She tried to pull away. Let's go for a walk, Viola continued. You and me? Yes, you and me. Alice looked around in terror. Come on, get a move on, Viola urged, they can't see us out here. But . . . Alice tried to object. Viola didn't let her finish; she pulled her harder by the sleeve and Alice had no choice but to follow, hobbling, as they ran to the bus stop.

They sat down side by side, Alice pressed against the window so as not to invade Viola's space. From one moment to the next she expected something to happen, something terrible. But Viola was radiant. She took a lipstick from her bag and ran it over her lips. Want some? she then asked. Alice shook her head. The school shrank in the distance behind them. My father will kill me, Alice mumbled. Her legs were shaking. Viola sighed. Come on, show me your attendance sheet. She studied Alice's father's signature and said it's easy . . . I'll sign it. She showed Alice her own sheet. She faked a signature whenever she didn't feel like going to class. Anyway first period tomorrow is Follini, she said, and she can't see a thing.

Viola started talking about school, about how she didn't give a damn about math because she was going to do law anyway. Alice

49

could hardly believe her ears. She thought about the day before, about the locker room, and didn't know what to call this sudden intimacy.

They got off in the square and started walking under the arcades. Viola stopped at a clothing shop with fluorescent windows where Alice had never even set foot. She was acting as if they were lifelong friends. She insisted they try on some clothes, which she picked out herself. She asked Alice her size, and Alice was ashamed to tell her. The shop assistants watched them suspiciously, but Viola paid no attention. They shared a dressing room and Alice surreptitiously compared her own body with her friend's. In the end they didn't buy anything.

They went to a café and Viola ordered two coffees, without so much as asking Alice what she wanted. Alice hadn't a clue what was going on, but a new and unexpected happiness was filling her head. Slowly she forgot all about her father and school. She was sitting in a café with Viola Bai and that time seemed theirs alone.

Viola smoked three cigarettes and insisted that Alice try one too. Viola laughed, showing her perfect teeth, every time her new friend exploded in a fit of coughing. She subjected her to a little quiz about the boys she hadn't had and the kisses she hadn't given. Alice replied with her eyes lowered. You want me to believe you've never had a boyfriend? Never ever ever? Alice shook her head. That's impossible. A tragedy, Viola exaggerated. We absolutely have to do something. You don't want to die a virgin!

So the next day, at ten o'clock break, they roamed the school in search of the boyfriend for Alice. Viola had dismissed Giada and the others, saying we've got things to do, and they watched her leave the classroom hand in hand with her new friend.

Viola had already organized everything. It would happen at her birthday party the following Saturday. They just had to find the right boy. As they walked down the corridor she pointed this and that out to Alice, saying look at the ass on that one, not bad at all, he certainly knows what to do.

Alice smiled nervously but couldn't make her mind up. In her head she imagined with unsettling clarity the moment when a boy would slip his hands under her shirt. When he would discover that, underneath the clothes that fell so well, there was nothing but chubby flesh and flabby skin.

Now they were leaning on the fire escape railing on the third floor, watching the boys play football in the courtyard with a yellow ball that seemed not to be blown up enough.

"What about Trivero?" Viola asked.

"I don't know who he is."

"What do you mean you don't know who he is? He's in the fifth year. He used to row with my sister. They say some interesting things about him."

"What sort of things?"

Viola gestured with her hands, indicating something long, and then laughed loudly, enjoying the disconcerting effect of her allusions. Alice felt her face flush with shame, but she also felt a marvelous certainty that her loneliness was truly over.

They went down to the ground floor and passed the snacks and drinks machines. Students had formed a chaotic line, chinking the coins in their jeans pockets.

"Okay, but you've got to decide," said Viola.

Alice spun on her heels. She looked around, disoriented.

"That one looks cute," she said, pointing at two boys in the distance, near the window. They were standing close together, but they weren't talking or looking at each other.

"Who?" Viola asked. "The one with the bandage or the other one?"

"The one with the bandage."

Viola stared at her. Her sparkling eyes were as wide as two oceans.

"You're crazy," she said. "You know what he did?"

Alice shook her head.

"He stuck a knife in his hand, on purpose. Right here at school."

Alice shrugged.

"He looks interesting," she said.

"Interesting? He's a psychopath. With a guy like that you'll end up chopped to pieces and stuffed in a freezer."

Alice smiled, but went on looking at the boy with the bandaged hand. There was something in the way he kept his head tilted down that made her want to go over to him, lift his chin, and say to him look at me, I'm here.

"Are you absolutely sure?" Viola asked her.

"Yes," said Alice.

Viola shrugged.

"So let's go," she said.

She took Alice by the hand and pulled her toward the two boys at the window.

8

Mattia was looking out the opaque windows of the atrium. It was a bright day, an anticipation of spring at the beginning of March. The strong wind that had cleared the air during the night seemed to sweep time away too, making it run faster. Mattia tried to estimate how far away the horizon was by counting the roofs of the houses that he could see from there.

Denis was surreptitiously staring at him, trying to guess his thoughts. They hadn't talked about what had happened in the biology lab. In fact, they didn't talk much at all, but they spent time together, each in his own abyss, held safe and tight by the other's silence.

"Hi," Mattia heard someone say, too close to him.

Reflected in the glass he saw two girls standing behind him, holding hands. He turned around.

Denis looked at him quizzically. The girls seemed to be waiting for something.

"Hi," Mattia said softly. He lowered his head, to protect himself from one of the girls' piercing eyes.

"I'm Viola and this is Alice," she continued. "We're in 2B."

Mattia nodded. Denis's mouth fell open. Neither of them said anything.

"Well?" Viola said. "Aren't you going to introduce yourselves?"

Mattia spoke his name in a low voice, as if just remembering it himself. He offered Viola a limp hand, the one without the bandage, and she shook it firmly. The other girl barely touched it and smiled, looking in another direction.

Denis introduced himself next, just as clumsily.

"We wanted to invite you to my birthday party the Saturday after next," said Viola.

Again Denis sought Mattia's eyes, but Mattia responded by staring at Alice's timid half-smile. Her lips seemed so pale and thin to him, as if her mouth had been carved by a sharp scalpel.

"Why?" he asked.

Viola looked at him askance and then turned to Alice, with an expression that said I told you he was mad.

"What do you mean why? Obviously because we feel like inviting you."

"No, thanks," said Mattia. "I can't come."

Denis, relieved, quickly added that he couldn't come either.

Viola ignored him and concentrated on the boy with the bandage.

"You can't? I wonder what could be keeping you so busy on a Saturday evening," she said provocatively. "Do you have to play video games with your little friend? Or were you planning on cutting your veins again?"

Viola felt a tremor of terror and excitement as she uttered those last words. Alice gripped her hand harder to make her stop.

Mattia reflected that he had forgotten the number of roofs and wouldn't have time to count them again before the bell.

"I don't like parties," he explained.

Viola forced herself to laugh for a few seconds, a sequence of piercing, high-pitched giggles.

"You really are strange," she teased, tapping her right temple. "Everyone likes parties."

Alice had withdrawn her hand and unconsciously rested it on her belly.

"Well, I don't," Mattia snapped back.

Viola stared defiantly at him and he blankly held her gaze. Alice had taken a step back. Viola opened her mouth to give some kind of reply, but the bell rang just in time. Mattia turned around and headed resolutely toward the stairs, as if to say that as far as he was concerned the discussion was over. Denis followed, pulled along in his wake.

9

Since entering the service of the Della Rocca family, Soledad Galienas had slipped up only once. Four years ago, one rainy evening when the Della Roccas were out to dinner at a friend's.

Soledad's wardrobe contained only black clothes, underwear included. She had spoken so often of her husband's death in a work accident that she sometimes even believed it herself. She imagined him standing on a scaffolding sixty feet off the ground, cigarette between his teeth, as he leveled a layer of mortar before laying another row of bricks. She saw him trip over a tool or perhaps a coil of rope, the rope with which he was supposed to make a harness and which instead he had tossed aside because harnesses are for softies. She imagined him wobbling on the wooden planks before plummeting without a sound. The image panned out so that her husband became like a little black dot waving its arms against the white sky. Then her artificial memory ended with an overhead shot: her husband's body splattered on the dusty ground of the building site, lifeless and two-dimensional, his eyes still open and a dark pool of blood oozing out from under his back.

Thinking of him like that gave her a pleasurable tremor of anguish, and if she dwelled on it long enough, she even managed to squeeze out a few tears, which were entirely for herself.

The truth was that her husband had walked out. He had left her one morning, probably to start his life over again with a woman she didn't even know. She had never heard anything more about him. When she arrived in Italy she made up the story of her widowhood to have a past to tell people about, because there was nothing to say about her real past. Her black clothes and the thought that others might see the traces of a tragedy in her eyes, a pain that had never been assuaged, gave her a sense of security. She wore her mourning with dignity, and until that evening she had never betrayed the memory of the deceased.

On Saturdays she went to six o'clock mass, in order to be back in time for dinner. Ernesto had been courting her for weeks. After the service he stood waiting for her in the courtyard and, always with the same precise degree of ceremony, offered to walk her home. Soledad shrank into her black dress, but in the end she gave in. He told her about the post office where he used to work, and how long the evenings were now, at home alone, with so many years behind him and so many ghosts to reckon with. Ernesto was older than Soledad and his wife really had died, carried off by pancreatic cancer.

They walked arm in arm, very composed. That evening Ernesto had shared his umbrella with her, allowing his head and coat to get soaked so as to shelter her better from the rain. He had complimented her on her Italian, which was getting better week by week, and Soledad had laughed, pretending to be embarrassed.

It was thanks to a certain clumsiness, a lack of coordination, that instead of saying good-bye to each other as friends, with two chaste kisses on the cheek, their mouths had met on the front step of the Della Rocca house. Ernesto apologized, but then he bent over her lips again and Soledad felt all the dust that had settled in her heart whirl up and get in her eyes.

She was the one to invite him in. Ernesto had to stay hidden in her room for a few hours, just long enough for her to give Alice something to eat and send her to bed. The Della Roccas would be going out soon and wouldn't be back till late.

Ernesto thanked someone up above for the fact that such things could still happen at his age. They entered the house furtively, Soledad leading her lover by the hand, like a teenager, and with her finger to her mouth she told him not to make a sound. Then she hastily made dinner for Alice, watched her eat it too slowly, and said you look tired, you should go to bed. Alice protested that she wanted to watch television and Soledad gave in, just to get rid of her, as long as she watched it up in the den. Alice went upstairs, taking advantage of her father's absence to drag her feet as she walked.

Soledad returned to her lover. They kissed for a long time, sitting side by side, not knowing what to do with their own hands, clumsy and out of practice. Then Ernesto plucked up the courage to pull her to him.

As he fiddled with the devilish hooks that fastened her bra, apologizing under his breath for being so clumsy, she felt young and beautiful and uninhibited. She closed her eyes, and when she opened them again she saw Alice, standing in the doorway.

"Coño," she blurted out. *"¿Qué haces aquí?"*

She slipped away from Ernesto and covered her bosom with one arm. Alice tilted her head to one side and observed them without surprise, as if they were animals in a zoo.

"I can't get to sleep," she said.

By some mysterious coincidence Soledad was remembering that very moment when, turning around, she saw Alice standing in the study doorway. Soledad was dusting the library. Three at a time she pulled the lawyer's encyclopedia, the heavy volumes with dark green binding and gilded spines, off the shelf. While she held them with her left arm, which was already beginning to ache, with her right she dusted the mahogany surfaces, even in the most hidden corners, because the lawyer had once complained that she only pushed the dust around.

It was years since Alice had entered her father's study. An invisible barrier of hostility kept her frozen in the doorway. She was sure that if she placed so much as a toe on the regular, hypnotic geometry of the parquet, the wood would crack under her weight and send her plunging into a black abyss.

The whole room was saturated with her father's intense smell. It had seeped into the papers stacked neatly on the desk, and drenched the thick, cream-colored curtains. When she was little, Alice would tiptoe in and call her father for dinner. She always hesitated for a moment before speaking, enchanted by her father's posture as he loomed over his desk studying complicated documents from behind his silver-framed glasses. When the lawyer realized his daughter was there, he slowly lifted up his head and frowned, as if to ask what she was doing there. Then he nodded and gave her a hint of a smile. I'm coming, he said.

Alice was sure that she could hear those words echoing against the wallpaper in the study, trapped forever in these four walls and inside her head.

"*Hola, mi amorcito,*" said Soledad. She still called her that, even though the pencil-thin girl standing in front of her was a far cry from the sleepy child she used to dress and walk to school every morning.

"Hi," replied Alice.

Soledad looked at her for a few seconds, waiting for her to say something, but Alice glanced away nervously. Soledad returned to her shelves.

"Sol," Alice said at last.

"Yes?"

"I have to ask you something."

Soledad set the books down on the desk and walked over to Alice.

"What is it, *mi amorcito?*"

"I need a favor."

"What sort of favor? Of course, tell me."

Alice rolled the elastic of her trousers around her index finger.

"On Saturday I have to go to a party. At my friend Viola's house."

"Oh, how lovely," said Soledad, smiling.

"I'd like to bring a dessert. I'd like to make it myself. Would you help me?"

"Of course, darling. What sort of dessert?"

"I don't know. A cake. Or a tiramisù. Or that one that you make with cinnamon."

"My mother's recipe," said Soledad with a hint of pride. "I'll teach you."

Alice looked at her pleadingly.

"So we'll go shopping together on Saturday? Even though it's your day off?"

"Of course, dear," said Soledad. For a moment she felt important, and she recognized in Alice's insecurity the little girl she had raised.

"Could you take me somewhere else as well?" Alice ventured.

"Where?"

Alice hesitated for a moment.

"To get a tattoo," she said hastily.

"Oh, *mi amorcito*." Soledad sighed, vaguely disappointed. "You know your father doesn't want you to."

"We won't tell him. He'll never see it," Alice insisted with a whine.

Soledad shook her head.

"Come on, Sol, please," she begged. "I can't get it done on my own. I need my parents' permission."

"So what can I do?"

"You can pretend to be my mother. You'll only have to sign a piece of paper, you won't have to say anything."

"But I can't, my dear, I can't. Your father would fire me."

Alice suddenly grew more serious. She looked Soledad straight in the eyes.

"It'll be our secret, Sol." She paused. "After all, the two of us already have a secret, don't we?"

Soledad looked at her, puzzled. At first she didn't understand.

"I know how to keep secrets," Alice continued slowly. She felt as strong and ruthless as Viola. "Otherwise he'd have fired you ages ago."

Soledad was suddenly unable to breathe.

"But—" she said.

"So you'll do it?" Alice cut in.

Soledad looked at the floor.

"Okay," she said quietly. Then she turned her back on Alice and arranged the books on the shelf while her eyes filled with two fat tears.

Mattia deliberately made all his movements as silently as he could. He knew that the chaos of the world would only increase, that the background noise would grow until it covered every coherent signal, but he was convinced that by carefully measuring his every gesture he would be less guilty of that slow ruin.

He had learned to set down first his toe and then his heel, keeping his weight toward the outside of the sole to minimize the amount of surface area in contact with the ground. He had perfected this technique years before, when he would get up in the night and stealthily roam about the house, the skin of his hands having become so dry that the only way to know they were still his was to pass a knife over them. Over time that strange, circumspect gait had become his normal way of walking.

His parents would often find themselves suddenly face-to-face with him, like a hologram projected from the floor, a frown on his face and his mouth always tightly shut. Once his mother dropped a plate with fright. Mattia bent down to pick up the bits, but resisted the temptation of those sharp edges. His mother, embarrassed, thanked him, and when he left she sat on the floor and stayed there for a quarter of an hour, defeated.

Mattia turned the key in the front door. He had learned that by turning the handle toward himself and pressing his palm over the keyhole, he could eliminate almost entirely the metallic click of the lock. With the bandage on it was even easier.

He slipped into the hallway, put the keys back in again, and repeated the operation from inside, like a burglar in his own home.

His father was already home, earlier than usual. When he heard him raise his voice he froze, unsure whether to cross the sitting room and interrupt his parents' conversation or go out again and wait until he saw the living room light go out from the courtyard.

"I don't think it's right," his father concluded with a note of reproach in his voice.

"Right," Adele shot back. "You'd rather pretend nothing is wrong, act as if nothing strange were going on."

"And what's so strange?"

There was a pause. Mattia could picture his mother lowering her head and wrinkling up one corner of her mouth as if to say it's pointless trying to talk with you.

"What's so strange?" she repeated emphatically. "I don't . . ."

Mattia kept a step back from the ray of light that spilled from the sitting room into the hall. With his eyes he followed the line of shadow from the floor to the walls and then to the ceiling. He realized that it formed a trapezoid, only one more trick of perspective.

His mother often abandoned her sentences halfway through, as if she had forgotten what she was going to say as she was saying it. Those interruptions left bubbles of emptiness in her eyes and in the air and Mattia always imagined bursting them with a finger.

"What's strange is that he stuck a knife in his hand in front of all his classmates. What's strange is that we were convinced those days were over but we were wrong once again," his mother went on.

Mattia had no reaction when he realized that they were talking about him, just a mild sense of guilt at eavesdropping on a conversation he wasn't supposed to hear.

"That's not reason enough to go and talk to his teachers without him," his father said, but in a more moderate tone. "He's old enough to have the right to be there."

"For God's sake, Pietro," his mother exploded. She never called him by name. "That's not the point, don't you understand? Will you stop treating him as if he were—"

She froze. The silence stuck in the air like static electricity. A slight shock made Mattia's back contract.

"As if he were what?"

"Normal," his mother confessed. Her voice trembled slightly and Mattia wondered if she was crying. Then again, she cried often since that afternoon. Most of the time for no reason. Sometimes she cried because the meat she had cooked was stringy or because the plants on the balcony were full of parasites. Whatever the reason, her despair was always the same. As if, in any case, there were nothing to be done.

"His teachers say he has no friends. He only talks to the boy who sits next to him and he spends the whole day with him. Boys his age go out in the evening, try to hook up with girls—"

"You don't think he's . . ." his father interrupted. "Well, you know . . ."

Mattia tried to complete the sentence, but nothing came to mind.

"No, that's not what I think. Maybe I wish that's all it was," said his mother. "Sometimes I think that something of Michela ended up in him."

His father let out a deep, loud sigh.

"You promised not to talk about that anymore," he said, vaguely irritated.

Mattia thought of Michela, who had disappeared into thin air. But only for a fraction of a second. Then he let himself be distracted by the faint image of his parents, who, he discovered, were reflected in miniature on the smooth, curved surfaces of the umbrella stand. He started scratching his left elbow with his keys. He felt the joint twitching from one tooth to the next.

"Do you know what really makes me shiver?" said Adele. "All those high grades he gets. Always the highest. There's something frightening in those grades."

Mattia heard his mother sniff, once. She sniffed again, but now it sounded as if her nose were pressed up against something. He imagined his father taking her in his arms, in the middle of the living room.

"He's fifteen," said his father. "It's a cruel age."

His mother didn't reply and Mattia listened to those rhythmic sobs rising to a peak of intensity and then slowly ebbing, finally growing silent again.

At that point he walked into the living room. He closed his eyes slightly as he entered the beam of light. He stopped two steps away from his hugging parents, who looked at him in alarm, like two kids caught necking. Stamped on their faces was the question, how long had he been out there?

Mattia looked at a point midway between them. He said, simply, I do have friends, I'm going to a party on Saturday. Then he continued toward the hall and disappeared into his room.

The tattoo artist had eyed suspiciously first Alice and then the woman with the too dark skin and the frightened expression whom the girl had introduced as her mother. He didn't believe it for a second, but it was none of his business. He was used to tricks of that kind, and he was used to capricious teenage girls. They were getting younger and younger: this one couldn't be as much as seventeen, he thought. But he certainly wasn't in a position to refuse a job for a question of principle. He'd shown the woman to a chair, and she'd sat down and hadn't said another word. She had gripped her purse tightly in her hands, as if ready to leave at any moment, and looked everywhere except in the direction of the needle.

The girl hadn't flinched. He had asked does it hurt, because that's something you have to ask, but she had said no, no through clenched teeth.

He had recommended that she keep the gauze on for at least three days and to clean the wound morning and evening for a week. He had given her a jar of Vaseline and stuffed the money in his pocket.

Back home in the bathroom, Alice took off the white tape that held the bandage on. Her tattoo had been in existence for only a few hours and she had already peeked at it a dozen times. Each time she looked, a bit of the excitement dispersed, like a pool of shimmering water that evaporates beneath the August sun. This time she thought only of how red her skin had turned, all the way around the design. She wondered if her skin would ever regain its natural color and for a moment her throat tightened with panic. Then she banished that stupid anxiety. She hated the fact that her every action always had

66

to seem so irremediable, so definitive. In her mind she called it *the weight of consequences,* and she was sure that it was another awkward piece of her father that had wormed its way into her brain. How she longed for the uninhibitedness of kids her age, their vacuous sense of immortality. She yearned for all the lightness of her fifteen years, but in trying to grasp it she became aware of the fury with which the time at her disposal was slipping away. The weight of consequences was becoming more and more unbearable and her thoughts began whirling faster and faster, in ever smaller circles.

She had changed her mind at the last moment. That was what she had said to the young man who had already turned on the whizzing machine and was bringing the needle to her belly: I've changed my mind. Unsurprised, he had asked her don't you want to do it anymore? Alice had said yes I want to. But I don't want a rose. I want a violet.

The tattooist had looked at her, puzzled. Then he had confessed that he didn't exactly know what a violet looked like. It's kind of like a daisy, Alice had explained, only with three petals at the top and two at the bottom. And it's violet in color. The tattooist had said okay and set to work.

Alice looked at the livid little flower that now framed her navel and wondered if Viola would understand that it was for her, for their friendship. She decided she wouldn't show it to her till Monday. She wanted to present it without any scabs, bright against her pale skin. She chided herself for not doing it earlier, so that it would have been ready for tonight. She imagined what it would be like to show it secretly to that boy she'd invited to the party. Two days before, Mattia had appeared in front of her and Viola, with that sunken air of his. Denis and I are coming to the party, he had said. Viola hadn't even had time to come up with an unpleasant remark before he was already at the far end of the hall, his back turned to them and head lowered.

She wasn't sure she wanted to kiss him, but it was all decided now and she would look like an idiot in front of Viola if she backed down.

She measured the precise point where the top of her underpants had to come to be able to see the tattoo but not the scar immediately below it. She slipped on a pair of jeans, a T-shirt, and a sweatshirt big enough to cover the lot—the tattoo, the scar, and the bumps of her hips—and then left the bathroom, to join Soledad in the kitchen and watch her make her special cinnamon dessert.

12

Denis took deep, long breaths, trying to fill his lungs with the smell of Pietro Balossino's car. A slightly sour smell of sweat, which seemed to emanate not so much from the people as from the fireproof seat covers, and from something damp that had been sitting there too long, perhaps hidden under the mats. Denis felt the mixture wrap around his face like a hot bandage.

He would happily have spent all night in that car, driving around the half-dark streets of the hill, watching the lights of the cars in the opposite lane strike his friend's face and then return it to the shadows, unharmed.

Mattia was sitting in the front, beside his father. To Denis, who had been secretly studying the absence of any expression on both their faces, it seemed that father and son had agreed not to utter a single word during the whole journey, and to ensure that their eyes didn't meet even by accident.

He noticed that they had the same way of holding objects, framing them with their fingers tensed, touching surfaces but not really resting on them, as if they feared deforming whatever they held in their hands. Mr. Balossino seemed to barely touch the steering wheel. Mattia's frightful hands traced the edges of the present that his mother had bought for Viola and which he now held on his knees.

"So you're in the same class as Mattia," Mr. Balossino forced himself to say, though without much conviction.

"Yeah," said Denis, in a shrill voice that seemed to have been trapped for too long in his throat. "We sit next to each other."

Mattia's father nodded seriously and then, his conscience assuaged, he returned to his thoughts. Mattia seemed not even to have noticed

69

that scrap of conversation and didn't take his eyes off the window, through which he was trying to work out whether his perception that the dotted white line in the middle of the road was in fact a continuous line was due merely to his eye's slow response or to some more complicated mechanism.

Pietro Balossino braked a few feet away from the big gate of the Bai family's property and put on the hand brake as they were on a slight incline.

"She's pretty well off, your friend," he observed, leaning forward to see over the top of the gate.

Neither Denis nor Mattia admitted that they barely knew the girl's name.

"So I'll come back for you at midnight, okay?"

"Eleven," Mattia replied quickly. "Let's make it eleven."

"Eleven? But it's already nine o'clock. What are you going to do for only two hours?"

"Eleven," insisted Mattia.

Pietro Balossino shook his head and said okay.

Mattia got out of the car and Denis did likewise, reluctantly. He was worried that Mattia might make new friends at the party, fun, fashionable friends who, in the bat of an eye, would take him away forever. He was worried that he would never get into that car again.

He politely said good-bye to Mattia's father and, to seem like a grown-up, held out his hand. Pietro Balossino performed a clumsy acrobatic maneuver to shake it without unfastening his seat belt.

The boys stood stiffly at the gate and waited for the car to turn around before deciding to ring the bell.

Alice was crouching at one end of the white sofa. A glass of Sprite in her hand, from the corner of her eye she was peeking at Sara Turletti's voluminous thighs, crammed into a pair of dark tights.

Squashed onto the sofa they became even bigger, almost twice as broad. Alice thought about the space she occupied compared to her classmate. The idea of being able to become so thin as to be invisible gave her a pleasant pang in the stomach.

When Mattia and Denis came into the room, she suddenly stiffened her back and looked around desperately for Viola. She noticed that Mattia wasn't wearing a bandage anymore and tried to see if he had a scar on his wrist. She instinctively ran her index finger along the trace of her own scar. She knew how to find it even under her clothes; it was like an earthworm lying against her skin.

The boys looked around like hunted prey, but in truth not one of the thirty or so kids scattered around the room paid them the least attention. No one except Alice.

Denis followed Mattia's movements, going where he went and looking where he looked. Mattia walked over to Viola, who was busy telling one of her made-up stories to a group of girls. He didn't even ask himself whether he'd ever seen those girls at school. He stood behind the birthday girl, holding the present stiffly to his chest. Viola turned around when she noticed that her friends had taken their eyes off her irresistible mouth and were looking instead over her shoulder.

"Ah, you're here," she said rudely.

"Here," said Mattia, placing the present in her arms. Then he added a mumbled happy birthday.

He was about to go when Viola shouted in an overexcited voice, "Alice, Alice, come quickly. Your friend's here."

Denis swallowed the lump in his throat. One of Viola's little friends cackled into another girl's ear.

Alice got up from the sofa. In the four paces that separated her from the group she tried to mask her syncopated gait, but she was sure that that was what they were all looking at.

She greeted Denis with a quick smile and then Mattia, bowing her head and saying hi in a faint voice. Mattia said hi back and his eyebrows jerked, making him appear even more spastic in Viola's eyes.

There followed an uncomfortably long silence that only she was able to break.

"I've discovered where my sister keeps the pills," she said, beaming. "Do you want some?"

She aimed her question at Mattia, certain that he wouldn't have the slightest idea what she was talking about. She was right.

"Girls, come with me, let's go get them," she said. "You too, Alice."

She took Alice by an arm and the five girls jostled one another as they disappeared down the hall.

Denis was alone with Mattia again and his heartbeat resumed its regular frequency. They both walked over to the drinks table.

"There's whiskey," Denis observed, slightly shocked. "And vodka too."

Mattia didn't reply. He took a plastic cup from the stack and filled it to the brim with Coca-Cola, trying to get as close as possible to that limit where the surface tension of the liquid prevents it from spilling over. Then he set it down on the table. Denis poured himself some whiskey, looking cautiously around and hoping secretly to impress Mattia, who didn't even notice.

Two rooms away, the girls had sat Alice down on Viola's sister's bed to instruct her about what to do.

"No blow jobs. Not even if he asks you, understand?" advised Giada Savarino. "The first time the max you can do is a hand job."

Alice laughed nervously and couldn't work out whether Giada was being serious.

"Now, you go back in there and start talking to him," explained Viola, who had a plan in mind and a very clear one. "Then you come up with an excuse to take him to my room, okay?"

"And what excuse am I supposed to come up with?"

"How do I know? Anything. Tell him you're fed up with the music and you want some peace and quiet."

"What about his friend? He's always glued to him," Alice said.

"We'll take care of him," said Viola with her most ruthless smile.

She climbed onto her sister's bed, trampling the light green cover with her shoes. Alice thought of her father, who wouldn't even let her walk on the carpet with her shoes on. For a second she wondered what he would have said if he had seen her there, but then she swallowed back the thought.

Viola opened a drawer in the cupboard above the bed. She rummaged around, not tall enough to see inside, and took out a little box covered with red fabric, adorned with gilded Chinese characters.

"Take this," she said. She held her hand out toward Alice. In the middle of her palm was a bright blue pill, square and with rounded corners. Carved in the center was a butterfly. For a second Alice saw the filthy fruit gumdrop she had accepted from that very same hand and felt it trapped in her throat again.

"What is it?" she asked.

"Take it. You'll have more fun."

Viola winked. Alice thought for a moment. They were all looking at her. She thought this must be another test. She took the pill from Viola's hand and placed it on her tongue.

"You're ready," Viola said with satisfaction. "Let's go."

The girls left the room single file, all looking down and with wicked smiles on their faces. Federica pleaded with Viola, please, let me have one too. And Viola brusquely told her wait your turn.

Alice was the last to leave. When all their backs were turned, she brought a hand to her mouth and spat out the pill. She put it in her pocket and turned out the light.

13

Like four beasts of prey, Viola, Giada, Federica, and Giulia surrounded Denis.

"Will you come with us?" Viola asked.

"Why?"

"We'll explain why later," Viola cackled.

Denis froze. He sought Mattia's help, but Mattia was still absorbed in the quivering Coca-Cola. The loud music that filled the room made the surface jerk with each beat of the bass drum. Mattia waited with strange trepidation for the moment when it would spill over the rim.

"I'd rather stay here," said Denis.

"God, how boring you are," Viola said, losing her patience. "You're coming with us and that's that."

She pulled him by the arm. Denis resisted feebly. Then Giada started pulling as well and he gave in. As they were pushing him into the kitchen, he looked once more at his friend, who was still motionless.

Mattia became aware of Alice's presence when she rested a hand on the table: the tension broke and a thin layer of liquid spilled over the rim and settled around the base in a dark ring.

He instinctively looked up and met her gaze.

"How's it going?" she asked.

Mattia nodded. "Fine," he said.

"Do you like the party?"

"Mmm."

"Music this loud gives me a headache."

Alice waited for Mattia to say something. She looked at him and it seemed to her that he wasn't breathing. His eyes were meek and pain-stricken. Like the first time, she suddenly wanted to draw those eyes toward her, to take Mattia's head in her hands and tell him everything would be okay.

"Will you come into the other room with me?" she ventured.

Mattia looked at the floor, as if he had been waiting for those very words.

"Okay," he said.

Alice headed down the hall and he followed a short distance behind. Mattia, as always, kept his head down and looked in front of him. He noticed that Alice's right leg bent gracefully at the knee, like every other leg in the world, and her foot brushed the floor without a sound. Her left leg, on the other hand, remained stiff. To push it forward she had to make it do a little arc outward. For a fraction of a second her pelvis was unbalanced, as if she were about to topple sideways. At last her left foot touched the ground as well, heavily, like a crutch.

Mattia concentrated on that gyroscopic rhythm, and without realizing it he synchronized his steps with hers.

When they got to Viola's room, Alice sidled up next to him and, with a daring that startled even her, closed the door. They were standing, he on the rug and she just off it.

Why doesn't he say anything? Alice wondered.

For a moment she wanted to drop the whole thing, to open the door again and leave, to breathe normally.

But what would I tell Viola? she thought.

"It's better in here, isn't it?" she said.

"Yeah," Mattia agreed, nodding. His arms dangled at his sides like a ventriloquist's dummy. With his right index finger he was folding a short, hard bit of skin that stuck out from beside his thumbnail. It was almost like piercing himself with a needle and the sting distracted him for a moment from the charged air in the room.

Alice sat on Viola's bed, balancing on the edge. The mattress didn't dip beneath her weight. She looked around, searching for something.

"Why don't you sit down here?" she asked Mattia at last.

He obeyed, sitting down carefully, about a foot away from her. The music in the living room sounded like the heavy, panting breath of the walls. Alice noticed Mattia's hands, clenched into fists.

"Is your hand better?" she asked.

"Nearly," he said.

"How did you do it?"

"I cut myself. In the biology lab. By accident."

"Can I see?"

Mattia tightened his fists still further. Then he slowly opened his left hand. A furrow, light in shade and perfectly straight, cut it diagonally. Around it, Alice made out scars that were shorter and paler, almost white. They filled the whole of his palm, intersecting like the branches of a leafless tree seen against the light.

"I've got one too, you know," she said.

Mattia clenched his fist again and trapped his hand between his legs, as if to hide it. Alice stood up, lifted her sweatshirt slightly, and unbuttoned her jeans. He was seized by panic. He turned his eyes to the floor, but still managed to see Alice's hands folding back the edge of her trousers, revealing a piece of white gauze framed by Scotch tape and, just below it, the top of a pair of pale gray underpants.

Alice lowered the elastic band a couple of inches and Mattia held his breath.

"Look," she said.

A long scar ran along her protruding pelvis bone. It was thick and in relief, and wider than Mattia's. The marks from the stitches, which intersected it perpendicularly and at regular intervals, made it look like the kind of scar children draw on their faces when they dress up as pirates.

Mattia couldn't think what to say. Alice buttoned up her jeans and tucked her undershirt inside them. Then she sat down again, a little closer to him.

The silence was almost unbearable for both of them, the empty space between their faces overflowing with expectation and embarrassment.

"Do you like your new school?" Alice asked, for the sake of saying something.

"Yes."

"They say you're a genius."

Mattia sucked in his cheeks and bit into them till he felt the metallic taste of blood filling his mouth.

"Do you really like studying?"

Mattia nodded.

"Why?"

"It's the only thing I know how to do," he said shortly. He wanted to tell her that he liked studying because you can do it alone, because all the things you study are already dead, cold, and chewed over. He wanted to tell her that the pages of the schoolbooks were all the same temperature, that they left you time to choose, that they never hurt you and you couldn't hurt them either. But he said nothing.

"And do you like me?" Alice went for it. Her voice came out rather shrilly and her face exploded with heat.

"I don't know," Mattia answered hastily, looking at the floor.

"Why?"

"I don't know," he insisted. "I haven't thought about it."

"You don't need to think about it."

"If I don't think, I can't understand anything."

"I like you," said Alice. "A bit. I think."

He nodded. He played at contracting and relaxing his retina, to make the geometric design of the carpet go in and out of focus.

"Do you want to kiss me?" Alice asked. She wasn't ashamed, but as she said it her empty stomach curled with terror that he might say no.

Mattia didn't move for a few seconds. Then he shook his head, slowly, still staring at the swirls in the carpet.

With a nervous impulse, Alice brought her hands to her hips and measured the circumference of her waist.

"It doesn't matter," she said quickly, in a different voice. "Please don't tell anyone," she added.

You're an idiot, she thought. Worse than a girl in kindergarten.

She stood up. Suddenly Viola's room seemed like a strange, hostile place. She felt herself becoming intoxicated by all the colors on the walls, the desk covered with makeup, the toe shoes hanging from the closet door, like a pair of severed feet, the big photo of Viola at the beach, lying on the sand looking beautiful, the cassettes stacked haphazardly beside the stereo, and the clothes piled up on the armchair.

"Let's go back," she said.

Mattia got up from the bed. He looked at her for a moment, apologetically, it seemed to her. She opened the door, letting the music flood the room. She walked partway down the hall alone. Then she thought of Viola's face. She turned around, took Mattia's stiff hand without asking his permission, and together they walked into the noisy living room.

14

The girls had trapped Denis in the corner, near the fridge, so as to have a little fun. They had arranged themselves in front of him, forming a barrier of excited eyes and flowing hair, through which he could no longer see Mattia in the other room.

"Truth or dare?" Viola asked him.

Denis shook his head timidly, to say that he didn't feel like playing this game. Viola rolled her eyes and then opened the fridge, forcing Denis to lean to the side to make room for the door. She pulled out a bottle of peach vodka and took a gulp, without bothering to find a glass. Then she offered him some, with a complicit smile.

He already felt dizzy and a little nauseated. The whiskey had left a bitter aftertaste suspended between his nose and his mouth, but there was something in Viola's behavior that prevented him from objecting. He took the bottle and took a sip. Then he passed it to Giada Savarino, who grabbed it greedily and started to pour it down her throat as if it were orangeade.

"So. Truth or dare?" repeated Viola. "Otherwise we'll choose."

"I don't like this game," Denis objected unconvincingly.

"Mmm, you and your friend really are a drag," she said. "Then I'll choose. Truth. Let's see."

She rested her index finger on her chin and with her eyes traced an imaginary circle on the ceiling, pretending to be deep in thought.

"I know!" she exclaimed. "You have to tell us which one of us you like best."

Denis shrugged, intimidated.

"Dunno," he said.

"What do you mean, dunno? You must like at least one of us, right?"

Denis thought he didn't like any of them, that he just wanted them to get out of his way and let him get back to Mattia. That he had only one more hour to be with him and watch him exist, even at night, when usually the only thing he could do was imagine him in his bedroom, sleeping under a sheet the color of which he didn't know.

If I choose one of them, they'll leave me alone, he thought.

"Her." He pointed to Giulia Mirandi, because she seemed the most harmless.

Giulia brought a hand to her mouth as if she'd just been elected prom queen. Viola turned up one corner of her mouth. The other two exploded into coarse laughter.

"Good," said Viola. "So now the dare."

"No, that's enough," protested Denis.

"You really are a bore. Here you are, surrounded by four girls, and you don't even want to play a bit. Certainly this doesn't happen to you every day."

"But now it's someone else's turn."

"And I say it's still your turn. You have to do the dare. What do you say, girls?"

The others nodded greedily. The bottle was once more in the hands of Giada, who at regular intervals threw back her head and took a swig, as if she wanted to finish it before the others noticed.

"See?" said Viola.

Denis snorted.

"What do I have to do?" he asked with resignation.

"Well, since I'm a generous hostess, I'm going to give you a nice dare," Viola said mysteriously. The other three hung on her words, eager to discover the new torture. "You have to kiss Giulia."

Giulia blushed. Denis felt a pang in his ribs.

"Are you crazy?" Giulia asked, shocked, perhaps pretending.

Viola gave a capricious shrug. Denis shook his head no, two, three times in a row.

"You were the one who said you liked her," she said.

"What if I don't do it?"

Suddenly dead serious, Viola looked him straight in the eyes.

"If you don't do it you'll have to choose truth again," she said. "You could tell us about your little friend, for example."

In her keen, bright stare Denis recognized all the things he had always thought were invisible. His neck stiffened.

His arms at his sides, he leaned his face toward Giulia Mirandi, narrowed his eyes, and kissed her. Then he tried to draw back, but Giulia held his head, her hand on the back of his neck. She forced her tongue through his pursed lips.

In his mouth Denis tasted saliva that wasn't his own and felt sick. In the middle of this, his first kiss, he opened his eyes just in time to see Mattia coming into the kitchen, hand in hand with the crippled girl.

15

The others were the first to notice what Alice and Mattia would come to understand only many years later. They walked into the room holding hands. They weren't smiling and were looking in opposite directions, but it was as if their bodies flowed smoothly into each other's, through their arms and fingers.

The marked contrast between Alice's light-colored hair, which framed the excessively pale skin of her face, and Mattia's dark hair, tousled forward to hide his black eyes, was erased by the slender arc that linked them. There was a shared space between their bodies, the confines of which were not well delineated, from which nothing seemed to be missing and in which the air seemed motionless, undisturbed.

Alice walked a step ahead of him and Mattia's slight drag balanced her cadence, erasing the imperfections of her faulty leg. He let himself be carried forward, his feet making not the slightest sound on the tiles. His scars were hidden and safe in her hand.

They stopped on the threshold of the kitchen, a little away from the cluster of girls and Denis. They tried to work out what was happening. They had a dreamy air about them, as if they had come from some distant place that only they knew.

Denis pushed Giulia violently away and their mouths separated with a smack. He looked at Mattia and sought in his expression the traces of the thing that terrified him. He thought that he and Alice had said something to each other, something he would never be able to know, and his brain filled with blood.

He ran out of the room, deliberately knocking into him, to destroy that equilibrium he loathed. For an instant Mattia met Denis's red and upset eyes. For some reason they reminded him of Michela's defenseless eyes that afternoon in the park. Over the years those two gazes would gradually merge in his memory into a single, indelible fear.

Mattia let go of Alice's hand. It was as if all his nerve endings were concentrated in that single point, and when he broke away, it seemed that his arm gave off sparks, as if from a bared cable.

"Excuse me," he whispered to her and left the kitchen to catch up with Denis.

Alice walked over to Viola, who was staring at her with eyes of stone.

"We—" she began.

"I don't care," Viola cut in. Looking at Alice and Mattia, she had remembered the boy at the beach, the moment when he had refused to hold her hand, while she would have loved to go back to the others on the beach holding hands just like that. She was jealous, a painful, violent jealousy. And she was furious, because the happiness she wanted for herself she had just given to someone else. She felt robbed, as if Alice had taken her share too.

Alice leaned over to say something in her ear, but Viola turned away.

"What do you want now?" she said.

"Nothing." Alice retreated in fear.

At that moment Giada bent forward, as if an invisible man had punched her in the stomach. With one hand she held on to the kitchen counter and with the other she gripped her belly.

"What's wrong?" Viola asked.

"I'm going to throw up," she moaned.

"Gross, go to the bathroom," Viola yelled.

But it was too late. With a jerk Giada emptied the contents of her stomach onto the floor, something reddish and alcoholic, a mixture of vodka and Soledad's dessert.

The others pulled back, horrified, while Alice tried to hold her up by the hips. The air immediately turned rancid.

"Well done, you idiot," said Viola. "What a fucking awful party."

She left the room, her fists clenched furiously, as if struggling to keep from smashing something. Alice looked at her anxiously and then went back to taking care of Giada, who was sobbing gently.

16

The other guests had scattered about in small groups around the living room. Most of the boys were bobbing their heads back and forth to the music, while the girls scanned the room. Some held drinks in their hands; six or seven were dancing to "A Question of Time." Mattia wondered how they could feel so at ease, moving around like that in front of everyone. Then he realized it was the most natural thing in the world, which was precisely why he was incapable of it.

Denis had disappeared. Mattia crossed the living room and went to look for him in Viola's room. He even looked in her sister's and her parents' rooms. He looked in both bathrooms and in one he found a boy and a girl from school. She was sitting on the toilet and he was on the floor in front of her, legs crossed. They both wore sad and questioning expressions and Mattia hastily closed the door.

He went back to the living room and out onto the balcony. The hill dropped away darkly and below them lay the entire city, a series of bright white dots arranged homogeneously, as far as the eye could see. Mattia leaned over the railing and looked through the trees of the grounds of Villa Bai, but he couldn't see anyone. He went back inside; anxiety began to shorten his breath.

A spiral staircase led from the sitting room to a dark attic. He climbed the first steps, then stopped.

Where has he gotten to? he thought.

He went on, up to the top. The light that filtered from below allowed him to make out the shadow of Denis, standing in the middle of the room.

He called to him. All through their friendship he had uttered his name only two or three times at the most. He had never needed to, because Denis was always right next to him, like a natural extension of his limbs.

"Go away," Denis replied.

Mattia looked for the switch and turned on the light. The room was enormous, lined with tall bookshelves. The only other furniture was a big, empty wooden desk. Mattia had the impression that no one had come up to this floor of the house for a long time.

"It's almost eleven. We have to go," he said.

Denis didn't reply. His back was turned, and he stood in the middle of a big rug. Mattia walked over to his friend. He saw that Denis had been crying. He was blowing through his teeth as he breathed, his eyes fixed straight ahead and his half-open lips trembling slightly.

It took Mattia a few seconds to notice a desk lamp that lay shattered at his feet.

"What have you done?" he asked.

Denis's breathing turned into a wheeze.

"Denis, what have you done?"

Mattia tried to touch his friend's shoulder, but Denis gave a violent start. Mattia shook him.

"What have you done?"

"I . . ." Denis began. Then he froze.

"You what?"

Denis opened his left hand and showed Mattia a fragment of the lamp, a splinter of green glass, grown opaque from sweat, that seemed to swallow up the light.

"I wanted to feel what you feel," he whispered.

Mattia didn't understand. He stumbled back, confused. A burning sensation exploded in his gut and filled his arms and legs.

"But then I couldn't do it," said Denis.

He held the palms of his hands upward, as if waiting for something.

Mattia was about to ask him why, but didn't. The music rose up, muffled, from below. The low frequencies passed through the floor, but the higher ones seemed trapped.

Denis sniffed. "Let's get out of here," he said.

Mattia nodded, but neither of them made a move. Then Denis turned and abruptly walked toward the stairs. Mattia followed him across the living room and then outside, where the cool night air was waiting to give them back their breath.

17

Viola decided if you were in or out. On Sunday morning Giada Savarino's father had phoned Viola's father, waking up the entire Bai household. It was a long phone call and Viola, still in pajamas, had pressed her ear to her parents' bedroom door, but she hadn't been able to catch a single word of the conversation.

When she heard the bed creak, she had run back to her room and hid under the blankets, pretending to be asleep. Her father had woken her up saying you can tell me what happened later, but for now let me tell you that there will be no more parties in this house and, in fact, you can forget about parties of any kind for a good long while. At lunch her mother had asked her to explain the broken lamp in the attic and her sister hadn't come to her defense, because she had noticed that Viola had laid her hands on her personal stock.

She locked herself away in her room all day, disheartened and banned from using the phone. She couldn't get Alice and Mattia, and their way of holding hands, out of her head. As she scratched away the last remnants of nail polish she decided: Alice was out.

On Monday morning, locked in her bathroom at home, Alice finally removed the gauze that covered her tattoo. She balled it up and then threw it in the toilet, along with the crumbled biscuits that she hadn't eaten for breakfast.

She looked at the violet reflected in the mirror and thought that, for the second time, she had changed her body forever. She shivered with a pleasant mixture of regret and trepidation. She thought that this body was hers alone, that if she felt like it she could even destroy it, lay waste to it with indelible marks, or let it dry out like a flower picked on a whim by a child and then left to die on the ground.

That morning she would show her tattoo to Viola and the others, in the girls' bathroom. She would tell them how she and Mattia had kissed for a long time. There was no need to invent anything more than that. If they asked her for details, she would merely go along with their fantasies.

In class she left her backpack on her chair and headed over to Viola's desk to join the others. As she approached, she heard Giulia Mirandi saying here she comes. She said hi to everyone, beaming, but no one replied. She leaned over to give Viola two kisses on the cheeks, as Viola had taught her to do, but her friend didn't move an inch.

Alice stood up again and found herself looking into four hostile faces.

"We were all ill yesterday," Viola began.

"Really?" Alice asked, with genuine concern. "What was wrong with you?"

"A terrible stomachache, all of us," Giada broke in aggressively.

Alice saw Giada vomiting on the floor again and felt like saying I'm not surprised with the amount you all drank.

"There was nothing wrong with me," she said.

"Of course," sneered Viola, looking at the others. "There was no doubt about that."

Giada and Federica laughed; Giulia lowered her eyes.

"What's that supposed to mean?" Alice asked, disoriented.

"You know very well what I mean," Viola retorted, suddenly changing her tone and fixing her with her marvelous, piercing eyes.

"No, I don't know," Alice defended herself.

Giada attacked. "You poisoned us."

"What are you saying? What do you mean 'poisoned'?"

Giulia butted in, timidly. "Come on, girls, that's not true."

"Yes, it is. She poisoned us," Giada repeated. "Who knows what disgusting things she put in that dessert."

She turned back toward Alice. "You wanted to make us all sick, didn't you? Well, it worked, well done."

Alice listened to the sequence of words, but it took her a few seconds to reconstruct their meaning. She looked at Giulia, who, with her big blue eyes, was saying sorry, there's nothing I can do. Then she sought shelter in Viola's eyes, but Viola returned an empty gaze.

Giada held a hand over her belly, as if she were still having convulsions.

"But I made it with Soledad. We bought all the ingredients at the supermarket."

No one replied. They looked in different directions, as if waiting for the murderer to leave.

"It wasn't Sol's dessert. I ate it too, and I didn't get sick," Alice lied.

"You're a liar," pounced Federica Mazzoldi, who hadn't said a word till then. "You didn't even taste it. Everyone knows that—"

She suddenly froze.

"Please, stop," Giulia begged. She looked as if she were about to burst into tears.

Alice put a hand over her flat stomach. She could feel her heart beating under her skin.

"Everyone knows what?" she asked them in a calm voice.

Viola Bai slowly shook her head. Alice stared at her former friend in silence, waiting for words that didn't come but that floated in the air like tongues of transparent smoke. She didn't even move when the bell rang. Ms. Tubaldo, the science teacher, had to call her twice before she finally went to sit in her place.

18

Denis hadn't come to school. On Saturday, on the way home, he and Mattia hadn't looked at each other once. Denis had responded to Mattia's father in monosyllables, and hadn't even said good-bye when he got out of the car.

Mattia rested a hand on the empty chair beside him. Now and again Denis's words in that dark attic ran through his head. Then they slipped away, too quickly for him to get to the bottom of their meaning.

He realized it didn't really matter to him to understand them. He merely wished Denis was there, to shield him from everything beyond his desk.

The day before, his parents had made him sit down on the sofa, in the living room. They had sat in the chairs opposite him. Then his father said so tell us about the party. Mattia had clenched his hands tightly, but then stretched them out on his knees so that his parents could see them. He had shrugged and replied in a quiet voice that there was nothing to tell. His mother had gotten nervously to her feet and disappeared into the kitchen. His father, on the other hand, had come over to him and clapped him twice on the shoulder, as if consoling him for something. Mattia remembered how, when he was little, on the hottest days of summer, his father would blow on his and Michela's faces in turn, to cool them down. He remembered what the sweat felt like as it evaporated from his skin, ever so lightly, and was filled with a searing nostalgia for a part of the world that had drowned in the river along with Michela.

He wondered if his classmates knew everything. Maybe even his teachers knew. He felt their furtive glances weaving together above his head like a fishing net.

He opened his history book at random and started learning by heart the whole sequence of dates that appeared from that page onward. The list of numbers, lined up without any logical meaning, formed an ever longer trail in his head. As he followed it, Mattia slowly moved away from the thought of Denis standing in the shadow and forgot the void that now sat in his place.

19

During break time Alice slipped into the infirmary on the second floor, a narrow white room furnished only with a hospital bed and a mirrored cabinet with the essentials for first aid. She had ended up there only once before, when she had fainted during PE because in the previous forty hours she had eaten only two whole-grain crackers and a low-calorie snack. That day the gym teacher, in his green Diadora tracksuit, his whistle, which he never used, around his neck, had said to her think carefully about what you're doing, think very carefully. Then he had gone out, leaving her alone under the fluorescent light, without anything to do or look at for the whole next hour.

Alice found the first-aid cabinet open. She took a wad of cotton wool the size of a plum and the bottle of rubbing alcohol. She closed the door and looked around for a heavy object. There was only the wastepaper basket, made of hard plastic, a dull color halfway between red and brown. She prayed that no one would hear the noise from outside and shattered the mirror of the little cupboard with the bottom of the basket.

Then, being careful not to cut herself, she picked up a big triangular splinter of glass. She caught the reflection of her own right eye and felt proud that she hadn't cried, not even a bit. She stuffed everything into the center pocket of the baggy sweatshirt she was wearing and went back to class.

She spent the rest of the morning in a state of torpor. She never even glanced at Viola and the others and didn't listen to a single word of the lesson on the theater of Aeschylus.

As she was leaving the class, behind all her classmates, Giulia Mirandi furtively took her hand.

"I'm sorry," she whispered into her ear. Then she kissed her on the cheek and ran after the others, who were already in the hallway.

Alice waited for Mattia in the atrium, at the bottom of the linoleum-covered staircase down which poured a chaotic stream of pupils headed for the exit. She rested a hand on the banister. The cold metal gave her a sense of tranquillity.

Mattia came down the stairs enveloped by that foot and a half of emptiness that no one other than Denis dared occupy. His black hair fell over his forehead in tousled curls. He watched carefully where he placed his feet, leaning slightly backward as he descended. Alice called out to him, but he didn't turn around. She called again, more loudly now, and he looked up, said an embarrassed hi, and made as if to head toward the glass doors.

Alice elbowed her way through the other students and joined him. She took him by the arm and he gave a start.

"You have to come with me," she said.

"Where?"

"You have to help me do something."

Mattia looked around nervously, in search of some kind of threat.

"My father's waiting for me outside," he said.

"Your father will wait. You have to help me. Now," said Alice.

Mattia snorted. Then he said okay but he couldn't have said why.

"Come."

Alice took him by the hand, as she had at Viola's party, but this time Mattia's fingers spontaneously closed around hers.

They left the crowd of students. Alice walked quickly, as if she were escaping from someone. They slipped into the deserted corridor on the second floor. The doors leading to the empty classrooms conveyed a sense of abandonment.

They went into the girls' bathroom. Mattia hesitated. He was about to say I'm not supposed to be here, but then he let her drag him in. When Alice took him inside a cubicle and locked the door they were so close that his legs started trembling. The space not taken up by the old-style hole-in-the-ground toilet was nothing more than a thin strip of tiles and there was barely room for their four feet. There were pieces of toilet paper scattered on the ground half-stuck to the floor.

Now she's going to kiss me, he thought. And all you have to do is kiss her back. It'll be easy; everyone knows how.

Alice unzipped her shiny jacket and started to undress, just as she had at Viola's house. She untucked her T-shirt and lowered the same pair of jeans halfway down her bottom. She didn't look at Mattia; it was as if she were there on her own.

In place of Saturday evening's white gauze she had a flower tattooed on her skin. Mattia was about to say something, but then fell silent and looked away. Something stirred between his legs and he tried to distract himself. He read some of the graffiti on the wall, without grasping its meaning. He noticed how none of the writing was parallel to the line of tiles. Almost all of it was at the same angle to the edge of the floor and Mattia worked out that it was somewhere between 30 and 45 degrees.

"Take this," said Alice.

She handed him a piece of glass, reflective on one side and black on the other, and as sharp as a dagger. Mattia didn't understand. She lifted his chin, just as she had imagined doing the first time they had met.

"You've got to get rid of it. I can't do it on my own," she said to him.

Mattia looked at the glass shard and then at Alice's right hand, which pointed at the tattoo on her belly.

She anticipated his protest.

"I know you know how to do it," she said. "I never want to see it again. Please, do it for me."

Mattia rolled the shard in his hand and a shiver ran down his arm.

"But—" he said.

"Do it for me," Alice interrupted him, putting a hand to his lips to shut him up and then removing it immediately.

Do it for me, thought Mattia. Those four words stuck in his ear and made him kneel in front of Alice.

His heels touched the wall behind him. He didn't know how to position himself. Uncertain, he touched the skin next to the tattoo, to stretch it better. His face had never been so close to a girl's body. The natural thing to do seemed to be to breathe in deeply, to discover its smell.

He brought the shard close to her flesh. His hand was steady as he made a little cut the size of a fingertip. Alice trembled and let out a cry.

Mattia recoiled and hid the piece of glass behind his back, as if to deny that it had been him.

"I can't do it," he said.

He looked up. Alice wept silently. Her eyes were closed, clenched in an expression of pain.

"But I don't want to see it anymore," she sobbed.

It was clear to him that she had lost her nerve, and he felt relieved. He stood up and wondered if it would be better to leave.

Alice wiped away the drop of blood trickling down her belly. She buttoned up her jeans, while Mattia tried to think of something reassuring to say.

"You'll get used to it. In the end you won't even notice it anymore," he said.

"How is that possible? It will always be there, right before my eyes."

"Exactly," said Mattia. "Which is precisely why you won't see it anymore."

THE OTHER ROOM

1995

20

Mattia was right: the days had slipped over her skin like a solvent, one after the other, each removing a very thin layer of pigment from her tattoo, and from both their memories. The outlines, like the circumstances, were still there, black and well delineated, but the colors had merged together until they faded into a dull, uniform tonality, a neutral absence of meaning.

For Alice and Mattia, the high school years were an open wound that had seemed so deep that it could never heal. They had passed through them without breathing, he rejecting the world and she feeling rejected by it, and eventually they had noticed that it didn't make all that much difference. They had formed a defective and asymmetrical friendship, made up of long absences and much silence, a clean and empty space where both could come back to breathe when the walls of their school became too close for them to ignore the feeling of suffocation.

But over time, the wound of adolescence gradually healed. The edges of skin met in imperceptible but continuous movements. The scab peeled off with each fresh abrasion, but then stubbornly re-formed, darker and thicker. Finally a new layer of skin, smooth and elastic, had replaced the missing one. The scar slowly turned from red to white, and ended up merging with all the others.

Now they were lying on Alice's bed, their heads at opposite ends, their legs bent unnaturally to avoid any contact between their bodies. Alice thought if she turned around she could make her toes touch Mattia's back but pretend not to notice. But she was sure he would immediately pull away and decided to spare herself that little disappointment.

Neither one of them had suggested putting on some music. Their only plans were to stay there and wait for Sunday afternoon to wear itself out all by itself and it would once again be time to do something necessary, like eating, sleeping, or starting yet another week. The yellow light of September came in through the open window, dragging with it the intermittent rustle of the street.

Alice stood up on the bed, making the mattress ripple very slightly under Mattia's head. She held her clenched fists by her sides and stared at him from above. Her hair fell over her face, concealing her serious expression.

"Stay right there," she said. "Don't move."

She stepped over him and jumped down from the bed, her good leg dragging the other one behind it like something that had been attached to her by mistake. Mattia bent his chin to his chest to follow her movements around the room. He saw her opening a cube-shaped box that sat in the middle of her desk, and which he hadn't noticed until that moment.

Alice turned around with one eye closed and the other hidden behind an old camera. Mattia started to pull himself up.

"Down," she commanded. "I told you not to move."

Click. The Polaroid spat out a thin white tongue and Alice waved it in the air to bring out the color.

"Where did you get that from?" Mattia asked.

"The cellar. It was my father's. He bought it God knows when but never used it."

Mattia sat up on the bed. Alice dropped the photograph on the carpet and snapped another one.

"Come on, stop," he protested. "I look stupid in photographs."

"You always look stupid."

She snapped again.

"I think I want to be a photographer," Alice said. "I've made up my mind."

"What about university?"

Alice shrugged.

"Only my father cares about that," she said. "He can go, then."

"You're going to quit?"

"Maybe."

"You can't just wake up one day, decide you want to be a photographer, and throw away a year's work. It doesn't work like that," said Mattia sharply.

"Oh, right, I forgot you're just like him," Alice said ironically. "You always know what to do. You knew you wanted to be a mathematician when you were five. You're all so boring. Old and boring."

Then she turned toward the window and snapped a picture at random. She dropped it on the carpet as well, near the other two, and stomped on them with both feet, as if she were treading grapes.

Mattia thought about saying something to make amends, but nothing came out. He bent over and slid the first photograph out from under Alice's foot. The outline of his arms, crossed behind his head, was gradually emerging from the white. He wondered what extraordinary reaction was happening on that shiny surface and decided to look it up in the encyclopedia as soon as he got home.

"There's something else I want to show you," Alice said.

She tossed the camera onto the bed, like a little girl who's grown tired of a toy because she's spotted another, more inviting one, and left the room.

She was gone for a good ten minutes. Mattia started reading the titles of the books leaning crookedly on the shelf above the desk. Always the same ones. He combined the first letters of all the titles, but couldn't come up with a sensible word. He would have liked to identify a logical order in the sequence. He would probably have arranged them according to the color of their spines, copying the electromagnetic spectrum maybe, from red to violet, or according to height, in decreasing order.

"Ta-daaaa." Alice's voice distracted him.

Mattia turned and saw her standing in the doorway, gripping the frame as if afraid she might fall. She was wearing a wedding dress, which must have been dazzlingly white once, but which time had turned yellow at the hem, as if some disease were slowly devouring it. The years spent in a box had made it dry and stiff. The bodice fell limply over Alice's nonexistent bosom. It wasn't especially low-cut, just enough for one of the straps to slip a few inches down her arm. In that position Alice's collarbone looked more pronounced; it broke the soft line of her neck and formed a little hollow, like the basin of a dried-up lake. Mattia wondered what it might be like, eyes closed, to trace its outline with the tip of his finger. The lace at the end of the sleeves was crumpled and on the left arm it stood up slightly. The long train continued out of sight down the hall. Alice was still wearing her red slippers, which peeked out from under the full skirt, creating a curious dissonance.

"Well? Aren't you going to say something?" she said without looking at him. She smoothed the outer layer of tulle on the skirt. It felt cheap, synthetic.

"Whose is it?" asked Mattia.

"Mine, obviously."

"Come on, seriously."

"Whose do you think it is? It's my mother's."

Mattia nodded and imagined Fernanda in that dress. He pictured her wearing the only expression she ever gave him when, before going home, he would stick his head in the living room where she'd be watching television: an expression of tenderness and profound commiseration, like the one usually bestowed upon the sick when people visit them in the hospital. A ridiculous expression, as she was the sick one, sick with an illness that was slowly crumbling her whole body.

"Don't stand there gawking like that. Come on, take a picture of me."

Mattia picked the camera off the bed. He turned it around in his hands to work out which button to press. Alice rocked from side to side in the doorway, as if moved by a breeze that only she could feel. When Mattia brought the camera to his eye, she stiffened her back and assumed a serious, almost provocative expression.

"There," said Mattia.

"Now one of us together."

He shook his head.

"Come on, don't be your usual pain in the ass. And for once I want to see you dressed properly. Not in that mangy sweatshirt that you've been wearing for a month."

Mattia looked down. The wrists of his blue sweater looked as if they'd been devoured by moths. He had a habit of rubbing them with his thumbnail to keep his fingers busy and to keep from scratching the hollow between his index and middle fingers.

"And besides, you wouldn't want to ruin my wedding day, would you?" added Alice with a pout.

She knew it was only a joke, a silly game to pass the time, just a bit of nonsense like so many other things they did. And yet, when she opened the closet door and the mirror inside framed her in that white dress next to Mattia, for a moment the panic took her breath away.

"Nothing in here will work," she said hastily. "Come with me."

Resigned, Mattia followed her. When Alice got like this his legs would itch and he was seized by a desire to leave. There was something in her way of behaving, something in the violence with which his friend satisfied her childish whims, that he found unbearable. It felt as if she had tied him to a chair and then called hundreds of people, showing him off like a possession of hers, some kind of funny pet. Most of the time he said nothing and allowed his impatience to emerge through gestures, until Alice tired of his apathy and gave up, saying you always make me feel like an idiot.

Mattia followed the train of Alice's dress all the way to her parents' room. He had never been in there before. The blinds were down almost entirely and the light entered in parallel lines, so clearly that they seemed drawn on the wooden floor. The air was more dense and tired here than in the rest of the house. Against the wall was a double bed, much higher than the one that belonged to Mattia's parents, and two matching bedside tables.

Alice opened the closet and ran her finger along her father's suits, all hanging in an orderly fashion, each one protected by its cellophane covering. She took out a black one and threw it on the bed.

"Put that one on," she ordered Mattia.

"Have you gone mad? Your father will notice, you know."

"My father never notices anything."

For a moment Alice seemed absorbed in thought, as if reflecting on the words that she had just spoken, or looking at something through that wall of dark clothes.

"Now I'm going to find you a shirt and tie," she added.

Mattia stood still, uncertain what to do. She noticed.

"Will you get a move on? Don't tell me you're ashamed to get changed here!"

As she said that her empty stomach flipped over. For a second she felt dishonest. Her words had been a subtle form of blackmail.

Mattia huffed, then sat down on the bed and started untying his shoes.

Alice kept her back turned, pretending to choose a shirt that she had already chosen. When she heard the metallic jingle of his belt buckle, she counted to three and then turned around. Mattia was taking off his jeans. Underneath he had on a pair of soft gray boxers, not the close-fitting ones she had imagined.

Alice thought that she'd already seen him in shorts dozens of times, it's not like there was much of a difference with underwear, and yet she still felt herself tremble slightly under the four white layers of her wedding dress. He tugged at the bottom of his undershirt to cover himself better and quickly slipped on the elegant trousers. The fabric was soft and light. As it ran over the hairs of his legs it gave them an electric charge, making them stand up like cat's fur.

Alice came over and handed him the shirt. He took it without looking up. He was annoyed and fed up with this pointless playacting. He was ashamed of showing his thin legs and the sparse hairs on his chest and around his navel. Alice thought he was doing everything possible to make the scene embarrassing, as usual. Then she thought that, for him, she was the one to blame, and she felt her throat tighten. Even though she didn't want to, she looked away and let him take off his undershirt without her watching him.

"And now?" Mattia called to her.

She turned around. Seeing him in her father's clothes, she had trouble breathing. The jacket was a little big, his shoulders weren't quite wide enough to fill it out, but she couldn't help thinking that he was incredibly handsome.

"All you need is the tie," she said to him after a moment.

Mattia took the bordeaux-colored tie from Alice's hands and instinctively ran a thumb over the shiny fabric. A shiver ran down his arm and spine. He felt that the palm of his hand was as dry as sand. He quickly brought it to his mouth and breathed on it, to moisten it with his breath. He couldn't resist the temptation to bite one of the joints of his fingers, trying not to be seen by Alice, who noticed anyway.

"I don't know how to tie it," he said, dragging out his words.

"Mmm, you really are hopeless."

The truth was that Alice already knew that. She couldn't wait to show him that she could tie it. Her father had taught her when she was little. In the morning he would leave a tie on her bed and then, before going out, he'd stop by her room and ask is my tie ready? Alice would run to him, with the knot already made. Her father would lower his head, his hands joined together behind his back, as if he were bowing before a queen. She would put the tie around his neck, and then would tighten it and adjust it slightly. *Parfait,* he would say. One morning after the accident, Alice's father found the tie still on the bed, just as he had left it. From then on he always tied it himself and that little ritual passed away, like so many other things.

Alice prepared the knot, fluttering her skeletal fingers more than necessary. Mattia followed her gestures, which struck him as complicated. He let her adjust the tie around his neck.

"Wow, you look almost respectable. Do you want to see yourself in the mirror?"

"No," said Mattia. He just wanted to leave, wearing his own clothes.

"Photograph," said Alice, clapping once.

Mattia followed her back into her room. She picked up the camera.

"It hasn't got a self-timer," she said. "We'll just have to guess."

She pulled Mattia to her, by the waist. He stiffened and she clicked. The photograph slipped out with a hiss.

Alice fell onto the bed, just like a bride after hours of celebration, and fanned herself with the picture.

Mattia stayed right where he was, feeling those clothes that weren't his, but with the pleasant sensation of disappearing into them. The light in the room suddenly changed. It turned from yellow to a uniform blue as the last sliver of light disappeared behind the building opposite.

"Can I get changed now?"

He said it on purpose, to make her understand that he had had enough of her game. Alice seemed absorbed in thought; she arched her eyebrows slightly.

"There's one last thing," she said, getting up again. "The groom carries the bride in his arms over the threshold."

"Meaning?"

"You've got to take me in your arms. And carry me over there." Alice pointed to the hall. "Then you're free."

Mattia shook his head. She came over to him and held out her arms like a child.

"Come on, my hero," she said, teasing him.

Mattia slumped his shoulders even farther, defeated. He bent awkwardly in order to pick her up. He had never carried anyone like that. He put one arm behind her knees and the other behind her back, and when he picked her up he was startled by how light she was.

He stumbled toward the hall. He felt Alice's breath penetrate the fine weave of his shirt, definitely too close, and heard the train rustling on the floor. When they crossed the threshold, the sound of a prolonged, dry rip made him stop short.

"Damn," he said.

He hastily set Alice down. The skirt had gotten caught on the door frame. The rip was about six inches long and looked like a sneering mouth. They both stopped and stared at it, slightly dazed.

Mattia waited for Alice to say something, to give up and lose her temper with him. He felt as if he ought to apologize, but she was the one who had been so insistent on this foolishness. She'd been asking for trouble.

Alice stared expressionlessly at the rip.

"Who cares?" she said at last. "It's not like anyone's going to use it anymore."

IN AND OUT OF THE WATER

1998

21

Prime numbers are divisible only by 1 and by themselves. They hold their place in the infinite series of natural numbers, squashed, like all numbers, between two others, but one step further than the rest. They are suspicious, solitary numbers, which is why Mattia thought they were wonderful. Sometimes he thought that they had ended up in that sequence by mistake, that they'd been trapped, like pearls strung on a necklace. Other times he suspected that they too would have preferred to be like all the others, just ordinary numbers, but for some reason they couldn't do it. This second thought struck him mostly at night, in the chaotic interweaving of images that comes before sleep, when the mind is too weak to tell itself lies.

In his first year at university, Mattia had learned that, among prime numbers, there are some that are even more special. Mathematicians call them twin primes: pairs of prime numbers that are close to each other, almost neighbors, but between them there is always an even number that prevents them from truly touching. Numbers like 11 and 13, like 17 and 19, 41 and 43. If you have the patience to go on counting, you discover that these pairs gradually become rarer. You encounter increasingly isolated primes, lost in that silent, measured space made only of ciphers, and you develop a distressing presentiment that the pairs encountered up until that point were accidental, that solitude is the true destiny. Then, just when you're about to surrender, when you no longer have the desire to go on counting, you come across another pair of twins, clutching each other tightly. There is a common conviction among mathematicians that however far you go, there will always be another two, even if no one can say where exactly, until they are discovered.

Mattia thought that he and Alice were like that, twin primes, alone and lost, close but not close enough to really touch each other. He had never told her that. When he imagined confessing these things to her, the thin layer of sweat on his hands evaporated completely and for a good ten minutes he was no longer capable of touching anything.

He came home one winter day after having spent the afternoon at her house, where she'd done nothing the whole time but switch from one television channel to another. Mattia had paid no attention to the words or the images. Alice's right foot, resting on the living room coffee table, invaded his field of vision, penetrating it from the left like the head of a snake. Alice flexed her toes with hypnotic regularity. That repeated movement made something solid and worrying grow in his stomach and he struggled to keep his gaze fixed for as long as possible, so that nothing in the frame would change.

At home he took a pile of blank pages from his ring binder, thick enough so that the pen would run softly over them without scratching the stiff surface of the table. He leveled the edges with his hands, first above and below and then at the sides. He chose the fullest pen from the ones on the desk, removed the cap, and slipped it on the end so as not to lose it. Then he began to write in the exact center of the sheet, without needing to count the squares.

2760889966649. He put the lid back on the pen and set it down next to the paper. "Twothousandsevenhundredsixtybillioneighthundredeightyninemillionninehundredsixtysixthousandsixhundredandfortynine," he read out loud. Then he repeated it under his breath, as if to take possession of that tongue twister. He decided that this number would be his. He was sure that no one else in the world, no one else in the whole history of the world, had ever stopped to consider that number. Probably, until then, no one had ever written it down on a piece of paper, let alone spoken it out loud.

After a moment's hesitation he jumped two lines and wrote

2760889966651. This is hers, he thought. In his head the figures assumed the pale color of Alice's foot, standing out against the bluish glare of the television.

They could also be twin primes, Mattia had thought. If they are . . .

That thought suddenly seized him and he began to search for divisors for both numbers. 3 was easy: it was enough to take the sum of the numbers and see if it was a multiple of 3. 5 was ruled out from the beginning. Perhaps there was a rule for 7 as well, but Mattia couldn't remember it so he started doing the division longhand. Then 11, 13, and so on, in increasingly complicated calculations. He became drowsy for the first time trying 37, the pen slipping down the page. When he got to 47 he stopped. The vortex that had filled his stomach at Alice's house had dispersed, diluted into his muscles like smells in the air, and he was no longer able to notice it. In the room there were only himself and a lot of disordered pages, full of pointless divisions. The clock showed a quarter past three in the morning.

Mattia picked up the first page, the one with the two numbers written in the middle, and felt like an idiot. He tore it in half and then in half again, until the edges were firm enough to pass like a blade beneath the nail of the ring finger of his left hand.

During his four years of university, mathematics had led him into the most remote and fascinating corners of human thought. With meticulous ritualism Mattia copied out the proofs of all the theorems he encountered in his studies. Even on summer afternoons he kept the blinds lowered and worked in artificial light. He removed from his desk everything that might distract his gaze, so as to feel truly alone with the page. He wrote without stopping. If he found himself hesitating too long over a passage or made a mistake when aligning an expression after the equals sign, he shoved the paper to the floor and started all over. When he got to the end of those pages stuffed with symbols, letters, and numbers, he wrote "QED," and for a moment he felt he had put a small piece of the world in order. Then he leaned against the back of the chair and wove his hands together, without letting them rub.

He slowly lost contact with the page. The symbols, which only a moment before flowed from the movement of his wrist, now seemed distant to him, frozen in a place that denied him access. His head, immersed in the darkness of the room, began to fill with dark, disorderly thoughts and Mattia would usually choose a book, open it at random, and begin studying again.

Complex analysis, projective geometry, and tensor calculus had not managed to diminish his initial passion for numbers. Mattia liked to count, starting from 1 and proceeding through complicated progressions, which he often invented on the spur of the moment. He allowed himself to be led by numbers and he seemed to know each one of them. And so, when it came time to choose his thesis topic, he went with no doubts to the office of Professor Niccoli, professor of discrete calculus, with whom he had never even sat an exam and about whom he knew nothing other than his name.

Francesco Niccoli's office was on the fourth floor of the nineteenth-century building that housed the mathematics department. It was a small room, tidy and odorless, dominated by the color white—the walls, shelves, plastic desk, even the cumbersome computer on top of it, were white. Mattia drummed softly on the door and from inside Niccoli wasn't sure if the knocking was for him or for the office next door. He said come in, hoping he had not made a fool of himself.

Mattia opened the door and stepped into the office.

"Hello," he said.

"Hello," replied Niccoli.

Mattia's eye caught sight of a photograph hanging behind the professor, which showed him, much younger and beardless, holding a silver plate and shaking hands with an important-looking stranger.

Mattia narrowed his eyes, but couldn't read what was written on the plate.

"Well, then?" Niccoli urged, studying him with a frown.

"I'd like to write a dissertation on the zeros of the Riemann zeta function," said Mattia, staring at the professor's right shoulder, where a dusting of dandruff looked like a little starry sky.

Niccoli made a face, an ironic smile.

"Excuse me, but who are you?" he asked without concealing his disdain and locking his hands behind his head as if wanting to enjoy a moment of fun.

"My name is Mattia Balossino. I've finished my exams and I'd like to graduate within the year."

"Have you got your record book with you?"

Mattia nodded. He slid his backpack off, crouched on the floor, and rummaged around in it. Niccoli stretched out his hand to take the book, but Mattia preferred to set it on the edge of the desk.

For some months the professor had been obliged to hold objects at a distance to get them properly into focus. He quickly ran his eyes over the sequence of high grades. Not one flub, not one hesitation, not one try that had gone wrong, perhaps on account of a love story that had ended badly.

He closed the book and looked more carefully at Mattia. He was dressed anonymously and had the posture of someone who doesn't know how to occupy the space of his own body. The professor thought he was another of those who do well in their studies because they are unable to make much headway in life. The ones who, as soon as they find themselves outside the well-trodden paths of the university, always reveal themselves to be good for nothing.

"Don't you think I should be the one to suggest a topic for you?" he asked, speaking slowly.

Mattia shrugged. His black eyes moved right to left, following the edge of the desk.

"I'm interested in prime numbers. I want to work on the Riemann zeta function," he replied.

Niccoli sighed. Then he got up and walked over to the white bookshelf. As he ran his index finger along the spines of the books he snorted rhythmically. He pulled out some typed pages stapled in one corner.

"Fine, fine," he said, handing them to Mattia. "You can come back when you've performed the calculations in this article. All of them."

Mattia took the stack of pages and, without reading the title, slipped it into his backpack, which leaned against his leg, open and slack. He mumbled a thank-you and left the office, pulling the door shut behind him.

Niccoli went and sat back down in his chair and thought about how over dinner he would complain to his wife about this new and unexpected annoyance.

22

Alice's father had taken this photography business as the whim of a bored little girl. Nonetheless, for his daughter's twenty-third birthday, he gave her a Canon SLR, with case and tripod, and she had thanked him with a beautiful smile, as impossible to grasp as a gust of icy wind. He had also paid for her to take evening classes, which lasted six months, and Alice hadn't missed a single lesson. The agreement was clear if implicit: university came before everything else.

Then, in a precise instant, like the line separating light and shade, Fernanda's illness had gotten worse, dragging all three of them into an increasingly tight spiral of new tasks, drawing them toward an inevitable cycle of apathy and mutual indifference. Alice hadn't set foot in the university again and her father pretended not to notice. A feeling of remorse, the origins of which belonged to another time, kept him from imposing his will on his daughter and almost kept him from talking to her at all. Sometimes he thought it wouldn't take much, all he would have to do was go into her room one evening and tell her . . . Tell her what? His wife was disappearing from life like a wet mark drying on a shirt and, with her, the thread that still connected him to his daughter was slackening—it was already scraping the ground—leaving her free to decide for herself.

With photography Alice liked the actions more than the results. She liked opening the back of the camera and unrolling the new film a couple of inches, just enough to catch it in the runner, and thinking that this empty film would soon become something and not knowing what, taking the first few snaps into the void, aiming, focusing, checking her balance, deciding whether to include or exclude pieces of reality as she saw fit, enlarging, distorting.

Every time she heard the click of the shutter, followed by that faint rustle, she remembered when she used to catch grasshoppers in the garden of their house in the mountains when she was a little girl, trapping them between her cupped hands. She thought that it was the same with photographs, only now she seized time and fixed it on celluloid, capturing it halfway through its jump toward the next moment.

During the course she had been taught that the strap of the camera is to be wrapped around the wrist twice. That way, if someone tries to steal it they're forced to tear your whole arm off along with it. Alice ran no such risk in the corridor of Our Lady's Hospital, where her mother was being cared for, but she was used to carrying her Canon like that anyway.

As she walked she grazed along the two-tone wall, brushing it with her right shoulder from time to time to avoid touching anyone. Lunchtime visiting hour had just begun and people were pouring into the hospital like a liquid mass.

Aluminum-and-plywood doors opened onto the wards, each with its own particular smell. Oncology smelled of disinfectant and gauze soaked in methylated spirits.

Alice entered her mother's room, which was the second to last. She was sleeping a sleep that wasn't her own and the gadgets to which she was connected didn't make a sound. The light was faint and drowsy. On the bedside table red flowers were arranged in a vase: Soledad had brought them the day before.

Alice rested her hands and the camera on the edge of the bed, where the sheet, lifted in the middle by her mother's outline, flattened out again.

She came every day to do nothing. The nurses already took care of everything. Her role was to talk to her mother, she imagined. Lots of people do that, acting as if the patients were capable of hearing their thoughts, able to understand who was standing there beside them, and conversing with them inside their own heads, as if illness could open up a different channel of perception between people.

It was not something that Alice believed in. She felt alone in that room and that was that. Usually she would just sit there, waiting for half an hour to pass, and then leave. If she met a doctor she asked for news, which was always the same anyway. Their words and raised eyebrows meant we're only waiting for something to go wrong.

That morning, however, she had brought a hairbrush. She took it out of her bag and delicately, making sure not to scratch her face, combed her mother's hair; at least the hair that wasn't squashed against the pillow. She was as inert and as submissive as a doll.

She arranged her mother's arms on top of the sheet, extended and parallel, in a relaxed pose. Another drop of the saline solution in the drip ran down the tube and disappeared into Fernanda's veins.

Alice moved to the end of the bed, resting the Canon on the aluminum bar. She shut her left eye and pressed the other to the viewfinder. She had never photographed her mother before. She pressed the shutter and then leaned a little farther forward, without losing the frame.

A rustling sound startled her and the room suddenly filled with light.

"Better?" said a male voice behind her.

Alice turned around. Beside the window a doctor was busying himself with the cord of the venetian blinds. He was young.

"Yes, thanks," said Alice, a little intimidated.

The doctor stuck his hands in the pockets of his white coat and went on looking at her, as if waiting for her to continue. She leaned forward and snapped again, more or less randomly, as if to please him.

He must think I'm crazy, she said to herself.

Instead the doctor came casually over to her mother's bed. He took a glance at her chart, narrowing his eyes as he read, reducing them to slits. He went over to the drip and moved a wheel with his thumb. The drops started to come down more quickly and he watched them with satisfaction. Alice thought there was something reassuring about his movements.

The doctor came over to her and grasped the bed rail.

"The nurses are obsessed," he remarked to himself. "They want darkness everywhere. As if it weren't already hard enough in here to tell day from night."

He turned and smiled.

"Are you the daughter?"

"Yes."

He nodded, without condescension.

"I'm Dr. Rovelli," he said. "Fabio," he added, as if he'd been thinking about it.

Alice shook his hand and introduced herself. For a few seconds they stared at the sleeping Fernanda, without exchanging a word.

Then the doctor tapped twice on the metal bed, which sounded hollow, and walked away. As he passed by Alice he leaned slightly toward her ear.

"Don't say it was me," he whispered, winking and pointing at the light-filled windows.

When visiting hours were over Alice descended the two flights of stairs, crossed the entrance hall, and left through the automatic glass doors.

She crossed the courtyard and stopped at the kiosk for a bottle of fizzy water. She was hungry, but was used to keeping the impulse in check until she had erased it almost entirely. Fizzy drinks were one of her tricks. They were enough to fill her stomach, at least long enough to overcome the critical moment of lunch.

She looked for her wallet in her purse, hampered slightly by the camera that hung from her wrist.

"It's on me," said someone behind her.

Fabio, the doctor whom she had met just half an hour before, held out a bill to the man in the kiosk. He smiled at Alice in a way that stripped her of her wish to protest. Instead of the white coat he wore a blue short-sleeved T-shirt and a strong aftershave that she hadn't noticed before.

"And a Coke," he added, turning to the man.

"Thanks," said Alice.

She tried to open the bottle, but the top slipped through her fingers without moving.

"May I?" said Fabio.

He took the bottle from her hand and opened it using only his thumb and index finger. Alice thought there was nothing special in the gesture, that she could have done it herself, like anyone else, if only her hands hadn't been so sweaty. And yet she found it strangely fascinating, like a small heroic feat performed specially for her.

Fabio gave her back the water and they drank, each from their own bottle, glancing stealthily at each other as if contemplating what to say next. Fabio's hair was short, with chestnut curls that shaded into red where the sun struck them directly. Alice had a sense that he was aware of the way the light played on his hair; that in some way he was aware of everything he was, and all the things around him.

They moved a few feet away from the kiosk, together, as if by common agreement. Alice didn't know how to say good-bye. She felt indebted to him, partly because he had given her the water and partly because he had helped her to open it. She wasn't even sure she wanted to go so quickly.

Fabio understood.

"Can I walk you to wherever you're going?" he asked cheekily.

Alice blushed.

"I'm going to the car."

"To the car, then."

She didn't say yes or no, but smiled, looking in another direction. Fabio made an obsequious gesture with his hand that meant after you.

They crossed the main road and turned into a smaller one, where the sidewalk was no longer sheltered by trees.

It was from Alice's shadow, as they walked side by side, that the doctor noticed the asymmetry of her gait. Her right shoulder, weighed down by the camera, acted as a counterpoint to the line of her left leg, which was as hard as a stick. Alice's unsettling grace was exacerbated in her oblong shadow, making it look one-dimensional, a dark segment branching out into two proportional and equal mechanical prostheses.

"Have you hurt your leg?" he asked.

"What?" said Alice, alarmed.

"I asked if you'd hurt yourself," he repeated. "I saw you were limping."

Alice felt her good leg contracting too. She tried to correct her walk, leaning on her faulty leg as much as she could, until it really hurt. She thought of the cruelty and precision of the word *lame*.

"I had an accident," she said. Then, as if by way of apology, she added, "A long time ago."

"Car?"

"No, skiing."

"I love skiing," Fabio said enthusiastically, sure that he had found an opportunity for a conversation.

"I hate it," Alice replied crisply.

"That's too bad."

"Yes, too bad."

They walked side by side not saying anything more. The young doctor was surrounded by an aura of tranquillity, a solid and transparent sphere of security. His lips were pursed in a smile even when he wasn't smiling. He looked at ease, as if he met a girl in a hospital room every day and chatted to her as he walked her back to her car. Alice, on the other hand, felt like a piece of wood. Her tendons were on the alert, she was aware of the creaking of her joints, the stiff muscles sticking to her bones.

She pointed to a parked blue Seicento, as if to say that's it, and Fabio spread out his arms. A car passed along the road behind them. From nothing, its noise grew and then faded away again, until it finally disappeared.

"So, are you a photographer?" said the doctor, to buy some time as much as anything else.

"Yes," Alice replied instinctively. She immediately regretted it. For the moment she was a girl who had quit university and was wandering around the streets snapping photographs more or less at random. She wondered whether that was enough to make her a photographer; what was the boundary between being and not being someone?

She bit her thin lip. "More or less," she added.

"May I?" the doctor said, opening his hand for the camera.

"Of course."

Alice unwound the strap from her wrist and held it out to him. He turned it around in his hands. He took off the lens cap and aimed the lens first in front of him and then upward, toward the sky.

"Wow," he observed. "It looks professional."

She blushed and the doctor made as if to give her back the camera.

"You can take a picture if you like," said Alice.

"No, no, please. I don't know how. You do it."

"Of what?"

Fabio looked around. He turned his head from side to side, dubiously. Then he shrugged.

"Of me," he replied.

Alice looked at him suspiciously.

"Why should I?" she asked him, with a slightly malicious inflection that escaped from her involuntarily.

"Because then you'd have to see me again, at least to show it to me."

Alice hesitated for a moment. She looked into Fabio's eyes, carefully for the first time, and couldn't hold their gaze for more than a second. They were blue and shadowless, as clear as the sky behind him, and she felt lost inside them, as if she were naked in a huge empty room.

He's handsome, thought Alice. He's handsome in the way a boy should be handsome.

She aimed the viewfinder at the middle of his face. He smiled, without a hint of embarrassment. He didn't even tilt his head, as people often do in front of the lens. Alice adjusted the focus and then pressed down with her index finger. The air was shattered by a click.

23

Mattia presented himself in Niccoli's office a week after their first meeting. The professor recognized his knock, a fact that curiously disturbed him. Seeing Mattia come in, he took a deep breath, ready to fly into a fury as soon as the boy said something along the lines of there are things I don't understand or I wanted to ask you if you could explain a few passages to me. If I'm forceful enough, Niccoli thought, I might be able to get rid of him.

Mattia asked may I, and, without looking the professor in the face, set down on the edge of his desk the article that he had given him to study. Niccoli picked it up and a little stack of pages slid out, numbered and neatly written, appended to the stapled ones. He quickly gathered them up and realized they were the calculations of the article, perfectly executed and with precise reference to the text. He quickly flipped through them but didn't need to examine them thoroughly to determine that they were correct: the order of the pages was enough to reveal their exactness.

He was a little disappointed, his fit of fury stuck halfway down his throat, like a sneeze that refused to come. He kept nodding as he reviewed Mattia's work, trying in vain to suppress a jolt of envy for this boy who seemed so unfit for existence but was doubtless gifted in this subject, something he himself had never really felt.

"Very good," he said at last, more to himself than with the intention of paying a genuine compliment. Then, with apparent boredom, "A problem is raised in the final paragraphs. It concerns the moments of the zeta function to—"

"I've done it," Mattia cut in. "I think I've solved it."

Niccoli looked at him with suspicion and then with deliberate disdain.

"Oh, really?"

"In the last page of my notes."

The professor licked his index finger and flipped through to the end. Frowning, he quickly read Mattia's demonstration, not understanding much of it, but not finding anything to object to either. Then he started from the beginning, more slowly, and this time the reasoning struck him as clear, quite rigorous, in fact, although marred here and there by amateur pedantry. As he followed the steps, his forehead relaxed and he unconsciously began stroking his lower lip. He forgot about Mattia, who was still frozen in the same position since he first arrived, looking at his feet and repeating in his head let it be right, let it be right, as if the rest of his life depended on the professor's verdict. As he said that to himself he didn't imagine, however, that it really would be.

Niccoli rested the pages on the table again, carefully, and dropped back into his chair, once again crossing his hands behind his head, his favorite position.

"Well, I'd say you're all set," he said.

He was to graduate at the end of May. Mattia asked his parents not to come. What? was all his mother could say. He shook his head, looking toward the window. The glass gave onto a wall of darkness and reflected the image of the three of them sitting around a four-sided table. In the reflection Mattia saw his father taking his mother's arm and gesturing to her to let it go. Then he saw the reflection of her getting up from the table with her hand over her mouth and turning on the tap to wash the dishes, even though they hadn't finished dinner yet.

Graduation day arrived just like any other, and Mattia got up before the alarm. His phantasms, which had filled his mind with scribbled sheets of paper during the night, took a few minutes to dissolve. No one was in the living room, just an elegant blue suit, brand-new, laid out beside a perfectly ironed pale pink shirt. On the shirt was a note with the words *To our graduate* and signed *Mom and Dad,* but in Dad's handwriting alone. Mattia put the clothes on and left the house without even looking at himself in the mirror.

He defended his thesis, looking the members of the committee straight in the eyes, devoting an equal amount of time to each of them and with a steady voice. Niccoli, sitting in the first row, nodded gravely and noted the growing amazement on the faces of his colleagues.

When the moment of the announcement came, Mattia arranged himself in a line with the other candidates. They were the only ones standing in the oversized space of the great hall. Mattia felt the eyes of the audience tingle on his back. He tried to distract himself by estimating the volume of the room, taking as his scale the height of the dean, but the tingle climbed up his neck and split in two directions, wrapping around to his temples. He imagined thousands of little insects pouring into his ears; thousands of hungry moths tunneling into his brain.

The words that the dean repeated identically for each candidate seemed longer each time, and were drowned out by a growing noise in his head, so loud that he couldn't make out his own name when the moment came. Something solid, like an ice cube, obstructed his throat. He shook the dean's hand and it was so dry to the touch that he instinctively sought the metal buckle of the belt that he wasn't wearing. The whole audience rose to its feet with the sound of a rising tide. Niccoli came over and clapped him twice on the shoulder, saying congratulations. Before the applause ended Mattia was out of the hall and walking hastily down the corridor, forgetting to put his toe down first to keep his footsteps from echoing on the way out.

I've done it, I've done it, he silently repeated to himself. But the

closer he got to the door the more aware he became of an abyss opening up in his stomach. Outside, the sunlight overwhelmed him, along
with the heat and the noise of the traffic. He staggered, as if from
fear of falling from the concrete step. There was a group of people on
the pavement; Mattia counted sixteen with a single glance. Many of
them were holding flowers, almost certainly waiting for his fellow
students. For a moment Mattia wished someone was there for him.
He felt the need to abandon his own weight onto someone else's body,
as if the contents of his head had suddenly become more than his two
legs alone could bear. He looked for his parents, he looked for Alice
and Denis, but there were only strangers looking nervously at their
watches, fanning themselves with sheets of paper they'd picked up
who knows where, smoking, talking loudly, and noticing nothing.

He looked at the degree that he held rolled up in his hand, on
which was written in beautiful cursive script that Mattia Balossino
was a graduate, a professional, an adult, that it was time for Mr.
Balossino, B.Sc., to face up to life, and that this meant he had reached
the end of the track that he had blindly followed from the first year
of primary school to graduation. He was still only half breathing,
as if the air didn't have enough momentum to accomplish the complete cycle.

What now? he wondered out loud.

A short, panting woman said excuse me, please, and he stepped
aside to let her in. He followed her inside, not even she could lead
him to the right answer, and walked reluctantly down the corridor
and climbed the stairs to the second floor. He stepped into the library
and went and sat down at his usual place, beside the window. He set
his degree down on the empty seat beside him and stretched his
hands out on the table. He concentrated on his own breathing, which
was still stuck in some backwash between his throat and the bottom
of his lungs. It had happened to him before, but never for such a
long time.

You can't forget how to do it, he said to himself. It's something you simply can't forget and that's that.

He exhaled all the air and was in a state of apnea for several seconds. Then he opened his mouth wide and inhaled as hard as he could, so much that the muscles in his chest hurt. This time his breath went all the way to the bottom of his lungs and Mattia thought he could see the molecules of oxygen, round and white, scattering around his arteries and beginning to swirl toward his heart once more.

He stayed in the same position for an indefinite amount of time, without thinking, without noticing the students coming in and out, in an absentminded state of numbness and agitation.

Then something flashed in front of his eyes, a red patch, and Mattia gave a start. He focused his eyes upon a rose wrapped in cellophane, which someone had slapped rudely onto the desk. Following the stem he recognized Alice's hand with its protruding knuckles, slightly reddened compared to her white fingers, and rounded nails cut down to the edge of the fingertip.

"You're a real jerk."

Mattia looked at her as one looks at a hallucination. He felt as if he were approaching the scene from a long way away, from a blurry place that he was already unable to remember well. When he was close enough, he made out on Alice's face a deep and unfamiliar sadness.

"Why didn't you tell me?" she went on. "You should have told me. You should have."

Alice slipped into the seat opposite Mattia, exhausted. She looked outside, toward the street, shaking her head.

"How did you . . . ?" Mattia began.

"Your parents. I found out from your parents." Alice turned and stared at him, her blue eyes boiling with rage. "Do you think that's right?"

Mattia hesitated and then shook his head, a dim and distorted outline moving with him over the wrinkled surface of the cellophane.

"I'd always imagined being there. I'd imagined it so many times. While you . . ."

Alice paused, the rest of the sentence trapped between her teeth. Mattia reflected once more on how that moment had suddenly become so real. He tried to remember where he had been until a few seconds before, but couldn't.

"You never did," Alice finished. "Never."

He felt his head sinking between his shoulders, felt the moths swarming inside his skull again.

"It wasn't important," he whispered. "I didn't want—"

"Shut up," she interrupted him abruptly. Someone at another desk said shhh and the silence of the next few seconds preserved the memory of that hiss.

"You're pale," said Alice. She looked at Mattia suspiciously. "Are you okay?"

"I don't know. I feel a bit dizzy."

Alice got to her feet. She brushed her hair from her forehead, along with a tangle of unpleasant thoughts. Then she bent over Mattia and gave him a kiss on the cheek, silent and light, which in a breath swept away all the insects.

"I'm sure you did brilliantly," she whispered into his ear. "I know you did."

Mattia felt her hair tickling his neck. He felt the soft hollow of air that separated them filling with her warmth and pressing lightly on his skin, like cotton wool. He became aware of an urge to pull her to him, but his hands remained motionless, as if asleep.

Alice straightened up, then she picked up his diploma from the chair, unrolled it, and smiled, reading it under her breath.

"Wow," she said at last. Her voice assumed a radiant tone. "We've got to celebrate. Come on, Mr. B.Sc., on your feet," she commanded.

She held out her hand to Mattia. He took it, rather uncertainly at first. He allowed himself to be led out of the library, with the same disarmed trust with which years before he had been dragged into the girls' bathroom. Over time the proportions between their hands had changed. Now his fingers wrapped completely around Alice's, like the rough halves of a seashell.

"Where are we going?" he asked her.

"For a drive. The sun's out. And you need to get some sun."

They left the building and this time Mattia wasn't afraid of the light, the traffic, and the people gathered around the entrance.

In the car they kept the windows lowered. Alice drove with both hands on the wheel and sang to "Pictures of You," imitating the sound of the words that she didn't know. Mattia felt his muscles gradually relaxing, adapting to the shape of the seat. He felt as if the car were leaving a dark and sticky trail in its wake, a trail of his past and all his worries. He gradually began to feel lighter, like a jar being emptied. He closed his eyes, and for a few seconds floated on the air that fanned his face, and on Alice's voice.

When he opened them again they were on the road leading to his house. He wondered if they might have organized a surprise party for him and prayed that it wasn't so.

"Come on, where are we going?" he asked again.

"Don't you worry," murmured Alice. "If you ever take me for a drive you'll have the right to choose."

For the first time Mattia was ashamed to be twenty-two and not have gotten his driver's license. It was another of the things he had left behind, another obvious step in a boy's life that he had decided not to take, so as to stay as far as possible from the machinery of life. Like eating popcorn at the movies, like sitting on the back of a bench, like not respecting your parents' curfew, like playing football with a ball of tinfoil, like standing naked in front of a girl. He thought that from this precise moment things would be different. He decided he would get his license as soon as possible. He would do it for her, to take her for a drive. Even though he was afraid to admit it, when he was with her it seemed it was worth doing all those normal things that normal people do.

Now that they were close to Mattia's house, Alice turned in another direction. She pulled onto the main road and parked the car a hundred yards down, opposite the park.

"*Voilà*," she said. She unfastened her seat belt and got out of the car.

Mattia stayed frozen in his seat, his eyes fixed on the park.

"Well? Are you getting out?"

"Not here," he said.

"Come on, don't be stupid."

Mattia shook his head.

"Let's go somewhere else," he said.

Alice looked around.

"What's the problem?" she insisted. "We're just going to take a walk."

She came over to the window on Mattia's side. He was stiff, as if someone were sticking a knife in his back. His hand gripped the handle of the door, which was half open. He stared at the trees a hundred yards away. The wide, green leaves covered their knotty skeletons and the fractal structure of the branches, hiding their horrible secret.

He had never been back here. The last time was with the police, that day that his father had told him give your mother your hand and she had pulled hers away and stuck it in her pocket. That day he had still had both his arms bandaged, from his fingers to his elbow, with a thick dressing rolled in so many layers that it took a saw blade to remove it. He had shown the policemen where

Michela had been sitting. They had wanted to know the exact spot and had taken pictures, first from far away and then from close up.

From the car, on the way back home, he had seen the dredging machines sinking their mechanical arms into the river and pulling out big piles of wet soil, then dropping them heavily on the bank. Mattia had noticed that his mother held her breath every time, until each pile disintegrated on the ground. Michela must have been in that slime, but they didn't find her. They never found her.

"Let's get out of here. Please," repeated Mattia. His tone wasn't pleading. Instead he seemed absorbed, annoyed.

Alice got back into the car.

"Sometimes I don't know whether—"

"That's where I abandoned my twin sister," he cut in with a flat, almost inhuman voice. He lifted his arm and with his right index finger pointed to the trees in the park. Then he left it hanging there in midair, as if he had forgotten about it.

"Twin sister? What are you talking about? You don't have a twin sister. . . ."

Mattia nodded slowly, still staring at the trees.

"She was my identical twin. Completely identical to me," he said.

Then, before Alice even had time to ask, he told her everything. He spilled out the whole story, like a dam collapsing. The worm, the party, the Legos, the river, the bits of glass, the hospital room, the judge, the television appeal, the shrinks, everything, in a way he had never done with anyone. He talked without looking at her, without getting excited. Then he lapsed back into silence. He felt around under the seat with his right hand, but found only blunt shapes. He calmed down, feeling remote again, alien to his own body.

Alice's hand touched his chin and delicately turned his face toward her. All Mattia saw was a shadow moving toward him. He instinctively closed his eyes and then felt Alice's hot mouth on his, her tears on his cheek, or maybe they weren't hers, and finally her hands, so light, holding his head still and catching all his thoughts and imprisoning them there, in the space that no longer existed between them.

24

They saw each other often over the next month, without ever making a real date but never really by chance. After visiting hours Alice always ended up wandering around Fabio's ward, and he always managed to run into her. They'd stroll around the courtyard, always taking the same route that they had decided by mutual agreement, without discussing it. That outer enclosure marked the confines of their story, carving out a space where there was no need to name that clear and mysterious thing flowing between them.

Fabio seemed to have a precise knowledge of the dynamics of courtship; he knew how to respect rhythms and moderate phrases as if following a set protocol. He sensed Alice's profound suffering, but remained beyond it, as if he were standing on the border. The excesses of the world, whatever form they might assume, didn't really concern him. They collided with his equilibrium and common sense and so he preferred to ignore them, simply pretending that they didn't exist. If an obstacle blocked his path, he walked around it, without altering his own pace in the slightest, and soon forgot it. He never had doubts, or hardly ever.

Nonetheless, he knew how to reach an objective, so he was attentive to Alice's moods in a way that was respectful, though slightly pedantic. If she didn't talk, he asked her if something was wrong, but never twice in a row. He showed interest in her photographs, in how her mother was, and filled the silences with stories from his own day, amusing anecdotes he picked up around the ward.

Alice allowed herself to be carried away by his self-confidence and gradually abandoned herself to it, as she had abandoned herself to the support of the water when as a little girl she played dead in the swimming pool.

They lived the slow and invisible interpenetration of their universes, like two stars gravitating around a common axis, in ever tighter orbits, whose clear destiny is to coalesce at some point in space and time.

Alice's mother's treatment had been suspended. With a nod of the head, her husband had finally given his consent to let her sink into painless sleep, under a heavy blanket of morphine. Alice merely waited for it to come to an end and couldn't bring herself to feel guilty. Her mother already lived within her as a memory, settled like a clump of pollen in a corner of her head, where she would stay for the rest of her life, frozen in the same pile of soundless images.

Fabio hadn't planned to ask her and wasn't the type for impulsive gestures, but that afternoon there was something different about Alice. A kind of nervousness emerged from the way she wove her fingers together and moved her eyes from side to side, always careful not to meet his own. For the first time since meeting her he was hasty and incautious.

"My parents are going to the beach this weekend," he said out of the blue.

Alice seemed not to have heard. At any rate, she let the sentence drop. Her head had been buzzing like a wasps' nest for days. Mattia hadn't called her since his graduation, more than a week before, and yet it clearly was his turn now.

"I thought you could come to dinner at my place," Fabio tossed out.

His confidence faltered for a moment in the middle of those words, but he immediately shook off his uncertainty. He plunged both hands into the pockets of his white coat and prepared to accept any kind of reply with the same kind of lightness. He knew how to build a shelter for himself even before he needed one.

Alice smiled faintly, slightly panic-stricken.

"I don't know," she said gently. "Perhaps it isn't—"

"You're right," Fabio interrupted her. "I shouldn't have asked you. Sorry."

They finished their walk in silence and when they reached Fabio's ward again he murmured okay, long and drawn out, as if speaking to himself.

Neither of them moved. They exchanged a quick glance and immediately lowered their eyes. Fabio started to laugh.

"We never know how to say good-bye to each other, you and me," he said.

"Yeah." Alice smiled at him. She brought a hand to her hair, hooked a lock with her index finger, and tugged on it slightly.

Fabio took a resolute step toward her and the gravel of the path crunched beneath his foot. He kissed her on her left cheek, with affectionate arrogance, and then stepped back.

"Well, at least think about it," he said.

He smiled broadly, with his whole mouth, eyes, and cheeks. Then he turned around and walked confidently toward the entrance.

Now he'll turn around, thought Alice when he went through the glass door.

But Fabio turned the corner and disappeared down the corridor.

25

The letter was addressed to Mr. Mattia Balossino, B.Sc., and to the touch it was so light and insubstantial it seemed impossible it could contain his whole future. His mother hadn't shown it to him until dinner, perhaps out of embarrassment at having opened it without permission. She hadn't done it on purpose, she hadn't even looked at the name on the envelope: Mattia never got any mail.

"This came," she said, holding the letter over the plates.

Mattia glanced quizzically at his father, who nodded at something vague. Before taking the letter he ran his napkin over his upper lip, which was already clean. Seeing the complicated circular logo, printed in blue next to the address, he had no idea what it might contain. He pressed on both sides of the envelope to take out the folded page inside it. He opened it and began to read, rather impressed by the thought that this letter was specifically for him, Mr. Mattia Balossino, B.Sc.

His parents made more noise than necessary with their silverware and his father repeatedly cleared his throat. After reading it, Mattia refolded the page with the reverse sequence of gestures with which he had opened it, so as to return it to its initial form, and slipped it back into its envelope, which he then set down on Michela's chair.

He picked up his fork again, but was momentarily bewildered at the sight of the sliced zucchini on the plate, as if someone had made them appear there by surprise.

138   "It sounds like a wonderful opportunity," said Adele.

"Yeah."

"Do you want to go?"

As she spoke, Mattia's mother felt heat flashing in her face. She was aware that it had nothing to do with the fear of losing him. On the contrary, she hoped with all her might that he would accept, that he would leave this house and the place that he occupied opposite her every evening at dinner, his black head dangling over his plate and that contagious air of tragedy surrounding him.

"I don't know," Mattia replied to his plate.

"It's a wonderful opportunity," his mother repeated.

"Yeah."

Mattia's father broke the silence that followed with random thoughts about the efficiency of northern Europeans, about how clean their streets were, putting it all down to the severe climate and the lack of light for much of the year, which limited distractions. He had never been anywhere of the kind, but from what he had heard that was clearly how it was.

When, at the end of dinner, Mattia began stacking up the dishes, collecting them in the same order as he did every evening, his father put a hand on his shoulder and said under his breath go on, I'll finish up. Mattia picked up the envelope from the chair and went to his room.

He sat down on the bed and began turning the letter around in his hands. He folded it backward and forward a few times, making the thin paper of the envelope crack. Then he examined the logo beside the address more carefully. A bird of prey, probably an eagle, held its wings open and its head turned to one side so as to show its pointed beak in profile. Its wing tips and claws were inscribed in a circle, which a printing error had turned slightly oval. Another circle, larger and concentric with the preceding one, contained the name of the university that was offering Mattia a place. The Gothic characters, all those *k*'s and *h*'s in the name and the *o*'s with a diagonal line running through them, which in mathematics indicated a null set, made Mattia imagine a tall, dark building, with echoing corridors and high ceilings, surrounded by lawns with grass cut to a few millimeters from the ground, as silent and deserted as a cathedral at the end of the world.

In that unknown and far-off place lay his future as a mathematician. There was a promise of salvation, an uncontaminated place where nothing was yet compromised. Here, on the other hand, there was Alice, just Alice, and all around her a swamp.

It happened as it had on the day he graduated. Once again his breath caught halfway down his throat, where it acted as a stopper. He gasped as if the air in his room had suddenly liquefied. The days had grown longer, and the dusk was blue and wearying. Mattia would wait for the last trace of light to fade, his mind wandering along corridors that he hadn't yet seen, now and then bumping into Alice, who would look at him without a word, without so much as a smile.

You've just got to decide, he thought. Go or don't go. 1 or 0, like a binary code.

But the more he tried to simplify things, the more confused he became.

Someone knocked on the door of his room. The sound reached him as if from the bottom of a well.

"Yes?" he said.

The door opened slowly and his father poked his head in.

"Can I come in?" he asked.

"Uh-huh."

"Why are you sitting in the dark?"

Without waiting for an answer, Pietro flipped the switch and 100 watts of light exploded in Mattia's dilated pupils, which contracted with a pleasant pain.

His father sat down on the bed next to him. They had the same way of crossing their legs, the left calf balanced on the right heel, but neither of them had ever noticed.

"What's the name of that thing you studied?" Pietro asked after a while.

"What thing?"

"That thing you wrote your dissertation on. I can never remember what it's called."

"The Riemann zeta function."

"Right. The Riemann zeta function."

Mattia rubbed his thumbnail under the nail of his little finger, but the skin there had become so hard and calloused that he didn't feel a thing. His nails slipped noisily over each other.

"I wish I'd had your mind," Pietro went on. "But I never understand a thing about math. It just wasn't for me. You have to have a special sort of brain for some things."

Mattia thought there was nothing good about having his mind. That he would happily have unscrewed it and replaced it with a different one, or even with a package of biscotti, provided it was empty and light. He opened his mouth to reply that feeling special is the worst kind of cage that a person can build for himself, but he didn't say anything. He thought about the time his teacher had sat him in the middle of the classroom, with everyone else staring at him like some exotic beast, and it occurred to him that it was as if he'd never moved from there in all those years.

"Did Mom tell you to come?" he asked his father.

The muscles in Pietro's neck stiffened. He sucked in his lips and then nodded.

"Your future is the most important thing," he said in a vaguely embarrassed voice. "You need to think about yourself now. If you decide to go we'll support you. We haven't got a lot of money, but enough if you need it."

There was another lengthy silence, in which Mattia thought about Alice, and about the share of money that he had stolen from Michela.

"Dad?" he said at last.

"Yes?"

"Could you leave, please? I have to make a phone call."

Pietro gave a long sigh that also contained a certain amount of relief.

"Of course," he said.

He got up, and before turning around he stretched a hand toward Mattia's face. He was about to caress his cheek, but stopped a few inches from the unruly tufts of his son's beard. He redirected his hand to his hair, which he barely touched. After all, it had been quite a while since they had done such things.

26

Denis's love for Mattia had burned itself out, like a forgotten candle in an empty room, leaving behind a ravenous discontent. When he was nineteen, Denis found an advertisement for a gay bar on the last page of a local newspaper and tore it out, keeping the scrap of paper in his wallet for two whole months. From time to time he unrolled it and reread the address, even though he already knew it by heart.

All around him, guys his age were going out with girls and by now they were used to sex, so much so that they'd stopped talking about it all the time. Denis felt that his only escape route lay in that piece of newspaper; in that address that had faded from the sweat of his fingertips.

He went one rainy evening, without really having made his mind up to go. He put on the first thing he pulled out of his closet and headed out, giving a quick shout to his parents in the other room. I'm going to the movies, he said.

He walked past the bar two or three times, circling the block every time. Finally he went in with his hands in his pockets and a confidential wink to the bouncer. He sat down at the bar, ordered a lager, and sipped it slowly, staring at the bottles lined up along the wall, waiting.

A guy came over to him a moment later and Denis decided he'd be okay, even before he looked him properly in the face. The man started talking about himself, or maybe about some film that Denis hadn't seen. He shouted in his ear but Denis didn't listen to a word. He brusquely interrupted him saying let's go to the toilet. The other guy was struck dumb and then he smiled, revealing bad teeth. Denis thought he was horrible, that his eyebrows almost joined up and he was old, too old, but it didn't matter.

In the toilet the guy pulled his T-shirt up over his belly and bent forward to kiss him, but Denis pulled away. Instead he knelt down and unbuttoned the other man's pants. Damn, he said, you're in a hurry. But then he let him get on with it. Denis shut his eyes and tried to finish as quickly as possible.

He didn't get a result with his mouth and felt completely hopeless. Then he used his hands, both of them, insistently. As the guy came he came too, in his pants. He almost ran from the toilet, without giving the stranger time to get his clothes back on. The same old sense of guilt took hold of him as soon as he was past the toilet door, and drenched him like a bucket of icy water.

Outside the bar he wandered about for half an hour in search of a fountain to wash the smell off him.

He went back to the bar on other occasions. Every time he talked to someone different and he always found an excuse not to give his real name. He never hooked up with anyone else. He collected the stories of people like himself, mostly keeping silent and listening. He slowly discovered that the stories were similar, that there was a process, and that the process involved immersion, putting your whole head under until you touched the bottom and only then coming up for air.

Every one of them had a love that had rotted alone in their heart, as his love for Mattia had done. Each of them had been afraid and many of them still were, but not when they were here, among others who could understand, protected by the "scene," as they put it. When he talked to those strangers Denis felt less alone and wondered when his moment would come, the day when he would touch bottom, resurface, and finally be able to breathe.

One evening someone told him about "the cemetery lamps." That's what they called the little path up behind the graveyard, where the only light, faint and trembling, was from the tombstone lamps filtering between the bars of the big cemetery gate. They would grope about there, it was the perfect place to empty themselves of desire without seeing or being seen, merely putting their bodies at the disposal of the dark.

It was at the lamps that Denis had touched bottom. He slammed into it with his face, chest, and knees, as though diving into shallow water. Afterward he never went back to the bar, locking himself away, more stubbornly than before, in his own denial.

Then, in his junior year at university, he went to study in Spain. There, far from the probing eyes of his family and friends, far from all the streets whose names he knew, love found him. His name was Valerio and he was Italian like him; young and scared to death like him. The months they spent together, in a little apartment a few blocks from the Ramblas, were quick and intense and they removed the useless cloak of suffering, as on the first clear evening after days of pouring rain.

Back in Italy they lost sight of each other, but Denis didn't suffer. With a completely new confidence, which he would never lose, he moved on to other affairs, which seemed to have been waiting for him for all that time, lined up in an orderly fashion just around the corner. The only old friendship he maintained was with Mattia. They spoke only rarely, mostly on the phone, and were capable of being silent for minutes at a time, each lost in his own thoughts, punctuated by the other's reassuring, rhythmical breathing at the other end of the line.

Denis was brushing his teeth when the call came. At his house they always answered after the second ring, the time it took to get to the nearest telephone from anywhere in the apartment.

His mother called Denis it's for you, and he took his time answering. He rinsed his mouth out well, passed the towel over it, and glanced once more at his two upper front incisors. Over the past few days he had had a sense that they were overlapping, because of his wisdom teeth pushing in from the sides.

"Hello?"

"Hi."

Mattia never introduced himself. He knew that his voice was unmistakable to his friend and anyway he didn't like saying his name.

"So, Mr. Graduate, how are you?" Denis said cheerfully. He wasn't upset about the graduation business. He had learned to respect the chasm that Mattia had dug around himself. Years previously he had tried to jump over that chasm, and had fallen into it. Now he contented himself with sitting on the edge, his legs dangling into the void. Mattia's voice no longer stirred anything in his stomach, but he was aware of the idea of him and always would be, as the only true benchmark for everything that had come afterward.

"Did I disturb you?" asked Mattia.

"No. Did I disturb you?" Denis teased.

"I was the one who called you."

"Of course, so tell me: I can tell from your voice that something's up."

Mattia remained silent. Something was up, it was there on the tip of his tongue.

"Well?" Denis pressed. "And this something would be?"

Mattia exhaled loudly into the receiver and Denis became aware that he was having difficulty breathing. He picked up a pen beside the telephone and started playing with it, passing it between the fingers of his right hand. Then he dropped it and he didn't bend down to pick it up. Mattia still wasn't speaking.

"Shall I start asking questions?" said Denis. "We could do it so that you—"

"I've been offered a position abroad," Mattia interrupted. "At a university. An important one."

"Wow," Denis observed, not surprised in the least. "That sounds fantastic. Are you going?"

"I don't know. Should I?"

Denis pretended to laugh.

"You're asking me that when I haven't even finished university? I'd go in a second. A change of air always does one good."

He thought of adding and what is there to keep you here? But he didn't say it.

"It's because something happened, the other day," Mattia ventured. "The day I graduated."

"Mmm."

"Alice was there and . . ."

"And?"

Mattia hesitated for a moment.

"Well, we kissed," he said at last.

Denis's fingers stiffened around the receiver. He was surprised by his reaction. He was no longer jealous of Alice, there was no point, but at that moment it was as if an undigested bit of the past had come back up his throat. For a moment he saw Mattia and Alice hand in hand in Viola's kitchen, and he felt Giulia Mirandi's invasive tongue forcing its way into his mouth like a rolled-up towel.

"Hallelujah," he remarked, trying to sound happy. "You two have finally done it."

"Yeah."

In the pause that followed both of them wanted to hang up.

"And now you don't know what to do," Denis struggled to say.

"Yeah."

"But you and she are now, what would you say . . . ?"

"I don't know. I haven't seen her since."

"Ah."

Denis ran the nail of his index finger along the curled wire of the telephone. At the other end Mattia did the same and as always he thought of a DNA helix, missing its twin.

"Numbers are everywhere," said Denis. "They're always the same, aren't they?"

"Yes."

"But Alice is only here."

"Yes."

"So you've already made up your mind."

Denis heard his friend's breath easing and becoming more regular.

"Thank you," said Mattia.

"For what?"

Mattia hung up. Denis spent another few seconds with the receiver pressed to his ear, listening to the silence inside it. Something within him went out, like one last ember that had stayed lit for too long under the ashes.

I said the right thing, he thought.

The busy signal sounded. Denis hung up and went back into the bathroom to check on those wretched wisdom teeth.

27

"¿Qué pasa, mi amorcito?" Soledad asked Alice, tilting her head slightly to catch her eye. Ever since Fernanda had been in the hospital she had eaten at the dinner table with them, because father and daughter facing each other, alone, was unbearable for both of them.

Alice's father had developed the habit of not changing when he came home from work. He had dinner in his jacket and tie, slightly loosened, as if he were merely passing through. He held a newspaper open on the table and looked up only to make sure that his daughter was gulping down at least the occasional mouthful.

The silence had become part of the meal and disturbed only Sol, who often thought back to the rowdy meals at her mother's house, when she was still very young and could never have imagined she would end up like this.

Alice hadn't even looked at the cutlet and salad on her plate. She took little sips of water, crossing her eyes as she drank and regarding the glass resting on her lips as seriously as if it held some kind of medicine. She shrugged and flashed a swift smile at Sol.

"Sorry," she said. "I'm not very hungry."

Her father nervously turned the page. Before setting the paper back down he gave it an impetuous shake and couldn't help glancing at his daughter's full plate. He didn't comment and started reading again, beginning a random article in the middle, without grasping its meaning.

"Sol?" asked Alice.

"Yes?"

"How did your husband win you? The first time, I mean. What did he do?"

Soledad stopped chewing. Then she started again, more slowly, to gain some time. The first image that ran through her head wasn't of the day she met her husband. Instead she thought back to that morning when she had gotten up late and wandered barefoot around the house, looking for him. Over the years all the memories of her marriage had become concentrated in those few moments, as if the time spent with her husband had been only the preparation for an ending. That morning she had looked at the previous night's dirty dishes and the cushions in the wrong place on the sofa. Everything was just as they had left it and the sounds in the air were the same as ever. And yet something, in the way things were arranged and the way the light clung to them, had left her frozen in the middle of the sitting room, dismayed. And then, with disconcerting clarity, she had thought he's gone.

Soledad sighed, feigning her usual nostalgia.

"He brought me home from work on his bicycle. Every day he came with his bicycle," she said. "And he gave me some shoes."

"What?"

"Shoes. White ones, high heels."

Soledad smiled and indicated the length of the heels with her thumb and index finger.

"They were very pretty," she said.

Alice's father snorted and shuffled in his chair, as if he found all this intolerable. Alice imagined Sol's husband coming out of the shop with the shoe box under his arm. She knew him from the photograph that Sol kept hung over the head of her bed, with a dry little olive branch slipped between the nail and the hook.

For a moment Alice felt light-headed, but her thoughts immediately turned to Mattia, and stayed there. A week had passed, and he still hadn't called.

I'll go now, she thought.

She slipped a forkful of salad into her mouth, as if to say to her father look I've eaten. The vinegar stung her lips slightly. She was still chewing as she got up from the table.

"I've got to go out," she said.

Her father arched his eyebrows.

"And might we know where you're going at this hour?" he asked.

"Out," said Alice defiantly. Then she added, "To a girlfriend's," to soften the tone.

Her father shook his head, as if to say do what you like. For a moment Alice felt sorry for him, left on his own like that behind his newspaper. She felt a desire to hug him and tell him everything and ask him what she should do, but a moment later the same thought made her shiver. She turned around and headed resolutely for the bathroom.

Her father lowered the newspaper and with two fingers he rubbed his weary eyes. Sol turned the memory of the high-heeled shoes around in her head for a few seconds, then put it back in its place and got up to clear the things away.

On her way to Mattia's house, Alice kept the music turned up, but if when she got there someone had asked her what she was listening to, she wouldn't have been able to say. All of a sudden she was furious and she was sure that she was about to ruin everything, but she no longer had any choice. That evening, getting up from the table, she had crossed the invisible boundary beyond which things start working by themselves. It was like when she was learning to ski, when she would move her center of gravity too far forward by an insignificant couple of millimeters, just enough to end up facedown in the snow.

She had been to Mattia's house only once before, and only as far as the living room. Mattia had disappeared into his room to change and she had had an embarrassing chat with his mother,

Mrs. Balossino, who observed her from the sofa with a vaguely worried air, as if Alice's hair were on fire or something, without even offering her a seat.

Alice rang the doorbell and the display beside it lit up red, like a final warning. After a few crackles Mattia's mother answered in a frightened voice.

"Who is it?"

"It's Alice, Mrs. Balossino. I'm sorry about the time, but . . . is Mattia there?"

From the other end she heard a thoughtful silence. Alice pulled her hair over her right shoulder, having the disagreeable impression of being observed through the lens of the intercom. The door opened with an electrical click. Before coming in, Alice smiled at the camera to say thank you.

In the empty hallway her footsteps echoed with the rhythm of a heartbeat. Her bad leg seemed to have lost all life, as if her heart had forgotten to pump blood into it.

The door to the apartment was ajar, but there was no one to welcome her. Alice pushed it open and said, "Hello?" Mattia emerged from the sitting room and stopped at least two meters away from her.

"Hi," he said, without moving his arms.

"Hi."

They stood looking at each other for a few seconds, as if they didn't know each other at all. Mattia had crossed his big toe over his second one, inside his slipper, and by squashing one over the other and against the floor he hoped he could break them.

"Sorry if I'm—"

"Won't you come in?" Mattia broke in automatically.

Alice turned to close the door and the round brass handle slipped from her sweaty palm. The door slammed, shaking the frame, and a shiver of impatience ran through Mattia.

What's she doing here? he thought.

It was as if the Alice he had been talking to Denis about only a few minutes before wasn't the same one who had just dropped by without warning. He tried to clear his mind of that ridiculous thought, but the irritation remained in his mouth like a kind of nausea.

He thought of the word *hunted.* Then he thought about when his father used to drag him onto the carpet and imprison him between his enormous arms. He tickled him on his tummy and on his sides and he exploded with laughter; he laughed so hard that he couldn't breathe.

Alice followed him into the sitting room. Mattia's parents stood waiting, like a little welcoming committee.

"Good evening," she said, shrinking back.

"Hi, Alice," replied Adele, without moving.

Pietro, on the other hand, came over and unexpectedly stroked her hair.

"You're getting prettier and prettier," he said. "How's your mother?"

Adele, behind her husband's back, held a paralyzed smile and bit her lip for not having asked the question herself.

Alice blushed.

"Same as usual," she said, so as not to appear overdramatic. "She's getting by."

"Say hello from us," said Pietro.

All four of them stood in silence. Mattia's father seemed to stare right through Alice and she tried to distribute her weight uniformly on her legs, so as not to look crippled. She realized that her mother would never meet Mattia's parents and she was a bit sorry about that, but she was even sorrier to be the only one thinking anything of the kind.

"You two go on," Pietro said at last.

Alice passed beside him with her head lowered after smiling once more at Adele. Mattia was already waiting in his room.

"Shall I close it?" asked Alice once she was inside, pointing to the door. All her courage had deserted her.

"Uh-huh."

Mattia sat on the bed, with his hands crossed on his knees. Alice looked around the room. The things that filled it seemed not to have been touched by anyone; they looked like articles that had been carefully and calculatedly displayed in a shopwindow. There was nothing useless, not a photograph on the wall or a stuffed animal from childhood, nothing that gave off that smell of familiarity and affection that teenagers' rooms usually have. With all the chaos that filled her body and her head, Alice felt out of place.

"Nice room," she said, without really meaning it.

"Thanks," said Mattia.

There was an enormous list of things to say floating over their heads and both of them tried to ignore it by looking at the floor.

Alice slid her back along the wardrobe and sat down on the ground with her working knee against her chest. She forced a smile.

"So, how does it feel to have graduated?"

Mattia shrugged and smiled very slightly.

"Exactly the same as before."

"You really don't know how to be happy, do you?"

"Apparently not."

Alice let an affectionate mmm slip through her closed lips and thought that this embarrassment between them made no sense and yet it was there, solid and ineradicable.

"But things have been happening to you lately," she said.

"Yes."

Alice thought about whether to say it or not. Then she said it, not a drop of saliva left in her mouth.

"Something nice, no?"

Mattia drew in his legs.

Here we go, he thought.

"Yes, actually," he said.

He knew exactly what he was supposed to do. He was supposed to get up and go and sit next to her. He was supposed to smile, look into her eyes, and kiss her. It was that simple. It was mere mechanics, a banal sequence of vectors that would bring his mouth to meet hers. He could do it even if at that moment he didn't feel like it; he could trust the precision of his movements.

He made as if to get up, but somehow the mattress kept him where he was, like a sticky morass.

Once again Alice acted in his place.

"Can I sit next to you?" she asked.

He nodded and, even though there was no need to, moved slightly to one side.

Alice pulled herself to her feet, with the help of her hands.

On the bed, in the space that Mattia had left free, there was a piece of paper, typed and folded in three like an accordion. Alice picked it up to move it and noticed that it was written in English.

"What's this?" she asked.

"It came today. It's a letter from a university."

Alice read the name of the city, written in bold in the top left-hand corner, and the letters dimmed under her eyes.

"What does it say?"

"I've been offered a grant."

Alice felt dizzy and panic turned her face white.

"Wow," she lied. "For how long?"

"Four years."

She gulped. She was still standing up.

"And are you going?" she asked under her breath.

"I don't know yet," said Mattia, almost apologizing. "What do you think?"

Alice remained silent, with the sheet of paper in her hands and her gaze lost somewhere on the wall.

"What do you think?" Mattia repeated, as if she really hadn't heard him.

"What do I think about what?" Alice's voice had suddenly hardened, so much that Mattia gave a start. For some reason she thought about her mother in the hospital, dazed with drugs. She looked expressionlessly at the sheet of paper and wanted to tear it up.

Instead she put it back down on the bed, where she had been about to sit down.

"It would be important for my career," Mattia said by way of self-justification.

Alice nodded seriously, with her chin thrust out as if she had a golf ball in her mouth.

"Fine. So what are you waiting for? Off you go. Besides, it doesn't seem to me that there's anything to keep you here," she said between clenched teeth.

Mattia felt the veins in his neck swelling. Perhaps he was about to cry. Ever since that afternoon in the park the tears were always there, like a lump that was hard to swallow, as if that day his tear ducts, clogged for so long, had finally opened and all that accumulated stuff had finally begun to force its way out.

"But if I went away," he began in a slightly quivering voice, "would you . . . ?" He stopped.

"Me?" Alice stared at him from above, as though he were a stain on the bedcover. "I'd imagined the next four years differently," she said. "I'm twenty-three and my mother's about to die. I . . ." She shook her head. "But none of that matters to you. Go ahead and worry about your career."

It was the first time she had used her mother's illness to wound someone, and she didn't particularly regret it. She saw Mattia shrink in front of her eyes.

He didn't reply and in his mind ran through the instructions for breathing.

"But don't you worry," Alice went on. "I've found someone it does matter to. In fact that's what I came here to tell you." She paused, her mind blank. Once again things were taking a course of their own; once again she was tumbling down the slope and forgetting to stick in her ski poles to brake. "His name's Fabio, he's a doctor. I didn't want you to . . . you know."

She uttered the phrase like a little actress, in a voice that wasn't hers. She felt the words scratching her tongue like sand. As she uttered them, she studied Mattia's expression, to pick up a hint of disappointment that she could cling to, but his eyes were too dark for her to make out any spark in them. She was sure none of it mattered to him and her stomach crumpled like a plastic bag.

"I'll be off," she said quietly, exhausted.

Mattia nodded, looking toward the closed window to eliminate Alice completely from his field of vision. That name, Fabio, had pierced his head like a splinter and he just wanted Alice to leave.

He saw that outside the evening was clear and he sensed a warm wind was about to blow through. The opaque pollen of the poplars, swarming under the beam from the streetlights, looked like big legless insects.

Alice opened the door and he got to his feet. He walked her to the front door, following a few steps behind. She distractedly checked in her bag that she had everything, to gain another moment. Then she murmured okay and left.

Before the elevator doors closed, Alice and Mattia exchanged a good-bye that meant nothing at all.

28

Mattia's parents were watching television. His mother sat with her knees curled up under her nightdress; his father with his legs stretched out, crossed on the coffee table in front of the sofa, the remote control resting on one thigh. Alice hadn't responded to their good-bye, she didn't even seem to have noticed that they were there.

Mattia spoke from behind the back of the sofa.

"I've decided to accept," he said.

Adele brought a hand to her cheek and, bewildered, sought her husband's eyes. Mattia's father turned slightly and looked at his son as one looks at a grown-up son.

"Fine," he said.

Mattia went back to his room. He picked up the sheet of paper from the bed and sat down at the desk. He perceived the universe expanding; he could feel it accelerating under his feet and for a moment he hoped that its stretching fabric would burst and let him come crashing down.

He groped around for the light switch and turned it on. He chose the longest of the four pencils lined up side by side, dangerously close to the edge of the desk. From the second drawer he took the sharpener and bent down to sharpen it into the wastepaper basket. He blew away the thin sawdust that was left on the tip of the pencil. There was already a blank sheet in front of him.

He placed his left hand on the paper, palm down and fingers spread wide. He ran the very sharp graphite tip over his skin. He lingered for a second, ready to plunge it into the confluence of the two big veins at the base of his middle finger. Then, slowly, he removed it, and took a deep breath.

On the sheet he wrote *To the kind attention of the Dean.*

29

Fabio was waiting for her by the front door, with the lights of the landing, the door, and the sitting room all on. As he took the plastic bag with the tub of ice cream from her hands, he linked his fingers with hers and kissed her on one cheek, as if it were the most natural thing in the world. He said that dress really suits you and he meant it, and then he went back to the stove to get on with cooking dinner, but without taking his eyes off her.

From the stereo came music that Alice didn't recognize, but it wasn't there to be listened to, just to complete a perfect scenario; there was nothing casual about it. Two candles were lit, the wine was already open, and the table was tidily set for two, with the blades of the knives turned inward, which meant that the guest was welcome, as her mother had taught her when she was little. There was a white tablecloth with no wrinkles and the napkins were folded into triangles with the edges perfectly aligned.

Alice sat down at the table and counted the empty plates stacked on top of one another to work out how much there would be to eat. That evening, before leaving the house, she had spent a long time locked in the bathroom staring at the towels that Soledad changed every Friday. In the marbled-topped chest of drawers she had found her mother's makeup and used it. She had made herself up in the semidarkness, and before running the lipstick over her lips, she had sniffed the tip. The smell hadn't reminded her of anything.

160 She had allowed herself the ritual of trying on four different dresses, even though it was obvious from the outset, if not from the previous day, that she had already decided on the one she had worn to the Ronconi boy's confirmation, the one that her father had said

was the most inappropriate because it left her back uncovered to below the ribs and her arms completely bare.

Still barefoot and wearing the little blue dress whose neckline against her pale skin looked like a smile of satisfaction, Alice had gone down to Sol in the kitchen and asked her apprehensively for an opinion. You look wonderful, Sol had said. She kissed her on the forehead and Alice had been worried about smudging her makeup.

In the kitchen Fabio moved with great agility and at the same time with the excessive care of someone who knows he's being watched. Alice sipped the white wine that he had poured and the alcohol produced little explosions in her stomach, which had been empty for at least twenty hours. The heat spread along her arteries, then rose slowly to her head and swept away the thought of Mattia, like the evening tide when it reclaims the beach.

Sitting at the table, Alice carefully assessed Fabio's silhouette, the clear line that separated his chestnut hair from his neck, his pelvis, which was not especially slender, and his shoulders, somewhat inflated under his shirt. She found herself thinking of how it would feel to be safely trapped in his arms, with no more possibility to choose.

She had accepted his invitation because she had told Mattia about him and because—she was sure of it now—what she could find here was more like love than anything else she would ever have.

Fabio opened the fridge and from a stick of butter cut a slice that Alice thought was at least 80 or 90 grams. He threw it into the pan to thicken the risotto and it melted, giving up all its saturated and animal fats. He turned off the flame and stirred the risotto with a wooden spoon for another few minutes.

"Dinner's ready," he said.

He dried his hands on a dishcloth hanging over a chair and turned toward the table, holding the frying pan.

Alice darted a terrified glance at the contents.

"Just a little for me," she said, gesturing a pinch with her fingers, right before he poured a hypercaloric ladleful onto her plate.

"You don't like it?"

"It's not that," lied Alice. "It's just that I'm allergic to mushrooms. But I'll try it."

Fabio looked disappointed and stood there with the frying pan in midair. He actually lost a little color from his face.

"Damn, I'm really sorry. I had no idea."

"It doesn't matter. Really." Alice smiled at him.

"If you want I can—" he went on.

Alice hushed him by taking his hand. Fabio looked at her as a child looks at a present.

"I can try it, though," said Alice.

Fabio resolutely shook his head.

"Absolutely not. What if it makes you ill?"

He took the pan away and Alice couldn't help smiling. For a good half hour they sat talking over the empty plates and Fabio had to open another bottle of white.

Alice had the pleasant sensation of losing part of herself with each sip. She was aware of the insubstantiality of her own body and at the same time of the massive bulk of Fabio's, sitting in front of her with his elbows resting on the table and his shirtsleeves rolled halfway up his forearms. The thought of Mattia, so incessant over the past few weeks, vibrated faintly in the air like a slightly slackened violin string, a dissonant note lost in the middle of an orchestra.

"Well, we can console ourselves with the main course," said Fabio.

Alice thought she was going to faint. She had hoped it was going to end there. Instead Fabio rose from the table and took from the oven a baking dish with two tomatoes, two eggplants, and two yellow peppers, stuffed with something that looked like ground beef mixed with bread crumbs. The composition of colors was cheerful, but Alice immediately thought of the exorbitant dimensions of those vegetables and imagined them, completely whole as they were now, in the middle of her stomach, like rocks at the bottom of a pond.

"You choose," Fabio said invitingly.

Alice bit her lip. Then she timidly pointed at the tomato and he transferred it onto her plate, using a knife and fork as pincers.

"And?"

"That's enough," said Alice.

"Impossible. You haven't eaten a thing. And with all that you've drunk!"

Alice looked at him and for a moment she hated him deeply, as much as she hated her father, her mother, Sol, and anyone else who had ever counted the things on her plate.

"That one," she said, giving in, pointing at the eggplant.

Fabio served himself one of each vegetable, and before attacking them he looked at them with satisfaction. Alice tried the stuffing, barely touching it with the tip of her fork. Apart from the meat she immediately recognized eggs, ricotta, and Parmesan and hastily calculated that a whole day of fasting wouldn't be enough to compensate.

"How is it?" Fabio asked, smiling, with his mouth half full.

"Delicious," she replied.

She summoned up the courage to bite into a mouthful of eggplant. She gulped back her nausea and went on, one bite after another, without saying a word. She finished the whole eggplant, and as soon as she had set her fork down next to her plate, she was assailed by a sudden urge to vomit. Fabio was talking and pouring more wine. Alice nodded and with each movement she felt the eggplant dancing up and down in her stomach.

Fabio had already shoveled everything down, while on Alice's plate there still lay the tomato, red and filled with that nauseating mixture. If she cut it into tiny pieces and hid it in her napkin he would notice immediately because there was nothing to hide her apart from the candles, which had already burned halfway down.

Then, like a blessing, the second bottle of wine was finished and Fabio struggled from the table to get a third. He held his head in his hands and said out loud to her stop, please stop. Alice laughed. Fabio looked in the fridge and opened all the cupboards, but he couldn't find another bottle.

"I think my parents must have finished all the wine," he said. "I'll have to go to the cellar."

He exploded with laughter for no reason and Alice laughed with him, even though it hurt her stomach.

"Don't you move from there," he commanded, pointing a finger at his forehead.

"Okay," Alice replied and the idea came to her straightaway.

As soon as Fabio was gone, she picked up the greasy tomato with two fingers and carried it to the bathroom, holding it at arm's length to avoid the smell. She locked herself in, lifted the seat, and the toilet smiled at her as if saying leave it to me.

Alice studied the tomato. It was big, perhaps it needed to be cut up into little pieces, but it was also soft, and she said to herself who cares and threw it in as it was. It dropped in with a plop, and a splash of water nearly stained her blue dress. The tomato settled on the bottom and disappeared halfway down the drain.

She flushed and the water came down like healing rain, but instead of disappearing down the hole, it started filling the bowl and a less than reassuring gurgle rose from the bottom.

Alice drew back in horror and her bad leg wobbled so much that she almost ended up on the floor. She watched the water level rise and rise and then suddenly stop.

The sound of the siphon kicked in. The bowl was full to the brim. The surface of the transparent water quivered slightly and there at the bottom, motionless, was the tomato, trapped in the same spot as before.

Alice stood and looked at it for at least a minute, frozen with panic and at the same time strangely curious. She was reawakened by the sound of the key turning in the front door. She took the toilet brush and plunged it into the water, her face contorted into a grimace of disgust. The tomato just wouldn't move.

"What do I do now?" she whispered to herself.

Then, almost unconsciously, she flushed again, and this time the water began to spill out and spread over the floor in a thin layer, until it licked at Alice's elegant shoes. She tried to flush again, but the water kept flowing and pouring out, and if Alice hadn't put the rug over it, it would have reached the door and from there the other room.

After a few seconds the water stopped again. The tomato was still down there, intact. The lake on the floor had ceased spreading. Mattia had once explained to her that there's a precise point at which water stops spreading, when the surface tension has become strong enough to hold it together, like a film.

Alice looked at the mess she had made. She closed the lid of the toilet, as if surrendering to disaster, and sat down on it. She brought her hands to her closed eyes and began to cry. She cried for Mattia, for her mother, for her father, for all that water, but mostly for herself. Under her breath she called Mattia, as if seeking his help, but his name remained on her lips, sticky and insubstantial.

Fabio knocked at the bathroom door but she didn't move.

"Ali, everything okay?"

Alice could see his outline through the frosted glass of the door. She sniffed quietly and cleared her throat to disguise her tears.

"Sure," she said. "I'll be there in a minute."

She looked around, lost, as if she really didn't know how she'd ended up in that bathroom. The water from the toilet bowl dripped onto the floor in at least three different places and Alice hoped, for a moment, that she could drown in those few millimeters of water.

GETTING THINGS IN FOCUS

2003

30

She had turned up at Marcello Crozza's studio at ten o'clock one morning and, feigning a determination that had cost her three walks around the block, had said I want to learn the trade, could you take me on as an apprentice? Crozza, who was sitting by the automatic developer, had nodded. Then he had turned around and, looking her straight in the eyes, had said I can't pay you. He hadn't wanted to say forget it, because he'd done the same thing himself many years before and the memory of the courage it had taken him was all that was left of his passion for photography. In spite of all his disappointments, he wouldn't have denied anyone that sensation.

They were mostly vacation photos. Families of three or four people, by the sea or in tourist destinations, hugging in the middle of St. Mark's Square or under the Eiffel Tower, with their feet cut off and always in the same pose. Photographs taken with automatic cameras, overexposed or out of focus. Alice didn't even look at them anymore: she developed them and then slipped them all into the paper envelope with the yellow and red Kodak logo.

It was mostly a matter of being in the shop, receiving rolls of twenty-four or thirty-six shots, shut away in their little plastic containers, of marking the customer's name on the slip and telling them they'll be ready tomorrow, of printing out receipts and saying thank you, good-bye.

Sometimes, on Saturdays, there were weddings. Crozza picked 169 her up from home at a quarter to nine, always in the same suit and without his tie, because in the end he was the photographer, not a guest.

In church they had to set up the two lights, and on one of the first occasions Alice had dropped one and it had smashed on the steps of the altar and she had looked at Crozza in terror. He had pulled a face as if one of the pieces of glass had gotten stuck in his leg, but then he had said never mind, just clean it up.

He was fond of her and didn't know why. Perhaps because he had no children, or because since Alice had been working there he was able to go to the bar at eleven o'clock and check his lottery numbers and when he came back to the shop she smiled at him and asked him so, are we rich? Perhaps because she had that bad leg and lacked a mother as he lacked a wife and all lacks are pretty much the same. Or because he was sure that she would soon get tired of him and in the evening he would pull down the security gate on his own again and set off for home where no one was waiting, with his head empty and yet so very heavy.

Instead, after a year and a half, Alice was still there. Now that she had the keys she arrived before him in the morning and Crozza found her on the sidewalk in front of the shop, chatting with the lady from the grocer's next door, with whom he had never exchanged more than a "Good morning." He paid her under the table, five hundred euros a month. If they did weddings together he would drop her outside the door of the Della Rocca house and, with the engine of his Lancia still running, take out his wallet and hand her an extra fifty, saying see you Monday.

Sometimes she brought him her own snapshots and asked his opinion, even though it was clear to both of them that he had nothing more to teach her. They sat down at the desk and Crozza looked at the photographs, holding them up to the light, and gave her some advice about exposure time, or how best to use the shutter. He let her use his Nikon whenever she wanted and had secretly decided that he would give it to her as a present the day she left.

"We're getting married on Saturday," said Crozza. It was his way of saying they had a job.

Alice was putting on her denim jacket. Fabio would be there to pick her up at any moment.

"Okay," she said. "Where?"

"At the Gran Madre. Then there's a reception in a private villa in the hills. Rich folks' stuff," commented Crozza with a touch of disdain, immediately regretting it because he knew that Alice came from that world too.

"Hmm," she murmured. "Do you know who they are?"

"They sent the invitation. I've put it over there somewhere," said Crozza, pointing to the shelf under the cash register.

Alice looked in her bag for a rubber band and pulled back her hair. Crozza watched from across the shop. Once he had masturbated thinking about her, kneeling in the gloom after they'd lowered the security gate, but then he had felt so dreadful that he hadn't eaten and the next day he had sent her home saying you've got the day off today, I don't want anyone underfoot.

Alice rummaged among the sheets of paper stacked under the counter, more to fill the time while waiting than out of genuine interest. She found the envelope with the invitation, stiff and imposingly large. She opened it and the name leaped off the page in a gilded cursive, full of flourishes.

Ferruccio Carlo Bai and Maria Luisa Bai are delighted to announce the marriage of their daughter Viola . . .

Her eyes darkened before she went any further. A metallic taste flooded her mouth. She swallowed and it was like gulping down that fruit candy from the locker room all over again. She closed the envelope and waved it in the air for a moment, thinking.

"Can I go alone?" she ventured at last, her back still turned to Crozza.

He shut the drawer of the cash register with a rattle and a ding. "What?" he asked.

Alice turned around and her eyes were wide open and bright with something and Crozza couldn't help smiling, they were so beautiful.

"I've learned how by now, haven't I?" said Alice, walking over to him. "I can do it. Otherwise I'll never be able to manage on my own."

Crozza looked at her suspiciously. She rested her elbows on the desk, right in front of him, and leaned toward him. She was only a few inches from his nose and that gleam in her eyes begged him to say yes and not to ask for explanations.

"I don't know if—"

"Please," Alice broke in.

Crozza stroked his earlobe and was forced to look away.

"All right, then," he gave in. He didn't understand why he was whispering. "But don't screw it up."

"I promise," Alice said, making her translucent lips disappear into a smile.

Then she pushed herself forward on her elbows and gave him a kiss, which tickled Crozza's three-day beard.

"Go on, go on," he said, dismissing her with his hand.

Alice laughed and the sound of it scattered through the air as she left with that sinuous, rhythmic gait of hers.

That evening Crozza stayed a little longer than usual in the shop, doing nothing. He looked at the things around him and noticed that they had more presence, as they had many years before when they seemed to be asking him to take their picture.

He took the camera out of the bag, where Alice always put it back after giving all the lenses and mechanisms a good clean. He screwed on the lens and aimed it at the first object that came into view, the umbrella stand by the entrance. He enlarged part of the rounded edge until it looked like something else, like the crater of an extinct volcano. But then he didn't take the picture.

He put the camera away, picked up his jacket, turned out the lights, and left. He closed the security gate with the padlock and headed in the opposite direction from his usual one. He couldn't seem to wipe the stupid smile from his face and he really had no desire to go home.

The church was decorated with two enormous bouquets of lilies and daisies, arranged on either side of the altar, and with dozens of miniature copies of the same bouquet at the end of each pew. Alice set up the lights and arranged the reflector panel. Then she sat in the first row and waited. A lady was running the vacuum cleaner over the red carpet that Viola would walk down in an hour. Alice thought about when she and Viola used to sit on the railings and talk. She couldn't remember what they had talked about, only that she had looked at her rapt from a place just behind her eyes, a place full of jumbled thoughts that she had kept to herself even then.

Over the next half hour all the pews filled up and people accumulated at the back, where they stood fanning themselves with the order of service.

Alice went outside and waited on the cobblestones for the bride's car to arrive. High in the sky the sun warmed her hands and its rays seemed to pass right through them. As a little girl she had liked looking at her palms against the light, the red peeking through her closed fingers. Once she had shown it to her father and he had kissed her fingertips, pretending to eat them.

Viola arrived in a gleaming gray Porsche, and the driver had to help her out and pick up her cumbersome train. Alice madly snapped away, more to hide her face behind the camera than anything else. Then, when the bride passed by, she lowered it deliberately and smiled at her.

They looked at each other for only a moment and Viola caught her breath. Alice couldn't study her expression, because the bride had already passed her and was entering the church on her father's arm. For some reason Alice had always imagined him taller.

She was careful not to lose so much as a moment. She took various close-ups of the happy couple and their families. She immortalized the exchange of rings, the reading of the promises, the communion, the kiss, and the signing of the register. She was the only one moving in the whole church. It seemed to Alice that Viola's shoulders stiffened slightly when she was near her. She increased the exposure time still further, to obtain the blurry quality that, according to Crozza, suggested eternity.

As the couple left the church, Alice walked ahead of them, limping backward, bending slightly so as not to alter her height with a low perspective. Through the lens she became aware that Viola was looking at her with a frightened half-smile, as if she were the only one who could see a ghost. Alice exploded the flash in her face at regular intervals, about fifteen times, until the bride was forced to narrow her eyes.

She watched them get into the car and Viola darted her a glance from behind the window. She was sure she would immediately start talking to her husband about her, about how strange it was to have come across her there. She would describe her as the class anorexic, the cripple, someone she had never hung out with. She wouldn't mention the candy or the party or all the rest. Alice smiled at the thought that it might be their first half-truth as a married couple, the first of the tiny cracks that would eventually converge into a gaping hole.

"Miss, the bride and groom are waiting on the riverbank for you to photograph them," said a voice behind her.

Alice turned around and recognized one of the witnesses.

"Certainly. I'll be right there," she replied.

She quickly went into the church to dismantle her equipment. She was still putting the various pieces of the camera in the rectangular case when she heard someone calling to her.

"Alice?"

She turned around, already sure who had been speaking.

"Yes?"

Standing in front of her were Giada Savarino and Giulia Mirandi.

"Hi," said Giada ostentatiously, approaching Alice to kiss her on both cheeks.

Giulia stayed where she was, staring at her feet as she had done at school.

Alice barely brushed Giada's cheek with her own pursed lips.

"What on earth are you doing here?" shrieked Giada.

Alice thought it was a stupid question and couldn't help smiling.

"I'm taking photographs," she replied.

Giada responded with a smile, showing the same dimples she had had at seventeen.

It was strange to find them here, still alive, with their shared bits of past that suddenly counted for nothing.

"Hi, Giulia," Alice forced herself to say.

Giulia smiled at her and struggled to speak.

"We heard about your mother," she said. "We're really sorry."

Giada nodded repeatedly, to show her agreement.

"Yeah," replied Alice. "Thanks."

She started hastily putting things away. Giada and Giulia looked at each other.

"We'll let you get on with your work," Giada said, touching her shoulder. "You're very busy."

"Okay."

They turned around and walked toward the exit, the crisp click of their heels echoing off the walls of the now empty church.

The couple was waiting in the shade of a big tree standing some feet apart. Alice parked next to their Porsche and got out with the shoulder bag. It was hot and she felt her hair sticking to the back of her neck.

"Hi," she said, walking over.

"Alice," said Viola. "I didn't think—"

"Neither did I," Alice cut in.

They pretended to hug, as if not wanting to rumple their clothes. Viola was even more beautiful than she had been at school. Over the years her features had grown milder, the outlines were softer, and her eyes had lost that imperceptible vibration that made them so terrible. She still had that perfect body.

"This is Carlo," said Viola.

Alice shook his hand and felt how smooth it was.

"Shall we start?" she asked, cutting her short.

Viola nodded and sought her husband's eyes, but he didn't notice.

"Where shall we stand?" she asked.

Alice looked around. The sun was at its zenith and she would have to use the flash to eliminate all the shadows from their faces. She pointed to a bench in full sunlight on the riverbank.

"Sit down there," she said.

She took longer than was necessary to set up the camera. She pretended to busy herself with the flash, mounted one lens and then swapped it for another one. Viola's husband fanned himself with his tie, while she used her finger to try to stop the little drops of sweat trickling down her forehead.

Alice left them to stew for a bit longer as she pretended to find the right distance to take the picture.

Then she started issuing brusque orders. Put your arms around each other, smile, now serious, take her by the hand, rest your head on his shoulder, whisper in her ear, look at each other, closer, toward the river, take your jacket off. Crozza had taught her that you mustn't let your subjects breathe, you mustn't give them time to think, because it takes only a minute for the spontaneity to evaporate.

Viola obeyed, two or three times asking apprehensively is that all right?

"Okay, now let's go into the field," said Alice.

"More?" asked Viola, startled. The red of her flushed cheeks was starting to show through her foundation. Her eyeliner was already slightly smudged, the edges were getting jagged, making her look tired and slightly shabby.

"You pretend to run away and let him chase you across the field," Alice explained.

"What? You want me to run?"

"Yes, run."

"But . . ." Viola began to protest. She looked at her husband and he shrugged.

She snorted, then lifted up her skirt and began running. Her heels sank a few millimeters into the ground, and kicked up little clumps that dirtied the inside of her white dress. Her husband ran after her.

"You're going too slowly," he said.

Viola turned around all of a sudden with a look that reduced him to ashes, a look that Alice remembered all too well. She let them run after each other for two or three minutes, until Viola freed herself clumsily from her husband's clutches, saying that's enough.

Her hair had come undone on one side and a lock fell down her cheek.

"Yes," said Alice. "Just a few more shots."

She took them to the ice-cream stand and bought two lemon ice pops, which she paid for herself.

"Hold these," she said, extending them to the couple.

They seemed not to understand, and unwrapped them suspiciously. Viola was careful not to get the sticky syrup all over her hands.

They had to pretend to eat them, arms crossed, and then offer the other a lick. Viola's smile was becoming increasingly tense.

When Alice told her to hold on to the street lamp and use it as a pivot to spin around, Viola exploded.

"This is ridiculous," she said.

Her husband looked at her, slightly intimidated, and then looked at Alice, as if to apologize.

Alice smiled. "It's part of the classic album," she explained. "That's what you asked for. But we can skip that sequence."

She forced herself to sound sincere. She felt her tattoo pulsating, as if it wanted to jump out of her skin. Viola stared at her furiously and Alice held her gaze until her eyes burned.

"Have we finished?" said Viola.

Alice nodded.

"Let's go, then," the bride said to her husband.

Before letting himself be dragged away, he came over to Alice and shook her hand politely once more.

"Thanks," he said.

"My pleasure."

Alice watched them climb back up the slight slope to the parking lot. Around her were the usual sounds of Saturday, the laughter of children on the swings and the voices of the mothers looking after them. There was music in the distance and the rush of cars on the road, like a carpet of sound.

She wanted to tell Mattia, because he would have understood. But he was far away now. She thought that Crozza would be furious, but he would forgive her in the end. She was sure of it.

She smiled. She opened the back of the camera, took out the film, and unrolled it completely under the white light of the sun.

WHAT REMAINS

2007

His father phoned on Wednesday evenings, between eight and a quarter past. They had seen each other rarely over the last nine years and it had been a long time since the last visit, but the phone call in Mattia's two-room apartment had become a ritual. In the long pauses between words the same old silence arose between the two of them: there were no televisions or radios on, never any guests rattling their cutlery.

Mattia could imagine his mother listening to the phone call from her armchair without changing her expression, with both arms on the armrests, as when he and Michela were in primary school and she sat there listening to them recite poetry by heart and Mattia always knew it while Michela said nothing, incapable of doing anything.

Every Wednesday, after hanging up, Mattia found himself wondering whether the orange floral pattern of that armchair was still the same or whether they'd replaced it, since it had been threadbare even back then. He wondered whether his parents had grown old. Of course they had, he heard it in his father's voice, which was slower and wearier, more like an attack of breathlessness.

His mother came to the phone infrequently and her questions were a matter of form, always the same. Is it cold? Have you had your dinner yet? How are your classes going? We eat dinner at seven over here, Mattia had explained the first few times. Now he merely said yes.

"Hello?" he said, speaking in Italian.

There was no reason to answer the phone in English. Only about ten people had his home number and none of them would have dreamed of calling him at that time of day.

"It's Dad."

The delay in his reply was only just perceptible. Mattia meant to get a stopwatch to measure it, to calculate how much the signal deviated from the straight line of more than 1,000 kilometers that connected him and his father, but he forgot every time.

"Hi. Are you well?" said Mattia.

"Yes. And you?"

"Fine. . . . And Mom?"

"She's right here."

The first silence always fell at that point, like a mouthful of air after swimming a lap underwater.

Mattia ran his index finger along the scratch in the pale wood of the round table, a few inches from the middle. He couldn't even remember whether he had scratched it or whether it had been the old tenants. Just under the enameled surface it was compressed chipboard, which got under his fingernail without hurting him. Each Wednesday he dug that furrow a few fractions of a millimeter deeper, but a lifetime wouldn't be enough for him to break through to the other side.

"So you saw the sunrise?" his father asked.

Mattia smiled. It was a joke they had between them, perhaps the only one. About a year before, somewhere in a newspaper Pietro had read that watching the dawn over the North Sea is an unforgettable experience, and in the evening he had read his son the clipping over the phone. You absolutely have to go, he had advised. Since that day he asked from time to time so have you seen it? Mattia always answered no. His alarm was set to seventeen minutes past eight and the shortest way to the university was not along the seafront.

"No, no dawn yet," he replied.

"Well, it's not going anywhere," said Pietro.

They had already run out of things to say, but they lingered for a few seconds, the receivers pressed to their ears. They both breathed in a little of the affection that still survived between them, diluted along hundreds of miles of coaxial cables and nourished by something whose name they didn't know and which perhaps, if they thought too carefully about it, no longer existed.

"I'll say good-bye, then," Pietro said at last.

"Sure."

"And try to keep well."

"Okay. Say hi to Mum."

They hung up.

For Mattia it was the end of the day. He walked around the table. He looked distractedly at the papers stacked up on one side, the work he'd brought back from the office. He was still stuck on the same step. No matter where they began the proof, he and Alberto always ended up banging their heads against it sooner or later. He was sure that the solution lay just beyond that final obstacle, and that once past it getting to the end would be easy, like rolling down a grassy slope with his eyes closed.

But he was too tired to go back to work. He went into the kitchen and filled a pan with water from the tap. He put it on the stove and lit the gas. He spent so much time on his own that a normal person would have gone crazy in a month.

He sat down on the folding plastic chair, without completely relaxing. He looked up toward the unlit bulb dangling in the middle of the ceiling. It had blown just a month after he'd arrived, and he'd never bothered to replace it. He ate with the light turned on in the other room.

If he had simply upped and left the apartment that very evening and not come back, no one would have found any sign of his presence, apart from those incomprehensible pages stacked on the table. Mattia had put nothing of himself into the place. He had kept the anonymous pale oak furniture and the yellowed wallpaper that had been stuck to the walls since the building was constructed.

He got to his feet. He poured boiling water into a cup and immersed a tea bag in it. He watched the water turn dark. The methane flame was still lit and in the gloom it was violently blue. He lowered the flame until it was almost out and the hiss faded. He held his hand over the burner. The heat exerted a faint pressure on his devastated palm. Mattia brought it down slowly, and closed it around the flame.

He had spent hundreds and thousands of identical days at the university, and consumed innumerable cafeteria lunches in the little low building on the edge of the campus, but even now he remembered the very first day when he had walked in and copied the sequence of gestures of the other people. He had joined the line and, taking small steps, had reached the pile of plastic imitation-wood trays. He had picked one up, set the paper napkin on it, and helped himself to cutlery and a glass. Then, once he was in front of the uniformed woman who served up the portions, he had pointed to one of the three aluminum tubs, at random, without knowing what was in them. The cook had asked him something, in her own language or perhaps in English, and he hadn't understood. He had pointed to the tub again and she had repeated the question, exactly the same as before. Mattia shook his head. I don't understand, he had said in English in a loud and nervy voice. She had raised her eyes to the sky and waved the empty plate in the air. She's asking you if you want sauce on that muck, said the young man next to him in Italian. Mattia had spun around, disoriented, and shook his head. The young man had turned toward the dinner lady and simply said no. She had smiled at him and finally filled Mattia's dish and handed it to him. The young man had chosen the same and had brought it up to his nose and sniffed it with disgust. This stuff is revolting, he had observed.

You've just got here, then? he had asked him after a while, still staring at the thick puree on the plate. Mattia had said yes and the young man had nodded with a frown, as if it were a serious matter. After paying, Mattia had frozen in front of the cash register, his hands gripping the tray. He had looked around for an empty table, somewhere he could avoid feeling people's eyes on him and eat alone. He had just taken a step toward the back of the room when the young man from before had overtaken him and said come on, over here.

Alberto Torcia had already been there for four years, with a permanent research post funded by the European Union for the quality of his most recent publications. He too had escaped from something, but Mattia had never asked him what. Neither of them, after so many years, could have said whether the other was a friend or just a colleague, in spite of the fact that they shared an office and had lunch together every day.

It was Tuesday. Alberto sat down opposite Mattia and, through the glass of water that he brought to his lips, glimpsed the new mark, pale and perfectly circular, on his palm. Alberto didn't ask any questions, but merely gave him a crooked glance to let him know that he understood. Gilardi and Montanari, sitting at the same table, were sniggering over something they had found on the Internet.

Mattia drained his glass in one gulp, then cleared his throat.

"Yesterday evening an idea came to me about the discontinuity that—"

"Please, Mattia," Alberto interrupted him, dropping his fork and flopping back in his seat. His gestures were always very exaggerated. "At least have pity on me when I'm eating."

Mattia looked at the table. The slice of meat on his plate was cut into identical little squares and he separated them with his fork, leaving between them a regular grill of white lines.

"Why don't you do something else with your evenings?" Alberto went on more quietly, as if he didn't want the other two to hear him. As he spoke he drew little circles in the air with his knife.

Mattia said nothing and didn't look at him. He brought a little square of meat to his mouth, chosen from the ones on the edge whose fringed borders disturbed the geometry of the composition.

"If only you'd come and have a drink with us every now and again," Alberto continued.

"No," Mattia said brusquely.

"But—" Alberto protested.

"Anyway, you know."

Alberto shook his head and frowned, defeated. After all this time he still insisted, even though in all the years they had known each other he had managed to drag him out of the house only a dozen or so times.

He turned to the other two, breaking into their conversation.

"Have you seen her over there?" he asked, pointing to a young woman sitting two tables away with an elderly gentleman. As far as Mattia knew, the man was a geology professor. "If only I wasn't married, Christ, what I could do to a woman like that."

The others hesitated for a moment, because it had nothing to do with what they were talking about, but then they shifted gears and joined in, speculating about what such a babe was doing with an old windbag like that.

Mattia cut all the little squares of meat along the diagonal. Then he reassembled the triangles so as to form a larger one. The meat was already cold and tough. He took a piece of it and swallowed it almost whole. The rest he left where they were.

Outside the dining hall Alberto lit a cigarette, to give Gilardi and Montanari time to move away. He waited for Mattia, who was following a rectilinear crack along the ground and thinking about something that had nothing to do with being there.

"What were you saying about discontinuity?" he said.

"It doesn't matter."

"Come on, don't be a dick."

Mattia looked at his colleague. The tip of the cigarette between his lips was the only color that brightened that entirely gray day, the same as the one before and doubtless the same as the one that would follow.

"We can't escape it," said Mattia. "We've convinced ourselves that it exists. But I may have found a way to get something interesting out of it."

Alberto came closer. He didn't interrupt Mattia until he had finished his explanation, because he knew that Mattia didn't talk much, but when he did it was worth shutting up and listening.

32

The weight of consequences had collapsed on her all at once one evening a few years before, when Fabio, as he pushed inside her, had whispered I want to have a baby. His face was so close to Alice's that she had felt his breath sliding along her cheeks and dispersing among the sheets.

She had pulled him to her, guiding his head into the hollow between her neck and shoulder. Once, before they were married, he had told her it was the perfect fit, that his head was made to slip into that space.

So what do you think? Fabio had asked her, his voice muffled by the pillow. Alice hadn't replied, but had held him a bit tighter. She hadn't had the breath to speak.

She'd heard him closing the drawer with the condoms in it and had bent her right knee a little more to make room for him. Rhythmically she stroked his hair, her eyes wide open.

That secret had crept after her since her school days, but it had never taken hold of her mind for more than a few seconds. Alice had set it aside, like something she would think about later on. Now, all of a sudden, there it was, like an abyss cut into the black ceiling of the room, monstrous and irrepressible. Alice wanted to say to Fabio stop for a moment, wait, there's something I haven't told you, but he moved with disarming trust and he certainly wouldn't have understood.

190   She felt him come inside her, for the first time, and imagined that sticky liquid full of promise that he deposited in her dry body, where it too would dry.

She didn't want a baby, or maybe she did. She hadn't ever really thought about it. The question didn't arise and that was that. Her menstrual cycle had stopped around the last time she had eaten a whole chocolate pudding. The truth was that Fabio wanted a baby and she had to give him one. She had to, because when they made love he didn't ask her to turn the light on, not since the first time at his house. Because when it was over he lay on top of her and the weight of his body canceled out all her fears and he didn't speak, just breathed, and anyway he was there. She had to, because she didn't love him, but his love was enough for both of them, enough to keep them safe.

From then on sex had assumed a new guise. It bore within itself a precise purpose, which had soon led them to abandon everything that wasn't strictly necessary.

For weeks and then months nothing had happened. Fabio had himself examined and his sperm count was good. That evening he told Alice, being very careful to hold her tightly in his arms as he spoke. He immediately added you don't have to worry, it's not your fault. She pulled away and went into the other room before bursting into tears, and Fabio hated himself because he thought—in fact he knew—that it was his wife's fault.

Alice started feeling spied on. She kept a fictitious count of days, drawing little lines on the calendar beside the phone. She bought tampons and then threw them away unused. On the right days she pushed Fabio away in the dark, telling him we can't today.

He kept the same count, without telling her. Alice's secret, slimy and transparent, wormed its way between them, forcing them further and further apart. Every time he hinted at doctors, treatments, or the cause of the problem, Alice's face darkened and he was sure that it wouldn't be long before she found a pretext for an argument, any random nonsense.

Exhaustion slowly defeated them. They stopped talking about it and, along with the conversations, sex too had grown less frequent, until it was reduced to a laborious Friday night ritual. They took turns washing, before and after doing it. Fabio would come back from the bathroom, the skin of his face still gleaming with soap, wearing fresh underwear. In the meantime Alice would already have slipped on her T-shirt and would ask can I go now? When she came back into the room she would find him already asleep, or at least with his eyes closed, facing the wall and with his whole body on his side of the bed.

There was nothing very different about that Friday, at least at first. Alice joined him in bed just after one, having spent the whole evening shut up in the darkroom that Fabio had given her as a third anniversary present. He lowered the magazine he was reading and watched his wife's bare feet walk toward him, sticking to the wooden floor.

Alice slipped between the sheets and pressed herself against his side. Fabio let the magazine fall to the floor and turned out the bedside light. He did everything he could to not make it look like a habit, a duty, but the truth was clear to both of them.

They followed a series of movements that had become consolidated into a routine over time, and which made everything simpler, then Fabio entered her, with the help of his fingers.

Alice wasn't sure that he was really crying, because he held his head tilted to one side to avoid contact with her skin, but she noticed that there was something different in his way of moving. He was thrusting more violently and more urgently than usual, then he would stop suddenly, his breath heavy, and start again, as though torn between the desire to penetrate more deeply and the desire to slip away from her and from the room. She heard him sniffing as he panted.

When he finished he quickly withdrew, got out of bed, and went and shut himself in the bathroom, without even turning on the light.

He stayed there for longer than usual. Alice moved toward the middle of the bed, where the sheets were still cool. She put a hand on her stomach, in which nothing was happening, and, for the first time, thought she no longer had anyone to blame, that all these mistakes were hers alone.

Fabio crossed the room in the semidarkness, climbed into bed, and turned his back to her. It was Alice's turn, but she didn't move. She felt that something was about to happen, the air was full of it.

It took him another minute, or perhaps two, before he spoke.

"Ali," he said.

"Yes?"

He hesitated again.

"I can't do this anymore," he said softly.

Alice felt his words gripping her belly, like climbing plants sprouting suddenly from the bed. She didn't reply. She let him go on.

"I know what it is," Fabio went on. His voice grew clearer. As it struck the walls it assumed a slight metallic echo. "You don't want to let me in, you don't even want me to talk about it. But this . . ."

He stopped. Alice's eyes were open. They were accustomed to the dark. She followed the outlines of the furniture: the armchair, the wardrobe, the chest of drawers and on top of it the mirror that didn't reflect anything. All those objects sitting there, motionless and terribly insistent.

Alice thought of her parents' room. She thought how similar they were, that all bedrooms in the world were similar. She wondered what she was afraid of, losing him or losing those things: the curtains, the paintings, the carpet, all that security folded carefully away in the drawers.

"You barely ate two zucchinis this evening," Fabio went on.

"I wasn't hungry," she replied automatically.

Here we go, she thought.

"The same yesterday. You didn't even touch the meat. You cut it up into little pieces and then hid it in your napkin. Do you really think I'm that stupid?"

Alice clenched the sheets. How could she have thought he would never notice? She saw again the hundreds, thousands of times in which the same scene had repeated itself before her husband's eyes. She was furious about all the things he must have thought in silence.

"I expect you also know what I ate the evening before and the evening before that," she said.

"Tell me what it is," he said, loudly this time. "Tell me what it is that you find so repellent about food."

She thought of her father bringing his face down to the plate when he ate soup, the sound he made, how he sucked the spoon rather than simply putting it in his mouth. She thought with disgust of the chewed-up pulp between her husband's teeth every time he sat in front of her for dinner. She thought of Viola's gumdrop, with all those hairs stuck to it and its synthetic strawberry flavor. Then she thought about herself, without her T-shirt, reflected in the big mirror in her old house, and the scar that made her leg something slightly apart, something detached from her torso and useless. She thought of the balance, so fragile, of her own silhouette, the thin strip of shadow that her ribs cast over her belly and which she was prepared to defend at all costs.

"What is it you want? Do you want me to start stuffing myself? To deform myself to have your baby?" She spoke as if the baby were already there, somewhere in the universe. She called it your baby on purpose. "I can do some sort of treatment if you're so keen on the idea. I can take hormones, medicine, all the junk necessary to let you have this child of yours. Maybe then you'll stop spying on me."

"That isn't the point," Fabio shot back. He had suddenly regained all his irritating self-confidence.

Alice moved toward the edge of the bed to get away from his

threatening body. He rolled onto his back. His eyes were open and his face was tense, as if he were trying to see something beyond the darkness.

"Isn't it?"

"You should think about all the risks, particularly in your condition."

In your condition, Alice silently repeated to herself. She instinctively tried to bend her weak knee, to demonstrate to herself that she was in full control, but it barely moved.

"Poor Fabio," she said. "With that wife of his, crippled and . . ."

She couldn't finish her sentence. That last word, already trembling in the air, caught in her throat.

"There's a part of the brain," he began, ignoring her, as though an explanation might make everything simpler, "probably the hypothalamus, which controls the body mass index. If that index falls too low, gonadotropin production is inhibited. The mechanism is blocked, and menstruation stops. But that's just the first of the symptoms. Other things happen, more serious. The density of minerals in the bones diminishes and osteoporosis ensues. The bones crumble like wafers."

He talked like a doctor, listing causes and effects in a monotonous voice, as if knowing the name of an illness were the same as curing it. Alice reflected that her bones had already crumbled once, and that these things didn't interest her.

"Raising that index is enough for everything to return to normal," Fabio added. "It's a slow process, but we still have time."

Alice lifted herself up on her elbows. She wanted to leave the room.

"Fantastic. I suppose you've had all this ready for a while," she remarked. "That's all there is to it. Easy as that."

Fabio sat up as well. He took her arm, but she pulled away. He stared into her eyes through the gloom.

"It's not only about you anymore," he said.

Alice shook her head.

"Yes, it is," she said. "Maybe it's what I really want, haven't you thought of that? I want to feel my bones crumbling, I want to block the mechanism. As you said yourself."

Fabio thumped the mattress, making her start.

"So now what do you want to do?" she said provocatively.

Fabio sucked in air through his teeth. The compressed violence in his lungs made his arms stiffen.

"You're just selfish. You're spoiled and selfish."

He threw himself on the bed and turned his back to her again. All of a sudden things seemed to return to their place in the shadows. There was silence again, but it was an imprecise silence. Alice noticed a faint whirring sound, like the rustle of old films in the cinema. She listened, trying to work out where it was coming from.

Then she saw the outline of her husband bobbing slightly up and down. She became aware of his suppressed sobs, like a rhythmical vibration of the mattress. His body asked her to stretch out a hand and touch him, to stroke his neck and his hair, but she didn't lift it. She got up from the bed and walked toward the bathroom, slamming the door behind her.

33

After lunch Alberto and Mattia headed down to the basement, where nothing ever changed and you measured the passing of time only by the heaviness of your eyes as they filled with the white light of the fluorescent bulbs on the ceiling. They went into an empty classroom and Alberto sat down on the teacher's desk. His body was massive, not exactly fat, but to Mattia it seemed as if it were constantly expanding.

"Fire away," said Alberto. "Tell me everything from the start."

Mattia picked up a piece of chalk and broke it in half. A fine white dust settled on the tips of his leather shoes, the same ones he had worn on the day of his graduation.

"Let's consider things in two dimensions," he said.

He started to write in his neat hand. He began at the top left corner and filled the first two blackboards. On the third he copied out the results that he would need later. It was as if he had performed this calculation hundreds of times, when in fact it was the first time he had pulled it out of his head. He turned toward Alberto every now and again, who nodded at him seriously, while his mind scampered to keep up with the chalk.

When he got to the end, after a good half hour, Mattia wrote "QED" next to the framed result, just as he had done when he was a boy. The chalk had dried the skin of his hand, but he didn't even notice. His legs were trembling slightly.

For about ten seconds they stayed there in quiet contemplation. 197 Then Alberto clapped his hands and the noise echoed through the silence like a whiplash. He got down off the desk and almost fell on the floor, because his legs had gone to sleep from dangling like that.

He put a hand on Mattia's shoulder and Mattia found it both heavy and reassuring.

"No bullshit this time," he said. "You're having dinner with me tonight; we've got something to celebrate."

Mattia smiled faintly.

"Okay," he said.

They cleaned the blackboard together. They took care that nothing legible was left, that no one would be able to make out so much as a shadow of what had been written on it. No one would really have understood it, but they were already jealous of the result, as one is of a beautiful secret.

They left the classroom and Mattia turned out the lights. Then they went upstairs, one behind the other, each savoring the little glory of that moment.

Alberto's house was in a residential area exactly like the one where Mattia lived, but on the other side of the city. Mattia took the bus, which was half empty, his forehead resting against the window. The contact between that cold surface and his skin soothed him, and made him think of the compress that his mother used to put on Michela's head, nothing but a damp cloth handkerchief, but enough to calm her in the evening when she had those attacks that made her tremble all over and grind her teeth. Michela wanted her brother to wear a compress too, she said so to her mother with her eyes, and so he would lie down on the bed and stay there, waiting for his sister to finish writhing.

He had showered and shaved, and had put on his shirt and black jacket. In a liquor store he had never entered before he had bought a bottle of red wine, choosing the one with the most elegant label. The lady had wrapped it up in a sheet of tissue paper and then put it in a silver-colored bag. Mattia rocked it back and forth like a pendulum as he waited for someone to open the door. With his foot he arranged the doormat in front of the door so that the perimeter aligned precisely with the lines of the paving.

Alberto's wife came to the door. She ignored both Mattia's outstretched hand and the bag with the bottle. Instead she drew him to her and kissed him on the cheek.

"I don't know what you two have been up to, but I've never seen Alberto as happy as he is tonight," she whispered. "Come in."

Mattia resisted the temptation to rub his ear against his shoulder to get rid of an itch.

"Albi, Mattia's here," she called.

Instead of Alberto, his son Philip appeared from the hall. Mattia knew him from the photograph that his father kept on his desk, in which Philip was still only a few months old, and round and impersonal like all newborn babies. It had never occurred to him that he might have grown. Some of his parents' features were forcibly making their way beneath his skin: Alberto's long chin, his mother's not-quite-open eyelids. Mattia thought about the cruel mechanism of growth, the soft cartilages subject to imperceptible but inexorable changes, and, just for a moment, about Michela and her features, frozen forever since that day in the park.

Philip came over, pedaling his tricycle like a boy possessed. When he noticed Mattia, he braked suddenly and stared at him in astonishment, as if he had been caught doing something forbidden. Alberto's wife gathered him in her arms, lifting him from the tricycle.

"Here's the horrid little monster," she said, burying her nose in his cheek.

Mattia gave him a forced smile. Children made him uneasy.

"Let's go in. Nadia's here already," Alberto's wife went on.

"Nadia?" said Mattia.

Alberto's wife looked at him, confused.

"Yes, Nadia," she said. "Didn't Albi tell you?"

"No."

There was a moment of embarrassment. Mattia didn't know a Nadia. He wondered what was going on and feared he already knew.

"Anyway she's in there. Come on."

As they walked toward the kitchen, Philip studied Mattia suspiciously, hiding behind his mother's back, his index and middle fingers in his mouth and his knuckles gleaming with saliva. Mattia was forced to look elsewhere. He remembered the time he had followed Alice down a longer hall than this one. He looked at Philip's scribbles hanging on the walls instead of paintings and was careful not to trample his toys scattered on the floor. The whole house, its very walls, was impregnated with a smell of vitality that he was unused to. He thought about his own apartment, where it was so easy to decide simply not to exist. He already regretted accepting the invitation to dinner.

In the kitchen Alberto greeted him, shaking his hand affectionately, and he responded automatically. The woman sitting at the table stood up and held out her hand.

"This is Nadia," Alberto said. "And this is our next Fields Medal winner."

"Nice to meet you," said Mattia, embarrassed.

Nadia smiled at him. She made as if to lean forward, perhaps to kiss him on the cheeks, but Mattia's motionlessness held her back.

"A pleasure," she said, and nothing more.

For a few seconds he remained absorbed by one of the big earrings that dangled from her ears: a gold circle at least five centimeters in diameter, which when she moved began swinging in a complicated motion that Mattia tried to decompose into the three Cartesian axes. The size of the earring and its contrast with Nadia's jet-black hair made him think of something shameless, almost obscene, that frightened and aroused him at the same time.

They sat down at the table and Alberto poured red wine for everyone. He grandly toasted the article they would soon write and obliged Mattia to explain to Nadia, in simple terms, what it was about. She joined in with an uncertain smile, which betrayed thoughts of a different kind and made him lose the thread of the conversation more than once.

"It sounds interesting," she observed finally, and Mattia looked down.

"It's much more than interesting," said Alberto, waving his hands around as if imitating the shape of an ellipsoid, which Mattia pictured in his mind.

Alberto's wife came in holding a soup tureen, from which emanated a strong smell of cumin. The conversation turned to food, a more neutral territory. A tension that they hadn't previously been aware of dissipated. Everyone, apart from Mattia, expressed nostalgia for some kind of delicacy that they couldn't get here in northern Europe. Alberto talked about the ravioli his mother used to make. His wife remembered the seafood salad they used to eat together in their university days, in that restaurant facing the beach. Nadia described the cannoli filled with fresh ricotta and dotted with tiny chips of dark black chocolate that the only pastry shop in her little village made. As she described them she kept her eyes closed and sucked in her lips as if she could still taste a little of that flavor. She caught her lower lip with her teeth for a moment and then let it go. Mattia fixed on that detail without realizing it. He thought there was something exaggerated about Nadia's femininity, in the fluidity with which she rolled her hands around, and the southern inflection with which she pronounced her labial consonants, almost doubling them when there was no need. It was as if she possessed a dark power, which depressed him and at the same time made his cheeks burn.

"You just need the courage to go back," Nadia concluded.

All four of them remained in silence for a few seconds, as if each were thinking about what it was that kept them so far from home. Philip banged his toys against one another a few feet away from the table.

Alberto was able to keep a tottering conversation alive all through dinner, often embarking on long monologues, his hands waving above an increasingly untidy table.

After dessert, his wife got up to collect the plates. Nadia made as if to help her, but she told her to stay where she was and disappeared into the kitchen.

They sat in silence. Lost in thought, Mattia ran an index finger along the serrated edge of his knife.

"I'll just go and see what she's up to in there," said Alberto, getting up as well. From behind Nadia's back he darted a glance at Mattia, which meant do your best.

He and Nadia were left on their own with Philip. They looked up at the same time, because there was nothing else to look at, and they both laughed with embarrassment.

"What about you?" Nadia said to him after a while. "Why did you choose to stay here?"

She studied him with her eyes half closed, as if trying to guess his secret. She had long, thick eyelashes and Mattia thought they were too still to be real.

He finished lining up the crumbs with his index finger. He shrugged.

"I don't know," he said. "It's as if there's more oxygen here."

She nodded reflectively, as if she had understood. From the kitchen came the voices of Alberto and his wife talking about ordinary things, about the tap that was leaking again and who would put Philip to bed, things that at that moment seemed tremendously important to Mattia.

Silence fell again and he forced himself to think of something to say, something that seemed normal. Nadia entered his field of vision wherever he looked, an awkward presence. The dark color of her low-cut top distracted him, even as he was staring at his empty glass. Under the table, hidden by the tablecloth, were their legs and he imagined them down there, in the dark, forced into a strained intimacy.

Philip came over and put a toy car in front of him, right on his napkin. Mattia looked at the miniature Maserati, then looked at Philip, who observed him in turn, waiting for him to decide to do something.

Rather hesitantly he picked up the toy car and made it go back and forth on the tablecloth. He felt Nadia's dense gaze upon him, assessing his embarrassment. With his mouth he imitated a shy vroom. Then he stopped. Philip stared at him in silence, slightly annoyed. He stretched out his arm, took the car back, and returned to his toys.

Mattia poured himself some more wine and drained it in one gulp. Then he realized that he should have offered some to Nadia first and asked her would you like some? She said no, no, drawing in her hands and hunching her shoulders, as people usually do when they're cold.

Alberto came back into the room and made a kind of grunt. He rubbed his face hard with his hands.

"Sleepy time," he said to the child. He lifted him up by the collar of his polo shirt as if he were a doll.

Philip followed him without protest. As he left he glanced back at his toys piled up on the floor as if he had hidden something in the middle of them.

"Maybe it's time for me to go too," said Nadia, not quite turning toward Mattia.

"Yeah, perhaps it's time," he said.

They both contracted their leg muscles as if to get up, but it was a false start. They stayed where they were and looked at each other again. Nadia smiled and Mattia felt pierced by her gaze, stripped to the bone as if he could no longer hide anything.

They got up, almost at the same time. They put their chairs next to the table and Mattia noticed that she too had the foresight to lift hers off the ground.

Alberto found them standing there, not knowing how to move.

"What's happening?" he said. "Are you off already?"

"It's late, you must be tired," Nadia replied for both of them.

Alberto looked at Mattia with a smile of complicity.

"I'll call you a taxi," he said.

"I'll take the bus," Mattia said quickly.

Alberto gave him a sidelong look.

"At this time of night? Come on," he said. "And besides, Nadia's place is on the way."

34

The taxi slipped along the deserted avenues on the edge of town, between identical buildings without balconies. Few windows were still lit. March days end early and people adapt their body clocks to the night.

"The cities are darker here," said Nadia, as if thinking out loud.

They sat at opposite ends of the backseat. Mattia stared at the changing numbers on the taxi's meter, and watched the red segments going off and on to compose the various figures.

Nadia thought about the ridiculous space of solitude that separated them and tried to find the courage to occupy it with her body. Her apartment was only a few blocks away and time, like the road, was being consumed in a great hurry. It wasn't just the time of that particular evening, it was the time of possibilities, of her nearly thirty-five years. Over the past year, since breaking up with Martin, she had begun to notice the foreignness of the place, to suffer from the chill that dried her skin and never really left her, even in the summer. And yet she couldn't make up her mind to leave. She depended on the place now; she had grown attached to it with the obstinacy with which people become attached only to things that hurt them.

She reflected that if anything was going to be resolved, it would be resolved in that car. Afterward she would no longer have the strength. She would finally abandon herself, without remorse, to her translations, to the books whose pages she dissected by day and night, to earn her living and fill the holes dug by time.

She found him fascinating. He was strange, even stranger than the other colleagues that Alberto had introduced her to, to no avail.

The subject they studied seemed only to attract sinister characters, or to make them so over the years. She could have asked Mattia whether Mattia had been attracted by math because he was weird or if math had made him weird, to ask something funny, but she didn't feel like it. And yet, "strange" conveyed the idea. And disturbing. But there was something in his eyes, a kind of shining molecule drowning in those dark pupils, which, Nadia was sure, no woman had ever been able to capture.

She could have turned him on, she was dying to. She had pulled her hair to one side so as to reveal her bare neck and she ran her fingers back and forth along the seams of the bag that she held on her lap. But she didn't dare to go any further and she didn't want to turn around. If he was looking elsewhere, she didn't want to find out.

Mattia coughed quietly into his clenched fist, to warm it up. He noticed Nadia's urgency, but couldn't make up his mind. And even if he did decide, he thought, he wouldn't know what to do. Once Denis, talking about himself, had told him that all opening moves were the same, like in chess. You don't have to come up with anything new, there's no point, because you're both after the same thing anyway. The game soon finds its own way and it's only at that point that you need a strategy.

But I don't even know the opening moves, he thought.

What he did was to rest his left hand in the middle of the seat, like the end of a rope thrown into the sea. He kept it there, even though the synthetic fabric made him shiver.

Nadia understood and in silence, without any abrupt movements, she slid toward the middle. She lifted his arm, taking it by the wrist as if she knew what he were thinking, and put it around her neck. She rested her head against his chest and closed her eyes.

She was wearing strong perfume and it nestled in her hair; it stuck to Mattia's clothes and forced its way into his nostrils.

The taxi pulled up on the left, in front of Nadia's house, with its engine running.

"Seventeen-thirty," said the taxi driver.

She sat up and they both thought how much trouble it would be to find themselves like this again, to break an old equilibrium and build a different one. They wondered if they'd still be able to do it.

Mattia rummaged in his pockets and found his wallet. He held out a twenty and said no change, thanks. She opened the door.

Now follow her, Mattia thought, although he didn't move.

Nadia was already on the sidewalk. The taxi driver watched Mattia in the rearview mirror, waiting for instructions. The squares on the taximeter were all illuminated and flashing oo.oo.

"Come on," said Nadia and he obeyed.

The taxi set off again and they climbed to the top of a steep flight of stairs, with the steps covered in blue carpet and so narrow that Mattia had to walk with his feet at an angle.

Nadia's apartment was clean and very well kept, as only the home of a woman living on her own can be. In the middle of a circular table there was a wicker basket full of dry petals, which had stopped giving off any perfume a long time ago. The walls were painted in strong colors, orange, blue, and egg-yolk yellow, so unusual here in the north that there was something disrespectful about them.

Mattia asked may I come in? and watched Nadia take off her coat and lay it on a chair with the confidence of someone moving in her own space.

"I'm going to get something to drink," she said.

He waited in the middle of the sitting room, his ravaged hands hidden in his pockets. Nadia came back a few moments later with two glasses half full of red wine. She was laughing at a thought of her own.

"I'm not used to all this anymore. It hasn't happened to me for a long time," she confessed.

"That's fine," replied Mattia, rather than say that it had never happened to him.

They sipped the wine in silence, looking cautiously around. Each time their eyes met they smiled faintly, like two children.

Nadia kept her legs folded on the sofa, so that she could get closer to him. The scene was set. All that was required was an action, a cold start, instant and brutal as beginnings always are.

She thought about it for another moment. Then she set her glass down on the floor, behind the sofa, so as not to risk knocking it with her foot, and stretched out resolutely toward Mattia. She kissed him. With her feet she slipped off her high heels, which fell resoundingly to the floor. She climbed astride him, not leaving him the breath to say no.

She took his glass from him and guided his hands to her hips. Mattia's tongue was rigid. She began rolling hers around his, insistently, to force it to move, until he began to do the same, in the opposite direction.

With a certain awkwardness they rolled onto one side and Mattia ended up underneath. One of his legs was dangled off the sofa and the other was extended straight, blocked by her weight. He thought of the circular movement of his own tongue, its periodic motion, but soon he lost concentration, as if Nadia's face squashed against his own had managed to obstruct the complicated mechanism of his thought, like that time with Alice.

He slid his hands under Nadia's top and contact with her skin didn't repel him. They got undressed slowly, without pulling apart or opening their eyes. There was too much light in the room and any interruption would have made them stop.

As he busied himself with the unfastening of her bra Mattia thought it happens. In the end it happens, in some way you couldn't imagine before.

35

Fabio had gotten up early. He had switched off the alarm clock so that Alice wouldn't hear it and had left the room, forcing himself not to look at his wife, lying on her side of the bed, with one arm out of the sheet and her hand stretched out as if she were dreaming about clutching on to something.

He had fallen asleep out of exhaustion and passed through a sequence of nightmares that gradually became more and more gloomy. Now he felt the need to do something with his hands, to get himself dirty, to sweat and wear out his muscles. He considered going to the hospital to do an extra shift, but his parents were coming for lunch, as they did every second Saturday of the month. Twice he picked up the phone with the intention of calling them and telling them not to come, that Alice wasn't feeling well, but then they would have phoned to find out how she was doing, and he would have had to talk to his wife again, and things would have gotten even worse.

In the kitchen he took off his T-shirt. He drank some milk from the fridge. He could pretend nothing was wrong, behave as if nothing had happened the night before and carry on like that, as he had always done, but deep in his throat he felt a completely new sense of nausea. The skin of his face was taut with the tears that had dried on his cheeks. He splashed his face with water at the sink and dried himself with the dish towel hanging next to it.

He looked out the window. The sky was overcast, but the sun would come out shortly. It was always like that at this time of year. On such a day he could have taken his son out for a bike ride, followed the track that ran along the canal all the way to the park.

There they would have drunk from the fountain and sat on the grass for about half an hour. Then they would have come back, on the road this time. They would have stopped at the bakery and bought some pastries for lunch.

He wasn't asking for much. Only for a normal life; the one that he had always deserved.

He went down to the garage, still in his underwear. From the top shelf he took down the box of tools and its heaviness brought him a moment of relief. He took out a screwdriver, a size 9 and a size 12 wrench, and started dismantling his bike, piece by piece, methodically.

First he smeared grease over the gears, then he polished the frame with a rag drenched in alcohol. With his fingernail he scraped away the spots of mud that were stuck to it and also cleaned thoroughly between the pedals, in the cracks that his fingers couldn't enter. He put the various pieces back together again and checked the brake cables, adjusting them so that they were perfectly balanced. He pumped up both tires, testing their pressure with the palm of his hand.

He took a step backward, wiped his hands on his thighs, and observed his work with a weary sense of detachment. He knocked the bike to the ground with a kick. It folded in on itself, like an animal. One pedal started spinning in midair and Fabio listened to its hypnotic swish, until silence fell once more.

He was about to leave the garage, but then he turned back. He lifted the bike and put it back in its place. He couldn't help checking to see if it was damaged. He wondered why he was incapable of leaving everything in a mess, of giving vent to the rage that flooded his brain, cursing and smashing things. Why he preferred everything to seem as if it were in its proper place even when it wasn't.

He turned out the light and climbed the stairs.

Alice was sitting at the kitchen table. She was sipping tea thoughtfully. There was nothing in front of her but the sweetener container. She raised her eyes and looked him up and down.

"Why didn't you wake me up?"

Fabio shrugged. He went over to the tap and turned on the water full blast.

"You were fast asleep," he replied.

He poured dishwashing soap onto his hands and rubbed them hard under the water to remove the black streaks of grease.

"I'll be late with lunch," she said.

Fabio shrugged again.

"We could just forget about lunch," he said.

"What's this, a new development?"

He rubbed his hands together even harder.

"I don't know. It's just an idea."

"It's a new idea."

"Yeah, you're right. It's an idiotic idea," Fabio shot back through clenched teeth.

He turned off the tap and left the kitchen, as if in a hurry. Shortly afterward Alice heard the thunder of water in the shower. She put the cup in the sink and went back to the bedroom to get dressed.

On Fabio's side the sheets were crumpled, full of wrinkles flattened by the weight of his body. The pillow was folded in half, as if he had kept his head underneath it, and the blankets were piled up at the end of the bed, kicked away by his feet. There was a faint smell of sweat, as there was every morning, and Alice threw the window open to let in some fresh air.

The pieces of furniture that the night before had seemed to her to have a soul, a breath of their own, were nothing but the same old pieces of bedroom furniture, as scentless as her tepid resignation.

She made the bed, stretching the sheets out properly and tucking the corners under the mattress. She turned down the top sheet so that it was halfway down the pillows as Sol had taught her and got dressed.

From the bathroom came the buzz of Fabio's electric razor, which for some time she had associated with drowsy weekend mornings.

She wondered whether the previous night's conversation had been different from the others or whether it would be resolved as always. Would Fabio, just out of the shower and still not wearing his T-shirt, hug her from behind and keep his head pressed against her hair, for a long time, long enough to allow the rancor to evaporate? There was no other possible solution, for the time being.

Alice tried to imagine what would happen otherwise. She was transfixed by the sight of the curtains swelling slightly in the draft. She became aware of a sharp sense of abandonment, like a presentiment, not unlike what she had felt in that snow-filled ditch, and then in Mattia's room, and which she felt every time, even now, as she looked at her mother's neatly made bed. She brought her index finger to the pointed bone of her pelvis, running it along the sharp outline that she was not prepared to give up, and when the buzz of the razor stopped she shook her head and went back into the kitchen, with the more solid and imminent worry of lunch.

She chopped up an onion and cut off a little chunk of butter, which she set aside in a small dish. All those things that Fabio had taught her. She was accustomed to dealing with food with ascetic detachment, following simple sequences of actions, the end result of which would not concern her.

She liberated the asparagus stalks from the red elastic band that kept them together, held them under the cold water, and laid them out on a chopping board. She set a panful of water on the burner.

She was alerted to the presence of Fabio in the room by a series of small approaching noises. She froze, waiting for contact with his body.

Instead he sat down on the banquette and started distractedly flipping through a magazine.

"Fabio," she called to him, not really knowing what to say.

He didn't reply. He turned a page, making more noise than necessary. He gripped one corner between his fingers, uncertain whether to tear it or not.

"Fabio," she repeated at the same volume, but turning around.

"What is it?"

"Can you get me the rice, please? It's in the top cupboard. I can't reach."

It was just an excuse, they both knew that. It was just a way of saying come here.

Fabio threw the magazine on the table and it struck an ashtray carved from half a coconut, which began to spin. He sat there for a few seconds with his hands resting on his knees, as if he were thinking about it. Then he suddenly rose to his feet and walked over to the sink.

"Where?" he asked angrily, taking care not to look at Alice.

"There." She pointed.

Fabio pulled a chair over to the fridge, making it squeak on the ceramic tiles. He climbed up on it with bare feet. Alice looked at them as if she hadn't seen them before, and found them attractive, but in a vaguely frightening way.

He picked up the box of rice. It was already open. He shook it. Then he smiled in a way that Alice found sinister. He tilted the box and rice started spilling onto the floor, like thin white rain.

"What are you doing?" said Alice.

Fabio smiled.

"Here's your rice," he replied.

He shook the box harder and the grains scattered all around the kitchen. Alice came over.

"Stop it," she said, but he ignored her. Alice repeated it more loudly.

"Like at our wedding, remember? Our damn wedding," shouted Fabio.

She gripped him by a calf to make him stop and he poured the rice over her head. A few grains stuck in her smooth hair. She looked up at him and said again stop it.

A grain hit her in the eye, hurting her, and with her eyes closed Alice slapped Fabio's shin. He reacted by shaking his leg hard, kicking her just below her left shoulder. His wife's bad knee did what it could to keep her upright, bending first forward and then backward, like a crooked hinge, but then it let her drop to the ground.

The box was empty. Fabio stayed standing on the chair, bewildered, with the box upside down in his hand, looking at his wife on the floor, curled up like a cat. A violent shock of lucidity flashed through his brain.

He got down.

"Ali, did you hurt yourself?" he said. "Let me see."

He slid a hand under her head to look at her face, but she squirmed away.

"Leave me alone!" she yelled.

"Darling, I'm sorry," he pleaded. "You are—"

"Go away!" shouted Alice, with a vocal power that neither of them could have suspected she owned.

Fabio pulled away. His hands trembled. He took two steps back, then stammered an okay. He ran toward the bedroom and came out wearing a T-shirt and a pair of shoes. He left the house without turning to look at his wife, who still hadn't moved.

36

Alice pushed her hair behind her ears. The cupboard door was still open above her head, the lifeless chair in front of her. She hadn't hurt herself. She didn't feel like crying. She couldn't manage to think about what had just happened.

She started picking up the grains of rice scattered over the floor. The first few she picked up one by one. Then she started sweeping them together with the palm of her hand.

She got up and threw a handful into the pan, in which the water was already boiling. She stood and looked at them, carried chaotically up and down by convective motions. Mattia had called them that once. She turned off the flame and went and sat on the sofa.

She wouldn't put anything away. She would wait for her in-laws to arrive and find her like that. She would tell them how Fabio had behaved.

But no one arrived. He must have warned them already. Or he had gone to their house and was telling them his version, saying that Alice's belly was as dry as a dried-up lake and that he was fed up with living like this.

The house was plunged into silence and the light seemed unable to find a place for itself. Alice picked up the telephone and dialed her father's number.

"Hello?" answered Soledad.

"Hi, Sol."

"Hi, *mi amorcito*. How's my baby?" said the housekeeper with her usual concern.

"So-so," said Alice.

"Why? *¿Qué pasa?*"

Alice remained silent for a few seconds.

"Is Dad there?" she asked.

"He's asleep. Shall I go and wake him up?"

Alice thought of her father, in the big bedroom that he now shared with only his thoughts, with the lowered blinds drawing lines of light on his sleeping body. The rancor that had always divided them had been absorbed by time; Alice could hardly remember it. What oppressed her most about that house, her father's serious, penetrating glance, was what she missed most now. He wouldn't say anything, he hardly ever spoke. Stroking her cheek, he would ask Sol to change the sheets in her room and that would be that. After her mother's death something had altered in him: it was as if he had slowed down. Paradoxically, since Fabio had entered Alice's life, her father had become more protective. He no longer talked about himself, he let her do the talking, losing himself in his daughter's voice, carried along by the timbre rather than the words, and responded with thoughtful murmurs.

His moments of absence had begun about a year before, when one evening he had confused Soledad with Fernanda. He had pulled her to him to kiss her, as if she really were his wife, and Sol had been forced to give him a gentle slap on the cheek, to which he had reacted with the whining resentment of a child. The next day he hadn't re- membered a thing, but the vague sense of there being something wrong, an interruption in the cadenced rhythm of time, had led him to ask Sol what had happened. She had tried not to reply, to change the subject, but he hadn't let it go. When the housekeeper had told the truth he had grown gloomy, had nodded and, turning around, had said I'm sorry, in a low voice. Then he had holed himself up in his study and stayed there until dinnertime, without sleeping or do- ing anything. He had sat down at his desk, with his hands resting on the walnut surface, and had tried in vain to reconstruct that miss- ing segment in the ribbon of his memory.

Episodes such as this were repeated with ever greater frequency and all three of them, Alice, her father, and Sol, tried to pretend nothing was wrong, waiting for the moment when that would no longer be possible.

"Ali?" Sol urged. "So shall I go and wake him up?"

"No, no," Alice said quickly. "Don't wake him. It's nothing."

"Really?"

"Yes. Let him rest."

She hung up and lay down on the sofa. She tried to keep her eyes open, directing them at the plastered ceiling. She wanted to be present at this very moment, in which she noticed a new, uncontrollable change. She wanted to be witness to the umpteenth little disaster, memorize its trajectory, but after a few minutes her breathing became more regular and Alice fell asleep.

37

Mattia was startled to find that he still had instincts, buried beneath the dense network of thoughts and abstractions that had woven itself around him. He was startled by the violence with which these instincts emerged and confidently guided his gestures.

The return to reality was painful. Nadia's foreign body had settled on his own. Contact with her sweat on one side and the crumpled fabric of the sofa and their squashed clothes on the other was suffocating. She was breathing slowly. Mattia thought that if the ratio between the intervals of their breath was an irrational number, there was no way of combining them to find a regularity.

He tried to take in some air by stretching over Nadia's head, but it was saturated with heavy condensation. He suddenly wanted to cover himself up. He twisted one leg because he felt his member, flaccid and cold, against her leg. He clumsily hurt her with his knee. Nadia gave a start and raised her head. She had already fallen asleep.

"Sorry," said Mattia.

"Doesn't matter."

She kissed him and her breath was too hot. He remained motionless, waiting for her to stop.

"Shall we go to the bedroom?" she said.

Mattia nodded. He would have liked to go back to his apartment, his comfortable void, but he knew it wasn't the right thing to do.

They both became aware of how embarrassing and unnatural the moment was, as they slipped beneath the sheets from opposite sides of the bed. Nadia smiled as if to say everything's fine. In the darkness she huddled up against his shoulder. She gave him another kiss and quickly fell asleep.

Mattia too closed his eyes, but was forced to open them again immediately, because a jumble of terrible memories lay in wait for him, piled up beneath his eyelids. Once again he had difficulty breathing. He reached his left hand under the bed and began rubbing his thumb against the iron netting, at the pointed juncture where two meshes met. In the darkness he brought his finger to his mouth and sucked it. The taste of blood calmed him for a few seconds.

He gradually became aware of the unfamiliar sounds of Nadia's apartment: the faint hum of the fridge, the heat that rustled for a few seconds and then stopped with a click of the boiler, and a clock, in the other room, that sounded to him as if it were going too slowly. He wanted to move his legs, to get up and out of there. Nadia was still in the middle of the bed, depriving him of the space he needed to turn around. Her hair stung his neck and her breathing dried the skin of his chest. Mattia thought that he would never manage to close his eyes. It was late already, perhaps after two. He had to teach the next day and was bound to make mistakes at the blackboard; he would look like a complete idiot in front of all his students. At his own place, on the other hand, he would have been able to sleep, at least for the few remaining hours.

If I'm quiet about it she won't notice, he thought.

He remained motionless for more than a minute, thinking. The sounds were becoming more and more apparent. Another sharp rattle from the boiler made him stiffen and he decided to leave.

With little movements he managed to free the arm that was underneath Nadia's head. In her sleep she felt the lack and moved to try to find him. Mattia drew himself upright. He rested first one foot on the floor and then the other. When he got up the bed squeaked slightly as it settled.

He turned to look at her in the semidarkness and vaguely

remembered the moment when he had turned his back on Michela in the park.

He walked barefoot to the sitting room. He picked up his clothes from the sofa and his shoes from the floor. He opened the door, as always, without a sound, and when he was in the corridor, still clutching his trousers, he finally managed to breathe deeply.

38

On the Saturday evening of the rice incident, Fabio had called her on her cell phone. Alice had wondered why he hadn't tried on the home phone first and then thought that perhaps it was because the home phone was an object that belonged to both of them and he didn't like the fact that there was something they shared at that moment any more than she did. It had been a short call, in spite of the drawn-out silences. He had said for tonight I'm staying here, like a decision that had already been made, and she had replied as far as I'm concerned you can stay there tomorrow as well and as long as you like. Then, once these tiresome details had been worked out, Fabio had added Alice, I'm sorry, and she had hung up without saying me too.

She hadn't answered the telephone again. Fabio's insistent calls soon abated, and she, in an attack of self-commiseration, had said to herself you see? Walking barefoot through the flat she had picked up at random a few things of her husband's, documents and a few items of clothing, and put them in a box, which she had then dumped in the hall.

One evening she had come back from work and found it wasn't there. Fabio hadn't taken away much else. The furniture was all in place and the closet still full of his clothes, but on the living room shelves there were now gaps among the books, black spaces that bore witness to the start of the breakup. Alice had stopped to look at them and for the first time the separation had assumed the concrete outlines of a hard fact, the massive consistence of a solid form.

With a certain relief she let herself go. She felt as if she had always done everything for someone else, but now there was just her and she could simply stop, surrender, and that was that. She had more time for the same things, but she was aware of an inertia in her actions, a weariness, as if she were moving through a viscous liquid. She finally gave up performing even the easiest tasks. Her dirty clothes piled up in the bathroom and, lying on the sofa for hours, she knew that they were there, that it wouldn't take much effort to pick them up, but none of her muscles considered this a sufficient motive.

She invented a case of the flu so as not to go to work. She slept much more than necessary, even in broad daylight. She didn't even lower the blinds; she had only to close her eyes to be unaware of the light, to cancel out the objects that surrounded her and forget her hateful body, which was growing weaker and weaker but still clung tenaciously to her thoughts. The weight of consequences was always there, like a stranger sleeping on top of her. It watched over her even when Alice plunged into sleep, a heavy sleep saturated with dreams, which was coming more and more to resemble an addiction. If her throat was dry, Alice imagined she was suffocating. If one of her arms tingled from being under the pillow too long, it was because a German shepherd was eating it. If her feet were cold because the blankets had fallen off them in her sleep, Alice found herself once more at the bottom of the crevasse, buried in snow up to her neck. But she wasn't afraid, or hardly ever. Paralysis allowed her to move only her tongue and she stretched it out to taste the snow. It was sweet and Alice would have liked to eat it all, but she couldn't turn her head. So she stayed there, waiting for the cold to rise up her legs, to fill her belly and spread from there to her veins, freezing her blood.

Her waking life was infested with half-constructed thoughts. Alice got up only when she had to, and her drowsy confusion faded slowly, leaving milky residues in her head, like interrupted memories, which mixed with the others and seemed no less true. She wandered through the silent apartment like the ghost of herself, unhurriedly following her own lucidity. I'm going mad, she thought sometimes. But she didn't mind. In fact, it made her smile, because at last she was the one making the choices.

In the evening she ate lettuce leaves, fishing them straight from the plastic bag. They were crunchy and made of nothing. They tasted only of water. She didn't eat them to fill up her stomach, but just to stand in for the ritual of dinner and somehow occupy that time, which she didn't know what else to do with. She ate lettuce until the flimsy stuff made her feel ill.

She emptied herself of Fabio and of herself, of all the useless efforts she had made to get where she was and find nothing there. With detached curiosity she observed the rebirth of her weaknesses, her obsessions. This time she would let them decide, since she hadn't been able to do anything anyway. Against certain parts of yourself you remain powerless, she said to herself, as she regressed pleasurably to the time when she was a girl. To the moment when Mattia had left and, shortly afterward, her mother too, on two journeys that were different but equally remote from her. Mattia. That was it. She thought of him often. Again. He was like another of her illnesses, from which she didn't really want to recover. You can fall ill with just a memory and she had fallen ill that afternoon in the car, by the park, when she had covered his face with her own to prevent him from looking on the site where that horror had taken place.

No matter how hard she tried, from all those years spent with Fabio she couldn't extract so much as one image that crushed her heart so powerfully, that had the same impetuous violence in its colors and which she could still feel on her skin and in the roots of her hair and between her legs. True, there had been that one time at dinner with Riccardo and his wife, when they'd laughed and drunk a lot. She'd been helping Alessandra wash the dishes and had cut the tip of her thumb on a glass that had shattered in her hands. And as she dropped it she had said ouch, not loudly—she had barely whispered it—but Fabio had heard and come running. He had examined her thumb under the light; leaning forward he had brought it to his lips and sucked a little of the blood, to make it stop, as if it had been his. With her thumb in his mouth he had looked up at her, with those disarming eyes that Alice couldn't resist. Then he had closed the wound in his hand and kissed Alice on the mouth. She had tasted her own blood in his saliva and imagined that it had circulated throughout her husband's body and come back to her cleaned, as though through dialysis.

There had been that time and there had been an infinite number of others, which Alice no longer remembered, because the love of those we don't love in return settles on the surface and from there quickly evaporates. What was left now was a faint red patch, almost invisible on her drawn skin, the spot where Fabio had kicked her.

Sometimes, particularly in the evening, she remembered what he had said. *I can't do this anymore.* She stroked her belly and tried to imagine what it would have been like to have someone in there, swimming in her cold liquid. *Tell me what it is.* But there was nothing to explain. There was no reason, or not only one. There was no beginning. There was her and that was that and she didn't want anyone in her belly.

Perhaps I should tell him that, she thought.

Then she picked up her cell phone and ran through her contact list till she got to *F*. She rubbed the keyboard with her thumb, as if hoping to activate the call by mistake. Then she pressed the red button. To see Fabio, talk to him, rebuild: it all seemed like an inhuman effort and she preferred to stay there, watching the furniture in the sitting room being covered with a layer of dust that was getting thicker by the day.

39

He hardly ever looked at the students. When he met their clear eyes directed at the blackboard and at him, he felt naked. Mattia wrote out his calculations and made precise comments, as if he were explaining them to himself as well as to everyone else. The classroom was too big for the dozen fourth-year students who were taking his course in algebraic topology. They arranged themselves in the first three rows, more or less always in the same places and leaving an empty seat between one and the next, as he himself had done in his university days, but in none of the students could he spot anything that reminded him of himself.

In the silence he heard the door at the back of the classroom close but he didn't turn around until the end of the proof. He turned a page in his notes, which he didn't really need, realigned the pages, and only then noticed a new figure in the topmost margin of his field of vision. He looked up and saw it was Nadia. She had taken a seat in the back row; dressed in white, she sat with her legs crossed and didn't greet him.

Mattia tried to conceal his panic, and moved on to the next theorem. He almost lost his thread, said I'm sorry, and tried to find the step in his notes, but was unable to concentrate. A barely perceptible murmur ran through the students; the teacher had never once hesitated since the beginning of the course.

He started over and made it to the end, writing quickly, his writing sloping more and more toward the bottom as it shrank toward the right-hand edge of the blackboard. He crammed the last two steps into a top corner because he had run out of space. Some of the students leaned forward to make out the exponents and subscripts that had gotten jumbled up with the formulas around them. There was still a quarter of an hour to go before the end of the lesson when Mattia said okay, I'll see you tomorrow.

He set down the chalk and watched the students get up, slightly puzzled, and give him a little wave before leaving the classroom. Nadia was still sitting there, in the same position, and no one seemed to notice her.

They were alone. They seemed very far apart. Nadia got up in the same instant as he stepped toward her. They met more or less halfway across the lecture hall and stayed a good meter apart.

"Hi," said Mattia. "I didn't think—"

"Listen," she broke in, looking resolutely into his eyes. "We don't even know each other. I'm sorry I just turned up like this."

"No, don't—" he tried to say, but Nadia didn't let him speak.

"I woke up and didn't find you, you could at least have . . ."

She stopped for a second. Mattia was forced to lower his gaze because his eyes stung, as if he hadn't blinked for more than a minute.

"But it doesn't matter," Nadia went on. "I don't chase after anybody. I don't feel like it anymore."

She held out a piece of paper and he took it.

"That's my number. But if you decide to use it don't wait too long."

They both looked at the floor. Nadia was about to lean forward, and wobbled slightly on her heels, but then suddenly turned around.

"Bye," she said.

Mattia cleared his throat instead of responding. He thought that it would take a finite amount of time for her to reach the door. Not enough time to make a decision, to articulate a thought.

Nadia stopped in the doorway.

"I don't know what's wrong with you," she said. "But whatever it is, I think I like it."

Then she left. Mattia looked at the piece of paper, on which there was merely a name and a sequence of numbers, mostly odd numbers. He picked up his papers from the desk, but waited for the hour to finish before leaving.

In the office Alberto was on the phone, the receiver pinched between his chin and his cheek, so he could gesticulate with both arms. He raised an eyebrow to Mattia in greeting.

When he hung up he leaned back into his chair and stretched his legs. He gave him a complicit smile.

"So?" he asked. "Were we up late last night?"

Mattia deliberately avoided his gaze. He shrugged. Alberto got up and went and stood behind Mattia's chair, massaging his shoulders like a trainer with his boxer. Mattia didn't like to be touched.

"I understand, you don't feel like talking about it. All right, then, let's change the subject. I've jotted down a draft for the article. Feel like casting your eye over it?"

Mattia nodded. He drummed gently with his index finger on the o of the computer, waiting for Alberto to take his hands off his shoulders. Some images from the previous night, always the same ones, ran through his head like faint flashes of light.

Alberto went back to his desk and slumped heavily into his chair. He started looking for the article amid a shapeless pile of papers.

"Ah," he said. "This came for you."

He tossed an envelope on Mattia's desk. Mattia looked at it without touching it. His name and the address of the university were written in thick blue ink, which must have soaked through to the other side of the paper. The *M* of Mattia started with a straight line, then, slightly detached from it, a soft, concave curve set off, continuing into the right-hand vertical. The two *t*'s were held together by a single horizontal line and all the letters were slightly sloped, piled up as if they had fallen on top of one another. There was a mistake in the address, a *c* too many. He would have needed only one letter, or nothing but the asymmetry between the two potbellied loops of the *B* in Balossino, to recognize Alice's handwriting straightaway.

He gulped and reached around for the letter opener, which was in its place in the second drawer down. He turned it nervously around in his fingers and slipped it into the flap of the envelope. His hands were trembling and he gripped harder on the handle to control himself.

Alberto watched him from the other side of the desk, pretending to be unable to find the papers that were already sitting in front of him. The trembling of Mattia's fingers was apparent even from that distance, but the piece of paper was hidden in the palm of his hand.

He watched his colleague close his eyes and stay like that for a good few seconds, before opening them again and looking around, as if lost and suddenly far away.

"Who's it from?" Alberto ventured.

Mattia looked at him with a kind of resentment, as if he didn't even recognize him. Then he got up, ignoring the question.

"I've got to go," he said.

"What?"

"I've got to go. I think . . . to Italy."

Alberto got up as well, as if to stop him.

"What are you talking about? What's happened?"

He instinctively walked over to him and tried once more to peer at the piece of paper, but Mattia kept it hidden between his hand and the rough fabric of his sweater, pressed against his stomach, like something secret. Three of the four white corners stuck out beyond his fingers, giving a clue to its rectangular shape and nothing more.

"Nothing. I don't know," Mattia shot back, with one arm already in the sleeve of his Windbreaker. "But I've got to go."

"And what about the article?"

"I'll look at it when I get back. You just go ahead."

Then he left, without giving Alberto time to protest.

40

The day Alice went back to work she turned up almost an hour late. She had switched off the alarm without even waking up and as she got ready to go out she had had to stop often, because every movement put an unbearable strain on her body.

Crozza didn't tell her off. He needed only to look at her face to understand. Alice's cheeks were hollow and her eyes, even though they seemed to pop too far out of her head, looked absent, veiled by an ominous sense of indifference.

"Sorry I'm late," she said as she walked in, without really meaning it.

Crozza turned the page of his newspaper and couldn't help glancing at the clock.

"There are some pictures to be printed by eleven," he said. "The usual crap."

He cleared his throat and lifted the newspaper higher. He followed Alice's movements from the corner of his eye. He watched her putting her bag in the usual place, taking off her jacket, and sitting down at the machine. She moved slowly and with excessive precision, which betrayed her efforts to make everything seem all right. Crozza watched her sitting lost in thought for a few seconds, with her chin resting on her hand, and at last, after brushing her hair back behind her ears, deciding to begin.

He calmly assessed her excessive thinness, hidden beneath her high-collared cotton sweater and in her far-from-skintight trousers, but apparent in her hands and even more in the outline of her face. He felt a furious sense of powerlessness, because he played no part in Alice's life, but by God she did in his, like a daughter whose name he hadn't been able to choose.

They worked until lunchtime without speaking. They exchanged only indispensable nods of the head. After all the years they had spent in there, every gesture seemed automatic and they moved with agility, sharing the space fairly. The old Nikon was in its place under the counter, in its black case, and they both sometimes wondered if it still worked.

"Lunch. Let's go—" the photographer said hesitantly.

"I've got something to do at lunchtime," Alice interrupted. "Sorry."

He nodded thoughtfully.

"If you don't feel well, you can go home for the afternoon," he said. "There isn't much to do, as you can see."

Alice looked at him in alarm. She pretended to rearrange the things on the counter: a pair of scissors, an envelope for photographs, a pen, and a roll of film cut into four equal segments. All she was doing was swapping them around.

"No, why? I—"

"How long is it since you've seen each other?" the photographer interrupted.

Alice gave a slight jump. She stuck one hand into her bag, as if to protect it.

"Three weeks. More or less."

Crozza nodded, then shrugged.

"Let's go," he said.

"But . . ."

"Come on, let's go," he repeated, more firmly.

Alice thought for a moment. Then she decided to follow him. They locked up the shop. The bell hanging from the door jangled in the shadow and then stopped. Alice and Crozza set off toward the photographer's car. He walked slowly, without showing it, out of respect for her laborious gait.

The old Lancia started only at the second attempt and Crozza muttered a curse between his teeth.

They drove down the avenue almost as far as the bridge, and then the photographer took a right and followed the road that ran along the river. When he changed lanes and switched on the right blinker to turn again, this time in the direction of the hospital, Alice suddenly froze.

"But where . . . ?" she tried to say.

He pulled up outside a shop with its security gate half closed, across from the entrance to the emergency room.

"It's none of my business," he said, without looking at Alice, "but you've got to go in there. To Fabio, or some other doctor."

Alice stared at him. Her initial puzzlement gave way to fury. The road was silent. Everyone was tucked away at home or in a restaurant for lunch. The leaves of the plane trees fluttered soundlessly.

"I haven't seen you like this since . . ." The photographer hesitated. "Since I've known you."

Alice considered that *like this* in her head. It sounded ominous and she glanced at herself in the mirror, but it showed only the side of the car. She shook her head, then unlocked the door and got out of the car. She slammed the door and without turning around she resolutely walked in the opposite direction of the hospital.

She walked quickly, more quickly than she really could, to get away from that place and Crozza's damned insolence, but after about a hundred meters she had to stop. She was out of breath and with each step she took her leg hurt more and more, pulsating as if asking her for mercy. The bone seemed to penetrate the living flesh, as if it had come out of joint again. Alice moved all her weight to the right and just managed to keep her balance, leaning one hand against the rough wall beside her.

She waited for the pain to pass, for her leg once more to become inert as usual and her breathing to become an unconscious action again. Her heart pumped blood slowly, without conviction, but she could hear it even in her ears.

You've got to go in there. To Fabio, or some other doctor, Crozza's voice echoed in her head.

And then? she thought.

She turned back, toward the hospital, walking with difficulty and without any precise intention. Her body chose the way as if by instinct and the passersby she met on the sidewalk stepped aside, because Alice was staggering a little, although she wasn't aware of it. Some of them stopped, unsure whether to offer to help, but then walked on.

Alice stepped into the courtyard of Our Lady's Hospital and didn't think back to the time when she had walked along the same little avenue with Fabio. She felt as if she didn't have a past, as if she had found herself in that place without knowing where she had come from. She was tired, with that tiredness that only emptiness brings.

She climbed the steps holding on to the handrail and stopped in front of the doorway. She wanted only to get there, to activate the sliding doors and wait for a few minutes, just long enough to collect her strength and leave. It was a way of giving chance a little push, nothing more, to find herself where Fabio was and see what happened. She wouldn't do what Crozza said, she wouldn't listen to anyone, and she wouldn't admit even to herself that she really hoped to find him.

Nothing happened. The automatic doors opened and when Alice took a step back they closed again.

What did you expect? she wondered.

She thought about sitting down for a few seconds, hoping it would pass. Her body was asking her something, every nerve was screaming it, but she didn't want to listen.

She was about to turn around, when she heard the electric swish of the doors again. She looked up at the sound, convinced that this time she would really find her husband standing in front of her.

The door was wide open, but Fabio wasn't there. Instead, on the other side of the doorway, a girl was standing. It was she who had activated the sensor, but she didn't come out. She stood right where she was, smoothing her skirt with her hands. At last she imitated Alice: she took a step back and the door closed again.

Alice studied her, curious about that gesture. She noticed that she wasn't all that young. She might have been the same age as Alice, more or less. She kept her torso bent slightly forward and her shoulders tightly curved, as if there wasn't enough room for them.

Alice thought there was something familiar about her, perhaps in her facial expression, but she couldn't place her. Her thoughts closed in on themselves; they spun in the void.

Then the girl did it again. She stepped forward, put her feet together, and a few seconds later stepped back.

It was then that she looked up and smiled at Alice from the other side of the glass.

A shiver ran down Alice's spine, vertebra by vertebra, before losing itself in her blind leg. She held her breath.

She knew someone else who smiled like that, merely arching her upper lip, barely revealing the two incisors, and leaving the rest of the mouth motionless.

It can't be, she thought.

She stepped forward to see better and the doors remained wide open. The girl looked disappointed and stared quizzically at her. Alice understood and stepped back to let her go on with her game. The other girl continued as if nothing was wrong.

She had the same dark hair, thick and wavy at the bottom, that Alice had managed to touch only a very few times. Her cheekbones protruded slightly and hid her black eyes, but as she looked at her

Alice recognized the same expression that had kept her up till late so many nights: the same opaque gleam as she had seen in Mattia's eyes.

It's her, she thought, and a feeling very like terror gripped her throat.

She instinctively fumbled for the camera in her bag, but she hadn't brought so much as a stupid Instamatic.

She went on looking at the girl, not knowing what else to do. She turned her head toward her and her vision dimmed from time to time, as if her crystalline lens couldn't find the right curvature. With her dry lips she pronounced the word *Michela,* but not enough air came from her mouth.

The girl didn't seem to tire of this. She played with the automatic door like a child. Now she was taking small jumps, back and forth, as if to catch the doors out.

An old lady walked over from inside the building. A big rectangular yellow envelope protruded from her bag, X-rays perhaps. Without saying a word, she took the girl by the arm and led her outside.

The girl didn't resist. When she passed by Alice, she turned for a moment to look at the sliding doors, as if to thank them for amusing her. She was so close that Alice was aware of the displacement of air produced by her body. By holding out a hand she could have touched her, but it was as though she were paralyzed.

She watched the two women as they walked slowly away.

Now people were coming in and out. The doors were constantly opening and closing, in a hypnotic rhythm that filled Alice's head.

As if suddenly coming to, she called Michela, this time out loud.

The girl didn't turn around and neither did the old lady who was with her. They didn't alter their pace by one iota, as if the name meant nothing to them.

Alice thought she should follow them, look at the girl from closer up, talk to her, understand. She put her right foot on the first step and drew her other leg forward, but it remained frozen where it was, fast asleep. She found herself toppling backward. With her hand she sought the handrail, but didn't find it.

She collapsed like a broken branch and slid down the two remaining steps.

From the ground she just had time to see the women disappearing around the corner. Then she felt the air becoming saturated with moisture and the sounds growing rounder and farther away.

Mattia had taken the three flights of stairs at a run. Between the second and the first he had bumped into one of his students, who had tried to stop him to ask something. He had brushed past him saying sorry, I've got to go, and in trying to avoid him he had almost stumbled. When he reached the entrance hall he had suddenly slowed down, to compose himself, but still walked quickly. The dark marble of the floor gleamed, reflecting things and people like a stretch of water. Mattia had given a nod of greeting to the doorman and gone outside.

The cold air had taken him by surprise and he had wondered what are you doing?

Now he was sitting on the low wall in front of the entrance and wondering why on earth he had reacted like that, as if all he had been doing all those years was waiting for a signal to go back.

He looked again at the photograph that Alice had sent him. It was of the two of them, by her parents' bed, dressed up as a bride and groom with those clothes that smelled of mothballs. Mattia looked resigned, while she was smiling. One of her arms was around his waist. The other held the camera and was partially out of the frame, as if she were now holding it toward him, as an adult, to caress him.

On the back Alice had written only one line and below it her signature:

You've got to come here.
Alice

Mattia tried to find an explanation for the message and, even more, for his own peculiar reaction. He imagined coming out of the arrivals zone of the airport and finding Alice and Fabio waiting for him on the other side of the barrier. He imagined greeting her, kissing her on the cheeks, and then shaking her husband's hand by way of introduction. They would pretend to argue about who should carry the suitcase to the car and on the way they would try in vain to tell each other how life had been, as if it could really be summed up. Mattia in the backseat, them in the front: three strangers pretending to have something in common and scratching the surface of things, just to avoid silence.

It's pointless, he said to himself.

That lucid thought brought him some relief, as if he were taking control of himself again after a moment of bewilderment. He tapped the photograph with his finger, already intending to put it away and go back to Alberto, to get on with their work.

While he was still lost in his thoughts, Kirsten Gorbahn, a postdoc from Dresden with whom he had recently written some articles, came over to peer at the photograph.

"Your wife?" she asked him cheerfully, pointing at Alice.

Mattia twisted his neck to look up at Kirsten. He was about to hide the photograph, but then he thought it would be rude. Kirsten had an oblong face, as if someone had pulled it hard by the chin. In two years spent studying in Rome she had learned a little Italian, which she pronounced with all the *o*'s closed.

"Hi," Mattia said uncertainly. "No, she isn't my wife. She's just . . . a friend."

Kirsten chuckled, amused by who knows what, and took a sip of coffee from the polystyrene cup that she was holding in her hands.

"She's cute," she remarked.

Mattia looked her up and down, slightly uneasily, and then looked back at the photograph. Yes, she really was.

42

When Alice came to, a nurse was taking her pulse. She still had her shoes on, and was lying at a slight angle on top of a white sheet on a hospital bed by the entrance. She immediately thought of Fabio, who might have seen her in that terrible state, and suddenly sat up.

"I'm fine," she said.

"Lie down," the nurse ordered her. "We're going to do a checkup."

"There's no need. Really, I'm fine," Alice insisted, overcoming the resistance of the nurse, who tried to keep her where she was. Fabio wasn't there.

"You fainted, young lady. You have to see a doctor."

But Alice was already on her feet. She checked that she still had her bag.

"It's nothing. Believe me."

The nurse raised her eyes to the sky but didn't stand in her way. Alice glanced around, lost, as if looking for someone. Then she said thank you and left in a hurry.

She hadn't hurt herself when she fell. She seemed merely to have banged her right knee. She felt the rhythmical pulsation of the bruise under her jeans. Her hands were a little scratched and dusty, as if she had dragged them along the gravel in the courtyard. She blew on them to clean them.

She walked over to the reception desk and bent down to the round hole in the glass. The lady on the other side looked up at her.

"Hello," said Alice. She had no idea how to explain herself. She 239 didn't even know how long she had been unconscious.

"A little while ago . . ." she said, "I was standing there . . ."

She pointed to the spot where she had been, but the lady didn't move her head.

"There was a woman, by the entrance. I didn't feel well. I fainted. Then . . . You see, I need to find out the name of that person."

The receptionist looked at her, bewildered, from behind the counter.

"I'm sorry?" she asked with a grimace.

"It sounds strange, I know," Alice insisted. "But you've got to help me. Perhaps you could give me the names of the patients who had appointments in this department today. Or examinations. Just the women, I only need those."

The woman looked at her. Then she smiled coldly.

"We aren't authorized to give out that kind of information," she replied.

"It's very important. Please. It's really very important."

The receptionist tapped with a pen on the register in front of her.

"I'm sorry. It really isn't possible," she replied irritably.

Alice snorted. She was about to pull away from the counter, but then she approached again.

"I'm Dr. Rovelli's wife," she said.

The receptionist sat up straighter in her chair. She arched her eyebrows and tapped the register with her pen again.

"I understand," she said. "If you like I'll let your husband know you're here."

She picked up the receiver but Alice stopped her with a gesture of her hand.

"No," she said, without controlling the tone of her voice. "There's no need."

"Are you sure?"

"Yes, thanks. Never mind."

———

She set off toward home. All the way there she couldn't think about anything else. Her mind was becoming clear again, but all the images that passed through it were obliterated by that girl's face. The details were already blurring, plunging fast into the midst of an ocean of other memories of no importance, but that inexplicable sense of familiarity remained. And that smile, the same as Mattia's, mixed with her own intermittent reflection on the glass.

Perhaps Michela was alive and she had seen her. It was madness, and yet Alice couldn't help believing it. It was as if her brain desperately needed that one thought. Clinging to it to stay alive.

She began to think, to formulate hypotheses. She tried to reconstruct how things might have gone. Perhaps the old lady had kidnapped Michela, had found her in the park and taken her away, because she had a violent desire for a little girl but couldn't have children. Her womb was defective or else she was unwilling to make a bit of room in it.

Just like me, thought Alice.

She had kidnapped her and then brought her up in a house a long way from there, with a different name, as if she were her own.

But in that case, why come back? Why risk being discovered after all those years? Perhaps she was being devoured by guilt. Or else she just wanted to tempt fate, as she herself had done outside the door of the oncology department.

On the other hand, perhaps the old woman had nothing to do with it. Maybe she had met Michela a long time afterward and knew nothing about her origins, her real family, just as Michela remembered nothing about herself.

Alice thought of Mattia, pointing from inside her car at the trees in front of him, his ashen, absent face that spoke of death. She was completely identical to me, he had said.

Suddenly it seemed to her that everything made sense, that the girl really was Michela, the vanished twin, and that every detail now fell into place: the blank expanse of her forehead, the length of her fingers, her circumspect way of moving them. And more than anything that childish game of hers, that more than anything.

But just a second later, she realized she was confused. All those details collapsed into a vague sense of weariness, orchestrated by the hunger that had clenched at her temples for days, and Alice feared losing her senses all over again.

At home, she left the door half open with the keys still in it. She went into the kitchen and opened the cupboard without even taking off her jacket. She found some tuna and ate it straight from the can without draining off the oil. The smell made her feel sick. She threw the empty can into the sink and picked up a can of peas. With her fork she fished them from the cloudy water and ate half of them, without breathing. They tasted of sand and the shiny skin stuck to her teeth. Then she pulled out the box of cookies that had sat open in the cupboard since the day Fabio had left. She ate five, one after the other, barely chewing them. They scratched her throat as she swallowed, like bits of glass. She stopped only when the cramps in her stomach were so strong that she had to sit down on the floor to withstand the pain.

When it had passed, she stood up and walked to the darkroom, limping openly, as she did when she was alone. She took one of the boxes from the second shelf. The word *Snapshots* was written on the side in indelible red pen. She spilled the contents onto the table and spread out the photographs with her fingers. Some were stuck together. Alice quickly inspected them and at last found the one she was looking for.

She studied it for a long time. Mattia was young, and so was she. His head was bent and it was hard to study his expression to determine the resemblance. A lot of time had passed. Perhaps too much.

That fixed image brought others to the surface and Alice's mind stitched them together to re-create movement, fragments of sounds, scraps of sensations. She was filled with searing but pleasurable nostalgia.

If she had been able to choose one point from which to start over, she would have chosen that one: she and Mattia in a silent room with their private intimacies, hesitant about touching each other but their outlines fitting precisely together.

She had to let him know. Only by seeing him could she be sure. If his sister was alive, Mattia had the right to know.

For the first time, she perceived all the space that separated them as a ludicrous distance. She was sure that he was still there, where she had written to him several times, many years before. If he had moved, she would have been aware of it somehow. Because she and Mattia were united by an invisible, elastic thread, buried under a pile of meaningless things, a thread that could exist only between two people like themselves: two people who had acknowledged their own solitude within the other.

She felt around under the pile of photographs and found a pen. She sat down to write, careful not to smudge the ink with her hand. At last she blew on it to dry it. She looked for an envelope, slipped the photograph inside, and sealed it.

Maybe he'll come, she thought.

A pleasant apprehension gripped her bones and made her smile, as if at that very moment time had begun again.

43

Before seeking the runway, the plane on which Mattia was traveling crossed the green patch of the hill, passed the basilica, and flew twice over the center of the city in a circular trajectory. Mattia took the bridge, the older one, as his point of reference and from there followed the road to his parents' house. It was still the same color as when he had left it.

He recognized the park nearby, bounded by the two main roads that flowed together into a broad curve bisected by the river. On so clear an afternoon you could see everything from up there: no one could have disappeared into nothingness.

He leaned farther forward, to look at what the plane was leaving behind it. He followed the winding road that climbed part of the way up the hill and found the Della Roccas' building, with its white façade and its windows all attached to one another, like an imposing block of ice. A little farther on there was his old school, with the green fire escapes, their surfaces, he remembered, cold and rough to the touch.

The place where he had spent the first half of his life, the half that was now over, was like an enormous sculpture made of colored cubes and inanimate shapes.

He took a taxi from the airport. His father had insisted on coming to collect him, but he had said no, I'll come on my own, in that tone that his parents knew well and that was pointless to resist.

After the taxi had driven off, he stood on the sidewalk on the other side of the street, looking at his old house. The bag that he carried over his shoulder wasn't very heavy. It contained clean clothes for two or three days at the most.

He found the entrance to the apartment block open and climbed to his floor. He rang the bell and heard no sound from inside. Then his father opened the door and, before they were able to say anything, they smiled at each other, each contemplating the passing of time in the changes that had occurred in the other.

Pietro Balossino was old. It wasn't just the white hair and the thick veins that stood out too much on the backs of his hands. He was old in the way he stood in front of his son, his whole body trembling almost imperceptibly, and leaned on the door handle, as if his legs were no longer enough on their own.

They hugged, rather awkwardly. Mattia's bag rolled off his shoulder and slipped between them. He let it fall to the floor. Their bodies were still the same temperature. Pietro Balossino touched his son's hair and remembered too many things. Feeling them all at the same time gave him a pain in his chest.

Mattia looked at his father to ask where's Mum? and he understood.

"Your mother's resting," he said. "She didn't feel very well. It must be the heat these past few days."

Mattia nodded.

"Are you hungry?"

"No. I'd just like a little water."

"I'll go and get you some."

His father quickly disappeared into the kitchen, as if looking for an excuse to get away. Mattia thought that that was all that was left, that parental affection resolves itself into small solicitudes, the concerns his parents listed on the telephone every Wednesday: food, heat and cold, tiredness, sometimes money. Everything else lay as if submerged at unreachable depths, in a mass of subjects never addressed, excuses to be made and received and memories to be corrected, which would remain unchanged.

He walked down the corridor to his bedroom. He was sure he

would find everything as he had left it, as if that space was immune to the erosion of time, as if all the years of his absence constituted only a parenthesis in that place. He felt an alienating sense of disappointment when he saw that everything was different, like the horrible feeling of ceasing to exist. The walls that had once been pale blue had been covered with cream-colored wallpaper, which made the room look brighter. Where his bed had been was the sofa that had been in the sitting room for years. His desk was still at the window, but on it there was no longer anything of his, just a pile of newspapers and a sewing machine. There were no photographs, of him or of Michela.

He stood in the doorway as if he needed permission to enter. His father came over with the glass of water and seemed to read his thoughts.

"Your mother wanted to learn to sew," he said, as if by way of justification. "But she soon got fed up with it."

Mattia drank the water down in one gulp. He rested his bag against the wall, where it wasn't in the way.

"I have to go now," he said.

"Already? But you've only just got here."

"There's someone I have to see."

He walked past his father, avoiding his eyes and sliding his back against the wall. Their bodies were too similar and bulky and adult to be so close to each other. He took the glass through to the kitchen, rinsed it, and set it upside down on the draining board.

"I'll be back this evening," he said.

He nodded good-bye to his father, who was standing in the middle of the living room, at the same spot where in another life he was hugging his mother, talking about him. It wasn't true that Alice was waiting for him, he didn't even know where to find her, but he had to get out of there as quickly as possible.

44

They wrote to each other during the first year. As with everything else that concerned them, it was Alice who had started it. She had sent him a photograph of a cake with a rather clumsy *Happy Birthday* written with strawberries cut in half. She had signed the back only with an *A*—and nothing more. She had made the cake for Mattia's birthday, and then had thrown the whole thing into the trash. Mattia had replied in a letter of four closely written pages, in which he told her how hard it was to start over in a new place without knowing the language, and in which he apologized for leaving. Or at least that was how it seemed to Alice. He hadn't asked her anything about Fabio, either in that letter or in the ones that followed, and she hadn't talked about him. Both of them were aware, however, of his strange and menacing presence, just beyond the edge of the page. Partly for that reason they soon began to reply to each other's letters coldly and at increasingly longer intervals, until their correspondence faded away entirely.

A few years later Mattia had received another card. It was an invitation to Alice and Fabio's wedding. He had stuck it on the fridge with a piece of tape, as if, hanging there, it would inevitably remind him of something. Each morning and each evening he found himself standing in front of it and each time it seemed to hurt him a little less. A week before the ceremony he had managed to send a telegram that said *Thank you for invitation must decline due to professional obligations. Congratulations, Mattia Balossino.* In a shop in the city center he had spent a whole morning choosing a crystal vase that he had sent to the couple at their new address.

It was not to this address that he went when he left his parents' house. Instead he headed for the hill, to the Della Roccas', where he and Alice had spent their afternoons together. He was sure he wouldn't find her there, but he wanted to pretend that nothing had changed.

He hesitated for a long time before pressing the buzzer. A woman replied, probably Soledad.

"Who is it?"

"I'm looking for Alice," he said.

"Alice doesn't live here anymore."

Yes, it was Soledad. He recognized her Spanish accent, still quite noticeable.

"Who is looking for her?" asked the housekeeper.

"It's Mattia."

There was an extended silence. Sol tried to remember.

"I can give you her new address."

"That's okay. I've got it, thanks," he said.

"Good-bye, then," said Sol, after another, shorter silence.

Mattia walked off without turning to look up. He was sure that Sol would be standing at one of the windows watching him, recognizing him only now and wondering what had become of him in all those years and what it was he had come back in search of. The truth was that even he didn't know.

45

Alice hadn't expected him so soon. She had sent the card only five days before and it was possible that Mattia hadn't even read it yet. At any rate she was sure that he would call first, that they would arrange to meet, perhaps in a bar, where she would prepare him calmly for the news.

Her days were filled with waiting for some kind of signal. At work she was distracted but cheerful and Crozza hadn't dared to ask her why, but in his heart he felt he deserved some credit for it. The void left by Fabio's departure had made way for an almost adolescent frenzy. Alice assembled and dismantled the image of the moment when she and Mattia would meet; she studied the scene from different angles and adjusted every detail. She wore away at the thought until it seemed not so much a projection as a memory.

She had also been to the local library. She had had to get a card, because she had never set foot in it before that day. She had looked for the newspapers that reported on Michela's disappearance. They were upsetting to read, as if all that horror were happening again, not far from where she was. Her confidence had wavered at the sight of a photograph of Michela on the front page, in which she was looking lost and staring at a point above the lens, perhaps the forehead of whoever was taking the picture. That image had instantly undermined the memory of the girl at the hospital, superimposing itself over her too precisely to seem believable. For the first time Alice had wondered if it might not all be a mistake, a hallucination that had lasted too long. Then she had covered the photograph with one hand and gone on reading, resolutely dispelling that doubt.

Michela's body had never been found. Not so much as an item of clothing, not a trace. The child had simply vanished. For months the line of a kidnapping had been pursued, but to no avail. No suspects were ever named. The news had gradually moved to the margins of the inside pages before finally disappearing altogether.

When the bell rang, Alice was drying her hair. She opened the door distractedly, without even asking who's there, as she arranged the towel on her head. She was barefoot and the first thing Mattia saw of her was her bare feet, the second toe slightly longer than the big one, as if pushing its way forward, and the fourth bent underneath, hidden away. They were details he knew well, which had survived in his mind longer than words and situations.

"Hi," he said, looking up.

Alice took a step back and instinctively closed both sides of her bathrobe, as if her heart might burst out of her chest. Then she focused on Mattia, took in his presence. She hugged him, pressing her inadequate weight against him. He circled her waist with his right arm, but kept his fingers raised, as if out of prudence.

"I'll be right there. I'll just be a moment," she said, rushing her words. She went back inside and closed the door, leaving him standing outside. She needed a few minutes on her own to get dressed and put on her makeup and dry her eyes before he noticed.

Mattia sat down on the front step, his back to the door. He studied the little garden, the almost perfect symmetry of the low hedge that ran along both sides of the path and the undulating shape that broke off halfway through a sine curve. When he heard the click of the lock he turned around and for a moment everything seemed as it had been: he waiting outside for Alice and she coming out, well dressed and smiling, then walking down the street together without having decided where they were going.

Alice bent forward and kissed him on the cheek. To sit down next to him she had to hold on to his shoulder, because of her stiff leg.

He moved over. They had nothing to rest their backs against, so they both sat leaning slightly forward.

"You were quick," said Alice.

"Your card arrived yesterday morning."

"So that place isn't so far away after all."

Mattia looked at the ground. Alice took his right hand and opened it palm side up. He didn't resist, because with her he had no need to be ashamed of the marks.

There were new ones, recognizable as darker lines in the middle of that tangle of white scars. None of them seemed all that recent, apart from one circular halo, like a burn. Alice followed its outline with the tip of her index finger and he was barely aware of her touch through all the layers of hardened skin. He calmly let her look, because his hand told much more than he could in words.

"It seemed important," said Mattia.

"It is."

He turned to look at her, to ask her to go on.

"Not yet," said Alice. "First let's get away from here."

Mattia got up first, then held out his hand to help her, just as they had always done. They walked toward the street. It was difficult to talk and think at the same time, as if the two actions canceled each other out.

"Here," said Alice.

She turned off the alarm of a dark green station wagon and Mattia thought it was too big for her alone.

"Do you want to drive?" Alice asked him with a smile.

"I don't know how."

"Are you joking?"

He shrugged. They looked at each other over the roof of the car. The sun sparkled on the bodywork between them.

"I don't need to drive there," he said by way of justification.

Alice tapped her chin with the key, thoughtfully.

"I know where we have to go, then," she said, with the same playfulness with which she announced her ideas as a girl.

They got into the car. There was nothing on the dashboard in front of Mattia, apart from two compact discs, one on top of the other with their spines facing him: Mussorgsky's *Pictures at an Exhibition* and a collection of Schubert sonatas.

"So you've become a fan of classical music?"

Alice darted a quick glance at the CDs. She wrinkled up her nose.

"No way. They're his. All they do is put me to sleep."

Mattia writhed against the seat belt. It scratched his shoulder because it was set for someone shorter, Alice probably, who sat there while her husband drove. They listened to classical music together. He tried to imagine it, then he allowed himself to be distracted by the words printed on the side-view mirror: *Objects in mirror are closer than they appear.*

"Fabio, right?" he asked. He already knew the answer, but he wanted to untie that knot, dissolve that awkward, silent presence that seemed to be studying them from the backseat. He knew that otherwise the conversation between them would stall right there, like a boat run aground on the rocks.

Alice nodded, as if making an effort. If she explained everything all at once, about the baby, the quarrel, and the rice that was still stuck in the corners of the kitchen, he would think that was the reason she had called him. He wouldn't believe the story about Michela, he would think of her as a woman having a crisis with her husband, trying to reestablish old relationships to keep from feeling so alone. For a moment she wondered whether that was actually the case.

"Do you have children?"

"No, none."

"But why—"

"Drop it," Alice cut in.

Mattia fell silent, but didn't apologize.

"What about you?" she asked after a while. She had hesitated to ask, for fear of his answer. Then her voice had come out all by itself, almost startling her.

"No," Mattia replied.

"No children?"

"I don't have . . ." He wanted to say *anyone*. "I'm not married."

Alice nodded.

"Still playing hard to get, then?" she said, turning to smile at him.

Mattia shook his head with embarrassment, and understood what she meant.

They had reached a large, deserted parking lot near the truck terminal, surrounded by huge prefabricated buildings, one after another. No one lived there. Three stacks of wooden pallets wrapped in plastic leaned against a gray wall, next to a lowered security gate. Higher up, on the roof, was a neon sign that must have shone bright orange at night.

Alice stopped the car in the middle of the parking lot and turned off the engine.

"Your turn," she said, opening the door.

"What?"

"Now you drive."

"No, no," said Mattia. "Forget it."

She stared at him carefully, with her eyes half closed and her lips pursed as if she were only now rediscovering a kind of affection that she had forgotten about.

"So you haven't changed that much," she said. It wasn't a reproach; in fact she seemed relieved.

"Neither have you," he said.

She shrugged.

"Okay, then," he said. "Let's give it a go."

Alice laughed. They got out of the car to switch seats and Mattia walked with his arms dangling exaggeratedly to demonstrate his total resignation. For the first time they each found themselves in the role of the other, each showing the other what they thought was their true profile.

"I don't know where to start," said Mattia, with his arms high on the steering wheel, as if he really didn't know where to put them.

"Nothing at all? You've never driven, not even once?"

"Practically never."

"So we're in a bit of a fix."

Alice leaned over him. For a moment Mattia stared at her hair falling vertically toward the center of the earth. Under the T-shirt that lifted slightly over her belly he recognized the upper edge of the tattoo, which he had observed close-up a long time ago.

"You're so thin," he blurted out, as if he were thinking out loud.

Alice jerked her head around to look at him, but then pretended nothing was wrong.

"No," she said, shrugging. "No different from usual."

She pulled back a little and pointed to the three pedals.

"Right, then. Clutch, brake, and accelerator. Left foot only for the clutch and right foot for the other two."

Mattia nodded, still somewhat distracted by the proximity of her body and the invisible smell of shower gel that lingered.

"You know the gears, right? And anyway they're written down here. First, second, third. And I have a feeling that'll do for now," Alice went on. "When you change gears, hold down the clutch and then slowly release it. And to start too: hold down the clutch and then release it while giving a bit of gas. Ready?"

"And if I'm not?" he replied.

He tried to concentrate. He felt as nervous as if he were about to take an exam. Over time he had become convinced that he no longer knew how to do anything outside of his element, the ordered and transfinite sets of mathematics. Normal people acquired self-confidence as they aged, while he was losing it, as if he had a limited reserve.

He assessed the space that separated them from the pallets stacked at the end of the parking lot. A good fifty meters, at least. Even if he set off at top speed he would have time to brake. He held the key turned too long, making the motor screech. He delicately released the clutch, but didn't press hard enough on the accelerator and the engine stalled with a gulp. Alice laughed.

"Almost. A bit more decisive this time though."

Mattia took a deep breath. Then he tried again. The car set off with a jerk and Alice told him to hit the clutch and put it in second. Mattia changed gears and accelerated again. They drove straight until they were almost ten meters from the factory wall, when he decided to turn the steering wheel. They did a 180-degree turn that threw them both to one side and returned them to the point they had started from.

Alice clapped her hands.

"You see?" she said.

He turned the car again and performed the same move. It was as if he knew how to follow only that narrow, oval trajectory, even though he had a huge lot all to himself.

"Keep going straight," said Alice. "Turn onto the road."

"Are you mad?"

"Come on, there's no one there. And besides, you've already figured it out."

Mattia adjusted the steering wheel. He felt his hands sweating from the plastic and the adrenaline stirring his muscles as it hadn't done for ages. For a moment he thought he was driving a car, the whole thing, with its pistons and greased mechanisms, and that he had Alice, so close, to tell him what to do. Just as he had imagined so often. Well, not exactly, but for once he resolved to ignore the imperfections.

"Okay," he said.

He steered the car toward the exit. Once there he leaned toward the windshield and looked in both directions. He delicately turned the steering wheel and couldn't help following its movements with his whole torso, as children do when they pretend to drive.

He was on the road. The sun, already low in the sky, was behind him and shone in his eyes from the rearview mirror. The arrow of the speedometer pointed to 30 kilometers an hour and the whole car vibrated with the hot breath of a domesticated animal.

"Am I doing okay?" he asked.

"Brilliantly. Now you can change into third."

The road went on for several hundred meters and Mattia looked straight ahead. Alice took advantage of the situation to observe him calmly from close-up. He was no longer the Mattia from the photograph. The skin of his face was no longer an even texture, smooth and elastic: now the first wrinkles, still very shallow, furrowed his brow. He had shaved, but new stubble was already emerging from his cheeks, dotting them with black. His physical presence was overwhelming; he no longer seemed to have any cracks through which one could invade his space, as she had often liked to do when she was a girl. Or else it was that she no longer felt she had the right to. That she was no longer capable of it.

She tried to find a resemblance to the girl from the hospital, but now that Mattia was here, her memory grew even more confused. All those details that seemed to coincide were no longer as clear as they had been. The color of the girl's hair was lighter, perhaps. And she didn't remember the dimples at the sides of her mouth, or those eyebrows, so thick at the outer ends. For the first time she was really worried that she had made a mistake.

How will I explain it to him? she wondered.

Mattia cleared his throat, as if the silence had gone on for too long or as if he had noticed that Alice was staring at him. She looked elsewhere, toward the hill.

"You remember the first time I came to pick you up in the car?" she said. "I'd had my license for less than an hour."

"Yeah. Of all the possible guinea pigs you chose me."

Alice thought that it wasn't true. She hadn't chosen him over all the others. The truth was that she hadn't even thought about anyone else.

"You spent the whole time clutching the door handle. You kept saying slow down, slow down."

She cried out with the shrill voice of a little girl. Mattia remembered that he had gone against his will. That afternoon he was supposed to be studying for his mathematical analysis exam, but in the end he had given in, because it seemed so damned important to Alice. All he did all afternoon was calculate again and again how many hours of study time he was losing. Thinking about it now, he felt stupid, as we all do when we remember all the time we waste wishing we were somewhere else.

"We drove around for half an hour in search of two free parking spaces because you couldn't get into a single one," he said, to banish those thoughts.

"It was just an excuse to keep you with me," Alice replied. "But you never understood anything."

They both laughed, to stifle the ghosts let loose by her words.

"Where do I go?" asked Mattia, becoming serious.

"Turn here."

"Okay. But then that's enough. I'll let you have your seat back."

He changed from third to second without Alice having to tell him, and took the curve well. He turned into a shady street, narrower than the other one and without the dividing line down the middle, squashed between two rows of identical, windowless buildings.

"I'll stop down there," he said.

They were almost there when a tractor trailer truck appeared from around the corner, heading straight toward them and taking up most of the road.

Mattia gripped the wheel tightly. His right foot didn't have the instinct to hit the brake, so he accelerated instead. With her good leg Alice searched for a pedal that wasn't there. The truck didn't slow down, but merely moved slightly to its side of the road.

"I can't get by," said Mattia. "I can't get by."

"Brake," said Alice, trying to seem calm.

Mattia couldn't think. The truck was a few meters away and only now did it show any sign of slowing down. He felt his foot contracting on the accelerator and thought about how he could pass it. He remembered how he used to ride his bike down the ramp of the bike path and how at the end he'd have to brake abruptly in order to get between the posts that blocked the cars entering. But Michela never slowed down, she'd go right between them on her bike with training wheels, but never once did she so much as brush them with the handlebars.

He turned the steering wheel to the right and seemed to be heading straight for the wall.

"Brake," Alice repeated. "The middle pedal."

He pressed it down hard, with both feet. The car jerked violently forward and came to a standstill just a few feet from the wall.

The recoil made Mattia bang his head against the left-hand window, but the seat belt held him in place. Alice rocked forward like a bending twig, but held on tightly to the door handle. The truck, two long, red segments, sped past them, indifferently.

———

They sat in silence for a few seconds, as though contemplating something extraordinary. Then Alice started laughing. Mattia's eyes stung and the nerves in his neck pulsed as if they had all been suddenly inflated and were about to explode.

"Did you hurt yourself?" Alice asked. It was as if she couldn't stop laughing.

Mattia was terrified. He didn't reply. She tried to become serious again.

"Let me see," she said.

She freed herself from her seat belt and stretched over him as he stared at the wall directly in front of them. He was thinking about the word *anelastic*. About how the kinetic energy now making his legs tremble would have been unleashed all at once on impact.

At last he took his feet off the brake and the car, its engine off, slipped backward slightly, down the almost imperceptible slope of the road. Alice pulled on the hand brake.

"You're fine," she said, brushing Mattia's forehead.

He closed his eyes and nodded. He concentrated to keep from crying.

"Let's go home and you can lie down for a bit," she said, as if home were their home.

"I have to go back to my parents' house," protested Mattia, but without much conviction.

"I'll take you back later. Now you need to rest."

"I have to—"

"Shut up."

They got out of the car to swap seats. The darkness had taken over the whole of the sky, apart from a thin, useless strip running along the horizon.

They didn't say another word the whole rest of the way. Mattia trapped his head in his right hand. He covered his eyes and pressed his temples with his thumb and middle finger. He read and reread the words on the side mirror: *Objects in mirror are closer than they appear.* He thought about the article he had left Alberto to write. He was bound to make a mess of it; Mattia had to get back as soon as possible. And then there were lessons to prepare, his silent apartment.

Alice turned to look at him, worried, taking her eyes off the road from time to time. She was doing all she could to drive gently. She wondered if it would be better to put on some music, but she didn't know what he would like. In truth she didn't know anything about him anymore.

In front of the house she went to help him out of the car, but Mattia got out by himself. He swayed on his feet as she opened the door. Alice moved quickly, but carefully. She felt responsible, as if it were all the unexpected consequence of a bad joke.

She threw the cushions on the floor to make room on the sofa. She said to Mattia lie down here and he obeyed. Then she went into the kitchen to make him some tea or chamomile or anything that she could hold in her hands when she came back into the sitting room.

As she waited for the water to boil she started tidying up, frantically. Every now and again she turned to glance at the sitting room, but all she could see was the back of the sofa, its bright, uniform blue.

Soon Mattia would ask her why she had summoned him there and she would have no escape. But now she was no longer sure of anything. She had seen a girl who looked like him. So? The world is full of people who look alike. Full of stupid and meaningless co-incidences. She hadn't even spoken to her. And she wouldn't have known how to find her again anyway. Thinking about it now, with Mattia in the other room, the whole thing seemed ridiculous and cruel.

The only certainty was that he had come back and that she didn't want him to go away again.

She washed the already clean dishes that were in the sink and emptied the potful of water sitting on the stove. A handful of rice had been lying on the bottom of it for weeks. Seen through the water, the grains looked bigger.

Alice poured the boiling water into a cup and dipped a tea bag in it. It gushed dark. She added two heaping spoonfuls of sugar and went back into the living room.

Mattia's hand had slipped from his closed eyes to his throat. The skin of his face had relaxed and his expression was neutral. His chest moved regularly up and down and he was breathing only through his nose.

Alice set the cup down on the glass table and, without taking her eyes off him, sat down in the armchair next to him. Mattia's breathing restored her calm. It was the only sound.

She slowly began to feel that her thoughts were regaining coherence. At last they slowed down, after dashing madly toward some vague destination. She found herself back in her own sitting room as if she had been dropped in it from another dimension.

Before her was a man whom she had once known and who was now someone else. Perhaps he really did look like the girl in the hospital. But they weren't identical, certainly not. And the Mattia who was sleeping on her sofa was no longer the boy she had seen disappearing through the elevator doors that evening when a hot, unquiet wind came down from the mountains. He was not the Mattia who had taken root in her head and blocked her path to everything else.

No, what she had in front of her was a grown-up person who had built a life around a terrifying abyss, on terrain that had already collapsed, and yet who had succeeded, far away from here, among people Alice didn't know. She had been prepared to destroy all that, to disinter a buried horror, for a simple suspicion, as slender as the memory of a memory.

But now that Mattia was there in front of her, with his eyes closed over thoughts to which she had no access, everything suddenly seemed clearer: she had looked for him because she needed to, because since the night she had left him on that landing, her life had rolled into a hole and hadn't moved from there. Mattia was the end of that tangle that she carried within herself, twisted by the years. If there was still some chance of untying it, some way of loosening it, it was by pulling that end that she now gripped between her fingers.

She felt that something was being resolved, like a long wait coming to an end. She sensed it in her limbs, even in her bad leg, which usually never noticed anything.

Getting up was a natural gesture. She didn't even wonder if it was appropriate or not, if it was really her right to do so. It was only time, sliding and dragging itself after more time. Only obvious gestures that knew nothing of the future and the past.

She bent over Mattia and kissed him on the lips. She wasn't afraid of waking him, she kissed him as you kiss someone who is awake, lingering over his closed lips, compressing them as if to leave a mark. He gave a start, but didn't open his eyes. He parted his lips and went along with her. He was awake.

It was different from the first time. Their facial muscles were stronger now, more conscious, and they sought an aggression having to do with the precise roles of a man and a woman. Alice stayed bent over him, without getting onto the sofa, as if she had forgotten the rest of her own body.

The kiss lasted a long time, whole minutes, long enough for reality to find a fissure between their clamped mouths and slip inside, forcing them both to analyze what was happening.

They pulled apart. Mattia gave a quick smile, automatically, and

Alice brought a finger to her damp lips, as if to make sure it had really happened. There was a decision to be made and it had to be made without speaking. They looked at each other, but they had already lost their synchronicity and their eyes didn't meet.

Mattia stood up, uncertainly.

"I'll just go . . ." he said, pointing to the corridor.

"Sure. At the end of the hall."

He left the room. He still had his shoes on and the sound of his footsteps seemed to be slipping away underground.

He locked himself in the bathroom and rested his hands on the sink. He felt stunned, groggy. He noticed a little swelling that was spreading slowly where he had hit his head.

He turned on the tap and put his wrists under the cold water, as his father had done when he wanted to stanch the blood gushing from Mattia's hands. He looked at the water and thought about Michela, as he did every time. It was a painless thought, like thinking about going to sleep or breathing. His sister had slipped into the current, dissolved slowly in the river, and through the river she had come back inside him. Her molecules were scattered all through his body.

He felt his circulation returning. Now he had to think, about that kiss and about what it was that he had come in search of after all that time. About why he had been prepared to receive Alice's lips and about why he had then felt the need to pull away and hide in here.

She was in the other room waiting for him. Separating them were two layers of brick, a few inches of plaster, and nine years of silence.

The truth was that once again she had acted in his place, had forced him to come back when he himself had always yearned to do it. She had written him a note and had said come here and he had jumped up like a spring. One letter had brought them together just as another had separated them.

Mattia knew what needed to be done. He had to get out of there and sit back down on that sofa, he had to take her hand and tell her I shouldn't have left. He had to kiss her once more and then again, until they were so used to that gesture that they couldn't do without it. It happened in films and it happened in reality, every day. People took what they wanted, they clutched at coincidences, the few there were, and made a life from them. He had either to tell Alice I'm here, or leave, take the first plane and disappear again, go back to the place where he had been hanging for all those years.

By now he had learned. Choices are made in brief seconds and paid for in the time that remains. It had happened with Michela and then with Alice and again now. He recognized them this time: those seconds were there, and he would never make a mistake again.

He closed his fingers around the jet of water. He caught some of it in his hands and bathed his face. Without looking, still bent over the basin, he stretched out an arm to take a towel. He rubbed it over his face and then pulled away. In the mirror he saw a darker patch on the other side. He turned it around. It was the embroidered initials *FR,* placed a few centimeters away from the corner, in a symmetrical position in respect to the bisecting line.

Mattia turned around and found another, identical towel. At the same point the letters *ADR* were sewn.

He looked around more carefully. In the water-stained glass there was a single toothbrush and next to it a basket of things all jumbled together: creams, a red rubber band, a hairbrush with hairs attached to it, and a pair of nail scissors. On the shelf under the mirror lay a razor, with tiny fragments of dark hair still trapped beneath the blade.

There had been a time when, sitting on the bed with Alice, he could scan her room with his eyes, identify something on a shelf and say to himself I bought that for her. Those gifts were there to bear witness to a journey, like little flags attached to stages of a voyage. They marked out the rhythm of Christmases and birthdays. Some he could still remember: the first Counting Crows record; a Galilean thermometer, with its different-colored bulbs floating in a transparent liquid; and a book on the history of mathematics that Alice had received with a snort but had actually read in the end. She preserved them carefully, finding an obvious position for them, so that it would be clear to him that she always had them before her eyes. Mattia knew it. He knew all that, but he couldn't move from where he was. As if, in yielding to Alice's call, he might find himself in a trap, drown in it, and be lost forever. He stayed there, impassive and silent, waiting until it was too late.

Around him now there was not a single object that he recognized. He looked at his own reflection in the mirror, his tousled hair, his shirt collar slightly askew, and it was then that he understood. In that bathroom, in that house as in his parents' house, in all those places, there was no longer anything of him.

He remained motionless, getting used to the decision he had made, until he felt that the seconds were over. He carefully folded the towel and with the back of his hand he wiped away the little drops that he had left on the edge of the sink.

He left the bathroom and walked down the hall. He stopped in the doorway of the living room.

"I have to go now," he said.

"Yes," replied Alice, as if she had prepared herself to say it.

The cushions were back in their place on the sofa and a big lamp lit everything from the middle of the ceiling. No trace of conspiracy remained. The tea had grown cold on the coffee table and a dark and sugary sediment had settled at the bottom of the cup. Mattia thought that it was merely someone else's house.

They walked to the door together. He touched Alice's hand with his as he passed close to her.

"The card you sent me," he said. "There was something you wanted to tell me."

Alice smiled.

"It was nothing."

"Before you said it was important."

"No. It wasn't."

"Was it something to do with me?"

She hesitated for a moment.

"No," she said. "Just with me."

Mattia nodded. He thought of a potential that had been exhausted, the invisible vector lines that had previously united them through the air and had now ceased to exist.

"Bye, then," said Alice.

The light was all inside and the darkness all outside. Mattia replied with a wave of his hand. Before going back in, she saw once again the dark circle drawn on his palm, like a mysterious and indelible symbol, irreparably closed.

46

The plane traveled in the dead of night and the few insomniacs who noticed it from the ground saw nothing but a little collection of intermittent lights, like a wandering constellation against the fixed black sky. Not one of them lifted a hand to wave to him, because that's something only children do.

Mattia got into the first of the taxis lined up in front of the terminal and gave the driver his address. As they passed along the seashore a faint glow was already rising from the horizon.

"Stop here, please," he said to the taxi driver.

"Here?"

"Yes."

He paid the fare and got out of the car, which immediately drove away. He walked across about ten meters of grass and approached a bench, which seemed to have been put there especially to look at the void. He dropped his bag on it but didn't sit down himself.

A strip of sun was already appearing on the horizon. Mattia tried to remember the geometrical name for that plane figure, bounded by an arc and a segment, but it wouldn't come to him. The sun seemed to be moving faster than it did in the daytime; it was possible to perceive its velocity, as if it were in a hurry to come up. The rays grazing the surface of the water were red, orange, and yellow and Mattia knew why, but knowing added nothing and didn't distract him.

The curve of the coast was flat and windswept and he was the 267 only one looking at it.

At last the gigantic red orb detached itself from the sea, like an incandescent ball. For a moment Mattia thought of the rotational motion of the stars and the planets, the sun that fell behind him in the evening and rose there in front of him in the morning. Every day, in and out of the water, whether he was there to look at it or not. It was nothing but mechanics, conservation of energy and angular momentum, forces that balanced one another, centripetal and centrifugal thrusts, nothing but a trajectory, which could not be anything other than what it was.

Slowly the tonalities faded away and the pale blue of morning began to emerge from the background of the other colors and took over first the sea and then the sky.

Mattia blew on his hands, which the brackish wind had made unusable. Then he drew them back into his jacket. He felt something in his right pocket. He pulled out a note folded in four. It was Nadia's number. He read the sequence of numbers to himself and smiled.

He waited for the last purple flame to go out on the horizon and, amid the dispersing mist, set off for home on foot.

His parents would have liked the dawn. Perhaps, one day, he would take them to see it and then they would stroll together to the port, to breakfast on smoked salmon sandwiches. He would explain to them how it happens, how the infinite wavelengths merge to form white light. He would talk to them about absorption and emission spectra and they would nod without understanding.

Mattia let the cold air of morning slip under his jacket. It smelled clean. Not far away there was a shower waiting for him, and a cup of hot tea and a day like many others, and he didn't need anything else.

47

That same morning, a few hours later, Alice raised the blinds. The dry rattle of the plastic slats rolling around the pulley was comforting. Outside the sun was already high in the sky.

She chose a CD from the stack next to the stereo, without thinking too much about it. She just wanted a little noise to clean the air. She turned the volume knob to the first red notch. Fabio would be furious. She couldn't help smiling as she thought about how he would say her name, shouting to make himself heard over the music and lingering too long over the *i,* jutting his chin.

She pulled off the bedsheets and piled them in a corner. She took clean ones from the closet. She watched them filling with air and then falling back down, undulating slightly. Damien Rice's voice broke slightly just before he managed to sing, *"Oh cuz nothing is lost, it's just frozen in frost."*

Alice washed calmly. She stayed in the shower for a long time, her face turned toward the jet of water. Then she got dressed and put a little makeup, almost invisible, on her cheeks and eyelids.

By the time she was ready the CD had been over for some time, but she didn't notice. She left the house and got into the car.

A block from the shop she changed direction. She would be a bit late, but it didn't matter.

She drove to the park where Mattia had told her everything. She felt as if nothing had changed. She remembered it all, apart from the pale wooden fence that now surrounded the grass.

She got out of the car and walked toward the trees. The grass crunched, still cold from the night, and the branches were full of new leaves. Some kids were sitting on the benches where Michela had sat so long before. In the middle of the table, cans were arranged on top of one another to form a tower. The kids were talking loudly and one of them was moving wildly around, imitating someone.

Alice walked over, trying to catch scraps of what they were saying, but before they could notice her she had walked on and headed for the river. Since the city council had decided to keep the dam open all year, hardly any water ran at that point. The river looked motionless in the elongated puddles, as if forgotten, exhausted. On Sundays, when it was hot, people brought their deck chairs from home and came down here to sunbathe. The bottom was made of white stones and a fine, yellowish sand. The grass on the bank was tall; it came up above Alice's knees.

She walked down the slope, checking with each step to make sure that the ground didn't yield. She continued on to the riverbed, to the edge of the water. In front of her was the bridge and farther away the Alps, which on clear days like this seemed incredibly close. Only the highest peaks were still covered with snow.

Alice lay down on the dry pebbles. Her bad leg thanked her by relaxing. The larger stones pricked her back, but she didn't move.

She closed her eyes and tried to imagine the water, all around and above her. She thought of Michela leaning over from the shore. Of her round face that she had seen in the papers reflected in the silver water. Of the splash that no one had been there to hear and the wet icy clothes dragging her down. Of her hair floating like dark seaweed. She saw her groping with her arms, waving them awkwardly and swallowing painful mouthfuls of that cold liquid, which dragged her farther down until she almost touched the bottom.

Then she imagined her movement becoming more sinuous, her arms finding the right gestures and describing circles that gradually became wider, her feet stretching out like two flippers and moving together, her head turning upward, where some light still filtered in. She saw Michela rising back up to the surface and breathing, finally. She followed her, as she swam on the surface of the water, in the direction of the current, toward somewhere new. All night long, all the way to the sea.

When she opened her eyes the sky was still there, with its monotonous and brilliant blue. Not a cloud passed across it.

Mattia was far away. Fabio was far away. The current of the river made a faint, somnolent swish.

She remembered lying in the crevasse, buried by snow. She thought of that perfect silence. Also now, like then, no one knew where she was. This time too, no one would come. But she no longer expected them to.

She smiled at the clear sky. With a little effort, she could get up by herself.

The Solitude of
Prime Numbers

A Penguin Readers Guide

ABOUT THE BOOK

Divisible only by one and themselves, prime numbers stand in stark contrast to natural numbers, upending the orderly logic of mathematics. They are strange, solitary, and disruptive. Like prime numbers, Mattia and Alice are also oddities, united in their loneliness, adrift in the normal world. Unable to fit in with anyone else, Alice and Mattia are kindred spirits, each bearing the burden of physical and psychological injuries from their childhood. Alice walks with a limp, the result of a skiing accident, and, painfully self-conscious of her body, nurses an eating disorder. Mattia's scars run deeper; devastated by the loss of his mentally handicapped twin sister and racked with guilt over his secret role in her disappearance, Mattia turns his emotional suffering into physical pain, deliberately cutting and burning himself. The relationship between these two damaged young people is the center of *The Solitude of Prime Numbers*, Paolo Giordano's brilliantly arresting debut novel.

Giordano's characters are provocative, even disturbing at times, and yet they have a fragility that evokes our sympathy. As Alice struggles to navigate the cruel and arbitrary rules of high school, she reaches out and retreats inward in equal measure, and when she is rebuked by her classmates, she turns to Mattia as her only friend. But while Alice is rejected by the world, Mattia, in turn, rejects the world itself, severing himself from any visible emotional contact with anyone else. He escapes into numbers, replacing the chaos of life with the peaceful structures of mathematics—and yet, even there, he finds Alice. Together they pass through adolescence into adulthood, and their private world expands to include a constellation of characters who love, desire, despise, and ignore them. Clinging together and yet never able to connect fully, Mattia and Alice are forced to question whether it's possible to unlock themselves from their painful pasts and overcome their deep loneliness by reaching out to each other. With artful precision, Giordano illustrates the bitter beauty of love and loss and how the two extremes are permanently intertwined. His novel is a brutally honest yet generous portrayal of two struggling souls. Mattia and Alice are neither good nor bad people, they are simply human, but they pay a deep price for the choices they make. Complex and compelling, *The Solitude of Prime Numbers* is an unsettling look at how the effects of a single moment can reverberate through a lifetime. ▪

AN INTERVIEW WITH PAOLO GIORDANO

Q: *The Solitude of Prime Numbers* has been translated into a number of languages. How involved were you in the process of translation? How does the spirit of your work shift from language to language?

Of course, there are only a few languages for which my contribution could be significant—English, French, German, Spanish. I read as much as I could of the translation, only to check whether the taste of the prose, its musicality and rhythm, were kept. For other languages, like Dutch or Chinese, I can't even read what is written. In the cases I could "taste," the translations were very good, though translation always slightly changed the overall feeling of the book—for instance, making it sound more literal or easier. I had to make very few changes. By the way, I usually trust translators a lot, as I often read foreign authors translated into Italian (even English-speaking ones, as I am quite lazy) and—at least in Italy—translations are excellent most of the time. ▪

Q: Your novel won the Strega Prize in Italy, an achievement for any author but especially for a first-time novelist. As the youngest author to win the award, how does it feel to be included with so many Italian literary giants? Are there any fellow winners whose work is meaningful to you, whether as a writer or as a reader?

At first, I felt very scared by winning the Strega Prize. I said to myself: Well, what am I to do now? I achieved the highest possible result that my mind could fancy with my first novel, so I was sure that everything in the future might only be less than that. That's why I chose to forget the prize somehow. It was a kind of removal mechanism, similar to what happens with traumas. Every time I think of the prize now, it looks like something that happened many years ago, maybe to another person. On the other hand, the prize gave me some self-confidence that I totally lacked and also, I hope, some credit with a lot of readers, which I will rely on in the future. Such big names have won the Strega Prize and many of those are important influences for me, some even from the time of high school. To name the most meaningful to me: Cesare Pavese, Alberto Moravia, Dino Buzzati, Primo Levi, Giuseppe Pontiggia, and Niccolò Ammaniti. I can relate an important part of my life as a reader to each of them. ▪

Q: Do you see the abuse that Mattia and Alice inflict on their bodies as an attempt to assert some measure of control over their lives or are their actions more a means of self-punishment?

I always try not to psychoanalyze my characters too much. The things they do and the way they behave never follow a strict psychological analysis, as this would tear out of them some humanity and some truth, which are the two things I care about the most. Nonetheless, especially for Mattia, it is obvious to see his scars as a way of punishing himself. But it's not only that. Both for him and for Alice, mortifying the body is a way to change the focus of the attention, from some pain that affects the mind to some pain that affects the flesh. It is a way for stopping painful, circular thoughts and to gain some control over things. After all, our body is one of the few things we can really name ours. ■

Q: ● What were your considerations in choosing anorexia and self-mutilation as the characters' methods of abuse? How do gender and class play into your choices?

I have to admit that I didn't really choose anorexia and self-mutilation. If I was aware at that time that I was entering those kinds of "social diseases" I would have escaped from them immediately. They slowly emerged from the story, in particular from some small gestures that Alice and Mattia did (she hid food in the napkin, he put his hands in the soil and found a cutting piece of glass). I hadn't thought of these gestures until they happened. Then, for the rest of the story, I tried to dodge them a little bit. That's why, for instance, the word "anorexia" is never used. On the other hand, gender and class definitely play a role. Let's consider anorexia, for example. In the 1990s, the time in which the adolescence of Alice takes place, anorexia was more specific of the upper class, the one she belongs to, and almost exclusively affected females. The situation's already changed. Now we know that anorexia is becoming a transversal problem, both for class and for gender (the number of males who suffer from anorexia is increasing very fast, as I read in a recent newspaper article). ■

Q: ● Some readers might claim to find your depiction of adolescence shocking while others might find it painfully familiar. In what ways do Alice and Mattia represent contemporary youth? Is there any of your own experience in either character?

I think that any honest description of adolescence has somehow to deal with fear. I think, for instance, of some of my favorite movies about teenagers: *Elephant* and *Paranoid Park* by Gus Van Sant, *Donnie Darko* by Richard Kelly, and the recent *Let the Right One In* by Thomas Alfredson. Adolescence is shocking. It's full of terror and ghosts and intoxicating joy. It's always been like this, I guess. And in that respect, my novel doesn't talk of a specific youth—not mine or the contemporary. Only the elements, the context, and the scenography suggest the atmosphere of the mid-1990s, the time of Nirvana and Smashing Pumpkins, my high school years. ■

Q: Pairs—or, more specifically, twins—appear a number of times within the novel: Mattia and Michela; Mattia and Alice; twin primes. What are twin primes and how does this apply to the two friends? What is the significance of the use of pairs in the novel?

Twin primes are couples of prime numbers, such as 11 and 13 or 17 and 19; namely, two primes separated by a single even number. Primes are those numbers that are not divisible by any other number other than 1 and themselves. Mattia and Alice are exactly like that: they seem not to combine with any other person; isolation seems a fundamental aspect of their lives. That is due to painful events that took place during their childhoods, but it is also due to their own specific personalities. Mattia is a sort of genius, introverted and incomprehensible; Alice is arrogant but deeply insecure. As they meet, they recognize something similar in the other. For the rest of the story, they desperately try to get closer and closer, but they never really succeed. There is always something in the way— that single even number between them. They are not the only pair in the book: Mattia has a twin, Michela, and he loses her when they are children. Alice constantly searches for someone to share her life with, but she ends up with the wrong choice.

The search for our twin is, after all, the search of our lives, at least for many of us. ∎

Q. Mattia and Alice find comfort, to whatever degree they can, by connecting with each other while being disconnected from the world around them. What kind of relief does this connection provide? What would have become of them without each other?

I think there are a few special relationships in life that are so strong and intense that they reject the rest of the world. In a way, they are based on the idea of rejecting the world. At least that's what happened to me a few times. They can be friendships or love affairs, but in both cases, what is shared is so special that we think nobody outside can understand it. The friendship between Alice and Mattia is at the same time magical, weird, and strong. It is a source of relief because it protects them from the outside world that seems to hate them, but it is also the source of a new burning pain: the difficulty—almost the impossibility—to really become a part of someone else. What I've noticed during my life is that such special relationships last for only the time the pain underneath them exists. As soon as things change or this pain fades out, they also vanish, incapable of finding a new definition within a more "normal" context. ∎

Q. Sex serves many purposes in the novel—as initiation, as empty experience, as measure of isolation—yet rarely as pleasure. Why do Alice and Mattia resist a physical expression of their emotions?

Sex is one of the situations where all things submerged in our subconscious come out, all fears, all desires, all the violence, and all the needs. That's why sex, in my opinion, is never as easy as television shows or jokes present it to be. We are often told that taking pleasure, especially from sex, and surrendering to it are things that happen naturally, gestures that come for free. I find it harder, instead, to learn how to surrender than to learn how to resist. That's exactly what my characters suffer from: the difficulty of covering the distance between desires and their fulfillments, the difficulty of doing "easy" things, such as kissing a girl or lying in bed with her, difficulties that are not only due to external causes, but also often to internal ones. ■

Q. Why did you decide to structure the novel in stages rather than as a continuous whole? What do the gaps between the years tell us?

I find that time gaps give a story a deeper breadth. Years and situations that are not told by the author give the reader a space where he/she can be free to make the story his/her own story. In my novel I also skipped some parts that could be seen as important, but I'm sure there are always sufficient elements for anyone to fill in the gaps with his own memories and emotions. And also a love story—this is a love story—always needs to travel across the years, even across an entire lifetime. ■

Q. What was the impulse behind the main metaphor of the novel? Have you always been fascinated by numbers?

The metaphor came by chance. I've always been fascinated by prime numbers because they are a very easy thing to define— they require only arithmetic. Also, an eight-year-old boy knows what they are, but still the mystery associated with them is unsolved, though all mathematicians have somehow dealt with it since the time of Archimedes. Nobody can predict what will be the next prime number discovered. So it was natural to me that

Mattia, who becomes a mathematician, was intrigued by prime numbers. That's why I started building the metaphor. Then I learned about the existence of twin primes: it was exactly what I needed. ▪

Q: Your readers might not realize that you are a physicist as well as an author. Could you tell us a little more about that side of your life?

After high school I found myself in a profound dilemma: I was mainly fascinated by literary studies (philosophy above all), but I was aware that a scientific background would help me understand the nowaday-world better. Then I chose the scientific subject that to me looked more similar to philosophy and I joined the university to study physics. I still think it was the right choice. During the years of university, I was totally embedded in physics and the further I went in learning the bigger my fascination became, especially for the microscopic world of elementary particles and of quantum physics. After graduation I started a PhD program in particle physics, which I'm finishing now. ▪

Q: How do you meld your scientific and artistic work? What prompted you to write a novel?

I wrote the novel during one of the busiest times of my life, as I was writing my thesis and then preparing for the admission exam to the PhD program. But it's always been my peculiarity to work better when I'm under pressure. I did physics during the day, often until 7 or 8 p.m. Then after dinner until late in the night I wrote the novel (only a couple of days a week, otherwise that would have been suicide). The reason I started writing was that, after five years of enthusiastic studies, I started to feel a bit bored with physics. I needed something different.

When I was younger I wanted to be a rock star, but I found out I didn't have the talent for that. I knew that writing was the only possibility left for doing something different, but I had to wait for that particular time to find the courage to start. Now that the book has had this huge success, things have turned the opposite way around: I write for most of the day and, when I have time, I go on with my research activity. ▪

DISCUSSION QUESTIONS

1. What pleasure or power do Mattia and Alice get from harming their bodies? Think about the moments in the novel when these acts occur. Do you think they are in response to something and, if so, what?

2. There is a brief moment at Viola's party where Alice and Mattia walk together and their respective scars seem to melt into one another and disappear. How? In what other ways are Mattia and Alice complementary?

3. Examine the relationship between Alice and Viola. Based on Alice's feelings toward Viola and Viola's treatment of Alice, what do you think about Alice's actions when they meet later in life?

4. What is it about adolescence that makes people so cruel? What was your own adolescence like? Did Mattia's and Alice's experience with their peers echo your own in any way?

5. Where are the parents in this novel? What presence or power do they assert? Why?

6. Was Mattia's action with his sister understandable? Was he aware of the possible consequences or not? Should children be held accountable when their actions have such severe consequences?

7. One of Alice's few pleasures in life is photography, an art that consists of capturing a moment and presenting

it according to one's own perspective. Why is this pursuit appropriate for Alice?

8. Mattia believes that "feeling special is the worst kind of cage that a person can build." What do you think he means by this?

9. Do you think Alice really sees Michela in the hospital or was she hallucinating? Why?

10. Examine the last paragraph of the novel. What is being said here? What happens to Alice? What happens to Mattia?